THOSE THREE WORDS

A BILLIONAIRE BOSS ROMANCE

ALEXIS WINTER

I NEVER THOUGHT GETTING FIRED FROM MY DREAM JOB WOULD CHANGE MY LIFE.

And I certainly never imagined three little words would be my undoing.

Trust me—they're not the words you're thinking.
Those three delicious, toe-curling words whispered by my boss were where it all changed.

When budget cuts at my local school leave me scrambling to find a job before I get evicted, I stumble upon the listing of a lifetime.
How hard can being a live-in nanny for a little five year old girl be?
Especially when it's double the salary and comes with a sexy, single dad.

But the moment I step inside Graham Hayes multi-million dollar estate and meet the grumpy billionaire—I know I'm in way over my head.

It's not just that he's quite possibly the most attractive man I've ever seen, it's the way he stares at me like it takes everything he has to keep from devouring me.

The way he curls his hands into fists to avoid touching me.
The way he reprimands me through gritted teeth while his lust filled
eyes burn through me.
The naughty things he whispers against my lips as his hands
explore me.

Way over my head.

Caring for his daughter is a dream—even his mother loves me.
Soon, I'm head over heels in this fantasy I'm living.
I'm even able to ignore the cryptic threats from his house-keeper
who's hellbent on getting me fired.

But I'm not prepared for the world of high-powered billionaires and
glitzy parties.
Besides, Graham isn't like these people—he's different.
At least, I think he is…until a shady character I've tried to leave in the
past reappears as Graham's new business partner and I'm reminded
that I don't belong in this world.

Sometimes life changing news comes in the form of just *three simple
words.*
Sometimes it comes in the form of an unexpected, heart-wrenching
secret and the fairytale is shattered.
Sometimes, it comes in the form of the opportunity of a fresh new
start.

**You just have to be willing to take the risk and walk away or
maybe…there's three little words that can fix it all.**

THANK YOU!

A wonderful thank you to my amazing readers for continuing to support my dream of bringing sexy, naughty, delicious little morsels of fun in the form of romance novels.

A special thank you to my amazing editors Michele Davine and Kimberly Dawn who without whom I would be completely lost!

Thank you to my fantastic cover designer Sarah Kil who always brings my visions to life in the most outstanding ways.

And lastly, to my ARC team and beta readers, you are wonderful and I couldn't do this without you.

XoXo,
Alexis

1

MARGOT

"I'm *fired?*"

The words feel so foreign rolling off my tongue. I've never been fired. I'm only twenty-six, but it still feels like a kick to the stomach.

"Not technically *fired*. It's not because of your performance, if that makes it any better. It's simply a matter of budget cuts." Mr. Diaz says the words with a sympathetic look on his face as if that will soften the blow of the situation.

It does not.

"I just don't understand. The music education program has grown so much in the last three years with me managing it. The ki—" My words hitch in my throat that is thick with emotion. "The kids. What about the kids? They love my class."

"Like I said, Miss Silver, regrettably, we just don't have the funding anymore to keep the program going. I'm sure you understand how all this bureaucratic red tape messes things up. Unfortunately, it's out of my hands."

I stare at the ground, my vision blurring through my tears.

"We can offer you two weeks' pay." He holds out an envelope to me, but I don't take it. "I'm sorry, Miss Silver. Truly, I am." Mr. Diaz places the envelope on the small table next to me before standing up and exiting the room.

Two weeks? That's it? I bounce my legs nervously, trying to divert my anxiousness into movement instead of having a full emotional breakdown in the teacher's lounge.

I've loved every second of being a music teacher. It was my dream job, what I went to school for. Both my parents were musicians. My mom taught me to read music and my dad taught me to feel it.

I pick up the envelope. Between this paycheck and my small savings, I'd say I have about enough money to live in my current Chicago studio for another month and a half before I'm evicted.

I let out a breath and gather my bag, then head back to my classroom. It's the end of the semester so it won't look strange that I'm carrying a box of items to my car. Most teachers clean out their classrooms for the summer.

"Bye, Miss Silver. See you next year!" Two of my students, Bryant and Adam, wave to me as I step into my classroom.

"Have a good summer, boys," I say as they both dart past me down the hallway and out the door.

I shut the door behind me and lean against it briefly. Already the pain of realizing I won't see Bryant and Adam next school year is threatening to break through. I push the thoughts aside, still probably a little numb from being fired.

I'll miss the smell of my classroom. That probably sounds weird but every classroom still has that same smell of pencil shavings and Lysol wipes from our childhood. Even though I'm pretty sure none of these kids have ever seen or used a number two pencil in their life.

I smile to myself, thinking about my favorite elementary teacher, Miss Nyguard. She was always so kind and sweet. Her wardrobe of pastel cardigans and floral skirts looked as though she'd borrowed them from someone twice her age. I wish I could tell her the impact she had on me. It was because of her that I wanted to be an educator.

Memories of her calm me as I pack up my final item, a small

succulent that my students bought me at the beginning of the year. I gather the box in my arms and walk to the door, not stopping to look around for a final time.

"Hey, Margot, I was looking for you."

I turn to see Hank Byers, the PE teacher, jogging toward me as he waves.

"Some of us are going to that karaoke bar over off Wabash tonight. Nothing crazy, just celebrating the end of another school year. You should come by."

I smile. Hank has been friendly to everyone here from day one. He's a big guy, tall and burly with a big mop of blond curls and cherubic cheeks with perfect dimples. He's the local man candy that all the single teachers have taken a shot at, but as far as I know, none have been successful.

"I dunno," I say, chewing on my bottom lip. I wasn't planning on telling anyone that my position was eliminated, and if I go out to a bar, odds are I'll wallow, have a few too many, and probably cry desperately to anyone who will listen to me.

"Come on. Just come out for one drink. I'll buy." He smiles and holds out his hands.

"Okay, one drink."

"Nice!" He claps his hands together. "I gotta get back in there." He points both thumbs over one shoulder. "Need to do some inventory on the sports equipment and see what I need to buy for next year."

"Sounds good and thanks for the invite."

"See you tonight," he says, turning to jog back toward the gymnasium. "And don't even think about bailing!" he shouts through cupped hands before disappearing inside.

I toss the box of items into my back seat and look around the mostly empty parking lot one last time before driving home.

* * *

"So what do you plan to do with your summer?"

Ah, the dreaded teacher question we all ask each other.

"I'll probably do private music lessons like I do every summer."

I swallow down my beer, my stomach uneasy at the thought that I should have reached out to parents weeks ago. Between end-of-year stuff and counting on the fact I'd still have a job next school year, I'd let it slip. I usually have about six or seven private students each summer, but that's nowhere near enough to cover even half my rent.

"What about you? Still coaching little league?"

"Yup. I'll be coaching again. Also do some umping for adult teams and playing in the over-thirty league. My uncle Roy needs some help with his painting business too so that'll be some nice extra cash." He spins his beer bottle on the bar in front of him.

Hank really is an attractive guy and he's clearly a man with drive, but I've never felt any sort of attraction to him. I'm not sure why. Maybe because we are coworkers I've never let myself even consider it.

"It's funny how everyone thinks being a teacher is this walk in the park because we get summers off. Nobody realizes we all pretty much have summer jobs to keep the lights on, especially in Chicago."

I nod in agreement, both of us chuckling.

"I, uh, I got fired today." The words are out of my mouth before I can stop myself from saying them.

"What?" Hank's head whips toward me, his expression shocked. "Why?"

"Budget cuts," I say, picking at the label on my beer bottle.

"Fuck, man, I'm so sorry." He shakes his head. I can feel pity radiating off him and I instantly regret saying anything.

"It's fine. I'll find something else." I'm trying to convince myself.

"No, it's not fine. You are an amazing teacher and those kids love you. It's more than a job, Margot; this is your life."

I purse my lips and nod my head, his words conveying exactly why it hurts so bad. I hang my head as the tears start to fall. No point in trying to fight them.

"I know that, Hank," I whisper as he stands up, reaching for my arm to pull me in for a hug.

"Let it out," he says, his large hands wrapping halfway around my back as my shoulders start to bob up and down.

I don't have the luxury of caring if I look pathetic right now. Maybe everyone will just think I've had too much to drink and can't keep it together. Anything is better than the humiliation of being fired, even if it's not my fault.

We stand there for several more moments before I excuse myself to freshen up in the restroom. By the time I've returned to my seat, Hank has ordered us another round.

"Thank you." I gesture toward the drink with my head as I reach into my purse for my wallet. "But I need to go home. It's been an emotional day."

His countenance falls a little as he nods. "I understand. This is on me," he says as I pull my wallet out.

"Thanks, Hank." I reach out and grab his hand, giving it a quick squeeze.

"Don't be a stranger, okay? You have my number. If you need someone to vent to or a job reference or anything, call me?" He raises his eyebrows with the question.

"Of course." I offer a polite nod before heading back home.

I'm almost to my apartment building when my phone vibrates in my pocket. I reach down and pull it out, looking at the screen to see who would be calling me at this time of night.

It's a name and number I haven't seen in the better part of four years. In fact, the last time I saw Warren Dorsey's name on my phone was right after my mother passed away.

I don't answer it. Instead, I hit the ignore button and shove the phone back in my pocket. The last thing I need right now is whatever the hell my biological deadbeat dad has brewing.

* * *

I SPEND the entire weekend combing through job postings. I apply to every job that is even remotely related to music first, then start in on the local cafés and stores.

I've checked my account balance a record forty-two times over a few days, staring at it like it's going to magically morph into enough money to save me from being evicted.

I also check my email at least a hundred times over the next week, hoping, praying for any kind of reply from my applications. A few are immediately returned with, *position has been filled* or *we regret to inform you...* I don't even bother reading past that point.

Exasperated, I open my last bottle of wine. It's not even one I bought. It's a dusty old table blend that was given out by our school administration during the holidays a few years back.

"Desperate times, desperate measures," I mutter as I pour myself a generous glass and open my laptop.

I scroll through Craigslist on the off chance anyone might need private music lessons. Over half the emails I sent out to parents about lessons over the summer were returned with explanations about traveling or not in the budget. Another blow to my nonexistent savings.

A listing catches my eye and I click the link to open it.

Needed: Live-in nanny. Full-time 5-6 days per week. All expenses covered. Dental, vision, and medical insurance. Competitive salary. Immediate hire.

"Whoa, what?" I pull the laptop screen closer to me as I read the salary. "That can't be right." I squint, reading it again.

How the hell can someone pay more than twice what I make as a teacher for a nanny and offer living expenses covered and health insurance?

My excitement builds as I read over the qualifications. Okay, now I see why they pay so well. They want someone with a preferred degree in childcare or related field, CPR certified, 5+ years' experience with children, no pets, can teach music.

"Holy shit!" I yelp as I hop up off the couch. I can't hold back the smile as my heart thuds wildly in my chest. I am literally a perfect candidate for this job, and they want someone who can start ASAP.

I open my email and copy the address. I attach my resume and spend the next thirty minutes crafting a perfectly worded cover letter and link to my LinkedIn profile. I hold my breath, hit send, and flop back against the couch.

Finally, a glimmer of hope.

* * *

"AND YOU HAVE A DEGREE IN EDUCATION?" Miss Perry, a willowy woman with a perfectly tight bun and beige skirt suit, reads over my resume. Her short-clipped nails are the softest shade of pink and her skin is smooth and shiny, like she's been freshly Botoxed.

"Yes, a double degree actually in music education as well as early childhood education."

I squeeze my fingers together in my lap, trying to calm my nerves.

"I see and your last job ended because?" She peers precariously over the glasses that are perched on her nose.

"Budget cuts unfortunately. I was there for three years but the funding for the music program wasn't renewed so... here I am." I plaster a nervous smile on my face as she returns her gaze back to the paper in her hands.

"Oh, and I brought a letter of recommendation from the school I just taught at." I reach into my bag and produce the document, handing it to her.

I resist the urge to recite my resume for her. I want to explain why I'm perfect for this position, but something about how uptight she is makes me lose my nerve. Not to mention the sheer monstrosity of a house that I drove up to, complete with a massive wrought iron gate. I had no idea places even existed like this in the Chicago suburbs.

"Great." She gives a tight-lipped smile and places the resume on the desk in front of her, along with the letter. "We'll call you." She stands and juts her hand out to me.

7

"Okay." I shake her hand. "Thanks again so much for taking the time to interview me. I'll be anxiously waiting to hear from you."

She walks me to the front door in silence, only the clicking of her heels on the marble floor echoing around us.

"Oh, and just so you know, my schedule is completely open. I have no obligations so if I got the job, I'd be fully committed." She stares at me blankly, her hand resting on the front door handle. "What I mean is no husband or kids or pets or anything. Not even a boyfriend," I say around a chuckle.

"Bye now," she says and I take the hint, stepping through the front door, and it closes behind me.

* * *

ONE FULL WEEK AND NOTHING.

No callback.

No email.

I pull my phone out of my pocket and double-check the ringer is on. I also make sure I don't have any missed calls or texts. I've left two voicemails and a follow-up email. I know I sound desperate, but I *am* desperate. I'm on my last month's rent and I have a total of $122 to my name.

A fleeting thought pops through my head. *Maybe now is the time to reach out to Warren Dorsey. He's a billionaire several times over.* I push the thought from my head as quickly as it enters.

"Still nothing?" Shelly, my coworker at the local café I managed to snag a barista job at, asks.

"Nope." I sigh, putting my phone back into my apron.

"Dammit, that sucks," she says as she hops off the counter and removes her apron.

I'm grateful for the cash tips we split each day at this place but it's still minimum wage and I won't get my first paycheck for another week.

I walk over to the neon open sign in the window and turn it off before locking the door. Because we're a café, we open early so I've been able to work a twelve-hour shift every day this week—four a.m. to four p.m.

"Have a great night, Shelly." I wave as we both walk our separate ways.

My phone rings and I jump, then dig my hand into my pocket and pull it out. I don't recognize the number but as someone who has just applied to dozens of jobs, I know it could be a possible employer.

"Hello, this is Margot."

"Miss Silver?" A deep, syrupy voice says my name on the other end.

"Yes, this is Margot Silver." I try to sound chipper and upbeat, as if that will help them determine if they want to hire me.

"This is Graham Hayes," the man's voice says. "The nanny position."

"Oh!" I say, surprised. Who is this calling me? It's certainly not Miss Uptight Perry. "Yes, how can I help you, Mr. Hayes?"

He clears his throat before speaking again, his voice doing weird things to my insides.

"I realize this is very unorthodox, but I'm kind of in a bind here. My housekeeper, Fiona Perry, who you interviewed with, is on vacation and didn't hire anyone yet. I found your resume in a pile and thought maybe you could help me?"

"Yeah, absolutely. What can I do for you?"

"I need a nanny to start right away."

"Okay, like how soon?"

"Tonight. Right now, actually. I'll pay cash."

I don't think twice. I accept the job, jump in my car, and rush to the Hayes' residence. I'm once again reminded just how imposing his residence is when I ring the buzzer at the front gate that is adorned with a massive *H*, for Hayes I assume.

"A little pretentious for my taste," I say as the gate opens and I zip up the driveway.

The moment I pull up to the house, I realize that if he's needing me to stay the night, I didn't bring anything other than the clothes I'm wearing and my wallet. I walk to the front porch and raise my hand to ring the bell when the door swings open and a tall, raven-haired man greets me. I jump back, startled.

Holy shit. Is this him?

I feel my mouth fall open and I instinctively bring my fingers to my lips to make sure I haven't actually just drooled on myself.

If James Bond and Henry Cavill had a baby, it would be Graham Hayes. His long, lean body is wrapped perfectly in what I can only assume is a custom-made tuxedo. He adjusts the cuff link on one of his wrists, his tanned fingers long enough they could probably encircle my waist if he put his hands together.

Suddenly my mouth feels dry and I'm very aware of my scuffed-up Converse and torn jeans, remembering that I just worked a twelve-hour shift and I look every bit the part. I tuck a piece of hair behind my ear that has fallen loose from my braid and try to stand up a little taller, like that's going to cover anything up.

"Miss Silver? Graham Hayes," he says curtly as he extends his hand toward me.

"I thought for sure you were gonna say Bruce Wayne." I laugh but his expression stays stoic. I reach my hand out to shake his and it's completely engulfed.

"Like Batman—never mind. Pleasure to meet you, sir."

"Please, come inside."

He gestures with his right hand, his left still holding the door. I step inside. The woodsy scent of his very expensive cologne envelops me and I have to remind myself to breathe.

But just as I'm almost clear of the doorway, my toe catches the lip and I catapult myself forward. I throw my hands out dramatically to catch myself, somehow making it worse and ending up doing a half somersault while falling into a crumpled pile of embarrassment at his feet.

In all those books and movies I've seen and read, this is the meet cute. This is the part where the handsome stranger gallantly thrusts his arms out and catches the heroine before she falls, their eyes drawn to each other's as her breasts smash against his body and he suddenly realizes she's everything he's been looking for.

But not in my case. Instead, Mr. Hayes makes zero effort to catch me and instead, he shoves his hands in his pockets and looks at me with exasperation, like I'm a bug that he's considering squishing.

2

GRAHAM

I catch myself staring a little too long at the small, impish woman standing on my front porch.

Is this the nanny?

She looks like she's barely bigger than a child herself.

Her strawberry-blond hair is swept up haphazardly in some sort of braid that has fallen, a few stray tendrils clinging to her slender neck. She thrusts her small hand into mine, a smile stretching across her face to her eyes. I feel the warmth of her fingers against the inside of my palm and instantly release it when my mind questions if the rest of her body is this soft and inviting.

I hold back a smile at her Bruce Wayne comment. It was certainly not the first time someone called me that.

I'm completely distracted by the smattering of freckles across her nose and cheeks that come into view once she steps over the threshold and into the entryway. Then suddenly she tumbles forward, landing in a heap at my feet.

"Are you alright, Miss Silver?"

I keep my hands in my pockets, too scared to reach out and touch her again.

"Yup." She stands, adjusting her shirt. "Only my pride is hurt."

I close the door behind her. "Please." I gesture for her to step into the parlor to the right of the entrance. I pick up her resume from the table where I placed it and we both take a seat opposite one another.

She looks nervous, her fingers knotting together in her lap as she sits up board straight.

"You can relax," I say, but she just offers a tight-lipped smile.

"I apologize for the out-of-the-blue call and fire drill request to have you work this evening, but my housekeeper, Miss Perry, is unfortunately on vacation and she failed to procure a new nanny before she left."

"I had assumed that the position had been filled when I didn't hear back from her."

I give her a questioning look and she continues. "Well, after I interviewed a week or so ago, I followed up with two phone calls and left her a voicemail, but I didn't hear anything back." She shrugs.

"Hmm." That is strange considering Miss Silver's impeccable background in education and her relevant work experience with young children. I'm not sure what Miss Perry's angle is recently; it's been like pulling teeth to get her to hire a new nanny ever since my last one had to return home to attend to some family business. I don't express any of this out loud; instead, I read over her resume again.

"Is there a reason you're not returning to teach music education at Jefferson Elementary? Or are you only looking for a summer position since you're a teacher?"

"I, uh, the position was downsized unfortunately. I was told that our funding wasn't renewed so they had to cut the program. Which is such a shame because I don't think people truly realize how important introducing music and teaching children to read music and play instruments really is. Such a transferable life skill if you ask me."

I didn't. I think it myself, but I can appreciate someone who is passionate about their career.

"Have you ever been a nanny or live-in caretaker before?" I lean back in my chair and watch as she shakes her head vigorously. She's young. Based on her graduation date, I'd guess she's barely over twenty-five.

"I haven't but I have spent my entire professional career wrangling children of all ages for several hours a day." She lets out another nervous laugh that wrinkles her nose and it's fucking adorable.

Nope. Get that thought out of your head.

"I love kids. I'm such a believer in enriching not only their lives with skills but also their day-to-day experiences, ya know? They're like little sponges; they just soak everything up so it's a waste to just stick them in front of a screen all day."

Her nervousness seems to have subsided. She's speaking animatedly, gesturing with her hands and laughing and smiling.

"Eleanor is five. It's just me and her. Her mother is not in the picture any longer. I need someone extremely reliable and the live-in portion is non-negotiable. I travel a lot for work. I'm gone early and often not home till late so I need someone that can really take the reins. I'm not looking for someone who needs babysitting themselves. Miss Perry is always around during the work hours to assist with anything, but to be clear, childcare and anything that goes along with it is not her job."

She nods her head vigorously as she pulls out her phone and taps around before holding it in front of her face and typing vigorously.

"Am I boring you, Miss Silver?" I can't hide the annoyance in my voice. Maybe it's a generational thing, but these damn phones are always in people's faces to the point it's exhausting.

"Oh, no. Sorry. I'm just taking notes on everything."

I nod and continue.

"As I was saying, all childcare-related responsibilities fall to you, including food preparation, meal times, laundry, classes, and schooling, etc. This position is six days a week. Sundays are yours and sometimes even Saturdays. There is an extensive outlined book detailing any and all preferences, allergies, likes and dislikes, contact information for doctors and teachers. Do you have any questions?"

She looks through her phone notes for a moment before her eyes dart upward to find mine.

"So, did you just want me for the night, or do I have the job?"

The words did you want me for the night shoot straight to my dick.

"The job is yours if you want it, Miss Silver." I toss her resume on the table next to me.

"Oh my God. Absolutely! Thank you so much, Mr. Hayes. I promise I won't let you down."

"Great. I'll sort out everything with Miss Perry when she's back. I assume she shared the compensation details. She'll have you fill out the proper tax documents and insurance information. As for tonight" —I glance at my watch and see that I need to leave in the next twenty minutes—"I have a work event that I cannot miss so I'll need you to watch Eleanor. I don't need you to spend the night. You can start work on Monday. That way you can move into your room this weekend. I'll have Miss Perry show you that on Saturday or Sunday. She'll call you."

I stand and she does as well, her big green eyes staring at me as she nods her head at what I'm saying.

"I'll introduce you to Eleanor."

I walk up the main staircase and down the hallway to Eleanor's room, Miss Silver on my heels. I raise my hand to knock when she shoots her hand out to grab my wrist. I stop and slowly turn my head to face her.

"Sorry, but, um, really quick question. Is she okay with a new nanny? I mean, is she onboard with this or is it going to be one of those situations where she's angry at me?" The nervousness is back as she grips my wrist.

I slowly maneuver myself out of her grip just as the bedroom door opens and Eleanor stands there, hip cocked.

"What's going on?" she says with her best suspicious look on her face. I squat down till I'm eye level with her.

"Eleanor, this is Miss Silver, your new nanny. She is a music teacher that loves kids and she's very excited to meet you and get to know you."

I turn to look back at Miss Silver. Her hands are knotted together as she smiles and then robotically waves at Eleanor.

"Hi, so lovely to meet you, Miss Eleanor. I'm Margot and I have to say your princess dress is by far the prettiest and most pink dress I've ever seen!"

I watch as Eleanor's eyes light up at the compliment and the way Miss Silver naturally charms her way into my little girl's heart instantly.

"It is?" Eleanor's big blue eyes almost bug out of her face as she twirls around. "I think so too!" she squeals.

Eleanor reaches for Miss Silver's hand, grabbing it and pulling her through the doorway and past me.

"Wanna see my matching shoes? They have a high heel!" She drags her toward her closet.

"Oh my goodness, those are prettier than anything I could have ever imagined. You look like you should be in a Disney movie with little birdies singing all around you and chipmunks and bunnies sitting at your feet."

"An, an, and cats? I love cats." Eleanor is instantly entranced.

I give Miss Silver a slight nod. "Eleanor, Daddy has to go to a work event. Please be on your best behavior."

"Bye, Daddy." She waves dismissively, her attention fully on showing Miss Silver her animal collection.

I close the door behind me and start back downstairs. It warms my heart that Eleanor is such a receptive little girl and that someone like Miss Silver can bring her the warmth and connection she needs.

Ever since her mom died when she was only six months old, I've struggled. I want to be engaged with her, to give her the kind of love and life she deserves and needs, but every time I look in her big, blue eyes, all I see is her mother, Meredith, and all the pain of that loss comes rushing back.

Some days it feels like just yesterday I was happy and fun-loving. I was ecstatic to be a father. I loved every second of Meredith's pregnancy cravings and mood swings. I know that sounds crazy, but nothing made me happier than running to three stores at eleven at night to find the very specific brand of cracker she was craving.

We met when the telecommunications company I had founded, landed a contract with the hospital she was a director at. I was instantly drawn to her, moth to the flame and all that, but she wasn't interested. She was focused on her career, had just gotten out of a toxic marriage, and was ready to dominate her thirties and travel the world. But I'm nothing if not persistent and after begging her for a first date that lasted a full twenty-six hours of just talking and sharing a bottle of wine, we both realized we were meant to be.

We were inseparable after that.

Nine months later we were married.

We enjoyed our time as newlyweds but after five years, we decided that our family of two was ready to be a family of three. Meredith got pregnant pretty easily, had no major complications, and was an instant natural at being a mother. She radiated pure joy and contentment.

Some of my favorite memories were those two and three a.m. feedings. She'd get Eleanor and come back to our bed and lean against me. We'd both sit there and just stare at our baby girl, gushing over how beautiful she was, who she looked like, how we both never thought love like this existed.

It was bliss... until two months later when Meredith's postpartum symptoms became strange and unbearable. After several tests, a CT scan revealed a large tumor on one of her ovaries. The biopsy came back as cancerous and unfortunately, it had already spread to her uterus and her other ovary. They did an emergency hysterectomy but it was too late. Within three months she had wasted away to nothing and the doctors had said there was nothing they could do.

One month later, she took her final breath as I held her hand and sobbed.

I grab my phone and wallet and head outside to meet my driver Phil and head to my work event.

"Good evening, Mr. Hayes."

"Evening, Phil," I say, ducking into the car as Phil closes the door behind me.

I glance up at the house, seeing the light in Eleanor's room still on, that image of Miss Silver at my feet dancing in my head, accompanied by her words, *Did you only want me for the night?* I shake the thoughts away just as quickly as they appear and attempt to make small talk with Phil to distract me.

"How are the kids, Phil? Gerald still pursuing biology at Northwestern?"

I stare out the window on the drive as Phil tells me about Gerald's first year in college. I do my best to push any filthy ideas about seeing Miss Silver on her knees in front of me out of my head.

I'm forty-two; the last thing I need to do is get involved with a twenty-something-year-old, especially since she's my nanny.

Even if it's torturous to have her living in my house.

Even if she stirs a desire in me that's been dormant for so long.

I refuse to be that cliché.

3

MARGOT

"The hands are the window to the dick."

"What?" I furrow my brow at Shelly's statement.

"Well, you know how they say the eyes are the window to the soul? My theory is that the hands are the window to a dude's dick." She says this very emphatically like it's a validated scientific theorem.

"I thought they myth-busted that rumor about the distance between the thumb and forefinger or whatever having a correlation to size?"

"Oh no, I'm not talking about size." She takes a bite of her panini as she continues to shake her head. She chews and swallows before finishing.

"I'm talking ability. Motion in the ocean, baby. I think if a man has nice manicured hands and knows how to subtly gesture with his hands, it directly correlates to his abilities in the bedroom. And don't even get me started on hand placement, like softly touching your waist or the small of your back or your wrist. It's enough to make me positively feral."

I can't help but laugh. Shelly and I hit it off the moment we met at the café I briefly worked at after getting fired. She's the epitome of an extrovert and very confidently speaks her mind. We're very much opposites of each other. She hates school, didn't go to college, and is perfectly content living day to day with no plan, just rolling with life's punches and having a blast.

She's one of those laid-back cool girls. I wish I was more like her.

"Where do you come up with this stuff?" I roll my eyes.

"I grew up on *Cosmo*. My mom had like five hundred of them in her basement and I'd sneak down there and read them after my parents went to bed. Also, TikTok." She smiles before taking another huge bite of her sandwich.

"Well, Mr. Hayes has gorgeous hands"—I draw out the syllable of the word for emphasis—"definitely manicured and he does those little movements like running his finger over his bottom lip or playing with his cuff link..." My words drift off as I picture the way he looked up at me from messing with the small gold bauble.

"Sounds like he knows *exactly* what he's doing." She laughs.

"But," I say, remembering how he failed to help me when I fell, "I stupidly tripped over the doorway and fell, or did like a small somersault thing, and landed at his feet, and he didn't even attempt to catch me or even help me up."

"Hey, I'm not saying guys with good hands are gentlemen or chivalrous. They just know how to fuck." She winks. "Oh, and they know how to fuck your life up too so be careful."

I just laugh and shake my head as thoughts of Graham float away while I drink my mimosa.

"So what's going on with your dating life? How are things with Karter with a *K*?"

"Don't do that." She gives me a pouty look that tells me she's still not fully over him.

"I'm sorry he was just so—" We both burst out laughing and she shakes her head.

"Yeah, he really was. We're not really a thing anymore. Turns out Karter with a *K* was not exactly into monogamy with an *M*."

She shrugs it off but I can see the disappointment in her eyes. I reach out and grab her hand. "Shit, I'm sorry."

"Don't be." She waves it off and picks up her mimosa. "Like I said, guys with good hands can fuck you up. I knew what I was getting into. Any guy that introduces himself like that is a walking red flag. Besides, there's a million more Karters I can fill my bed with."

"Still, you didn't deserve that, especially since he was hyper jealous of you even spending time with me."

"Screw him. I have a new outlook, a new plan for my twenty-fifth year." She wipes her hands on her napkin as her eyebrows bounce up and down. Classic Shelly, always coming up with some harebrained idea to get over one guy and on to the next.

"Oh yeah? What's that?"

"This will be my year of just fun sex. No strings, no attachments, no expectations. If I like someone and we're attracted to each other, then we can hang out and hook up. I'm not saying I'm going to hook up with everyone, just that there's no need for me to be out there looking for someone to settle down with when the reality is, I'm still so young. I'm not ready for shared bank accounts and babies and peeing with the door open." She wrinkles her nose like she's disgusted.

"I think that's great. I feel like that plan suits you. You're good at not catching feelings. I could stand to learn a few lessons from you."

I think about my last *relationship.* If you can even call it that.

Jake Dearborn. The editor of the university newspaper. Captain of the debate team. Star soccer player. Graduated summa cum laude. Only to turn around and give it all up to live in a van and travel across America sharing his experience via YouTube.

It sounds noble and amazing, a talented and gifted young man who gives it all up to pursue his dream and passion for traveling and sharing his experiences with the world.

At least, that was the image he portrayed to everyone.

The reality was, after graduation, his daddy handed him a trust fund that had more money in it than most of us will see in five lifetimes. So he had no obligations, no bills, and no reason to slum it with me anymore. I was merely a distraction for him while he was in college.

Actually, his words were, "You were a challenge and you know I can't back down. I had an amazing time with you, Margot Dargo." One day, he made up the stupid and pointless nickname that had zero backstory. "But this is my quest. I need to go experience life and all her hardships to become the man I need to be. I need to find who I really am beneath all these accomplishments and accolades. Life has been too easy. I need another challenge. I want to be self-made, like my father."

A challenge? Self-fucking-made? His dad was born a millionaire. I wouldn't exactly call living in a $150,000 custom van complete with every luxury plus some that my tiny studio didn't even have, a hardship. He wouldn't know hardship if it bit him in his mediocre dick. He had all his bills paid, no debt, and an empire to fall back on once his new quest bored him.

Did I scream all of that at him? No, of course not. I smiled and hugged him, wishing him well, and then I went home and cried my eyes out because while I was just a boring challenge to pass the time to him... I loved him.

It wasn't so much of a relationship and more like a sad Taylor Swift ballad about realizing too late that you were just another notch in his belt, but it still meant something to me at the time.

I just can't stand being led to believe that something is more than it is. If someone doesn't want forever with me or doesn't want a relationship, that's okay. Just don't make me believe there's potential when there isn't.

"Well, I need to be heading to the Hayes' estate to move into my new room." I glance at my phone. I didn't receive a call from Miss Perry about what time I should come by this weekend. Instead, she sent me a curt email that simply stated, *Saturday, 1 p.m.*

"Send me pictures of this place," Shelly says as we both hand our credit cards to the waiter. "Oh, and what happened with your apartment since you're not going to be living there anymore?"

"I'm not sure. When I explained my situation to the landlord, he wasn't very sympathetic. He said if I want to break my lease early, I have to pay the entire five months in rent up front which I can't afford to do. I can afford the monthly rent though." I sign my receipt and stand up to walk outside with Shelly.

"That's annoying."

"I know but I don't blame him. He'd be out all that money if I just bailed on the last five months. With my new salary I'll be able to afford to pay out the remaining months, but I really don't want to keep two places. I'll have to work a few weeks in order to save up enough to pay that big chunk of change. I'll figure it out." I turn to face her. "Thanks again for hanging with me this morning and don't worry, I'll make sure to send you pictures of my fancy new digs."

We give each other a hug goodbye and I climb behind the wheel of my car to head out to the suburbs.

"Miss Silver." Miss Perry opens the front door and ushers me inside. "I must say I was surprised to return from my vacation to see that you had been hired on. This way to your quarters."

Her snooty attitude is grating, I won't lie, but I give her my best smile anyway. I want to tell her that I was just as surprised to not get a callback, but I keep it to myself.

"I hope you had a great vacation, Fiona," I say as I follow her down the large marble entryway.

She stops dead in her tracks and I almost run into the back of her. She spins around slowly on her heel and I half expect her to have morphed into a zombie or ghost or something. Her face is firm as she crosses her bony arms over her chest. She's wearing another skirt suit, this one a pale pink that matches her nails.

"It's Miss Perry," she hisses the S sound at the end of her name as she gives me a positively vile look.

"Oh, so sorry. My apologies, Miss Perry. I didn't mean to offend," I say, taken aback as I stumble a bit over my words. She acts like someone with a noble title who I've just offended.

Relax, lady. We're in Illinois, not eighteenth-century England.

She turns back around and continues down the hall, her nude, square-toed heels echoing against the floor.

"Phil, Mr. Graham's driver, will bring your things in. He'll also show you where you can park in the garage."

"Is Mr. Graham home today?" I don't know why I ask it. I have no reason to interact with him, but I'd be lying if I didn't admit he seemed to have an instant effect on me.

"Mr. Graham is at the country club," she says as we enter an elevator and ride up to the second floor.

We exit and walk down another long hallway. The walls are adorned with beautiful paintings, most of which I don't recognize, but if I had to bet, I'd say they cost as much as a car and then some. The floors upstairs are a beautiful deep mahogany.

"This"—Miss Perry motions with her arm like she's Vanna White— "is your quarters."

I step around her and peer into the large room and gasp. There's a fireplace, some built-in bookshelves across from a couch, and a few chairs. The ceilings are vaulted and there's massive windows that look out over the grounds. This space alone is bigger than my entire studio apartment.

"This is your private sitting room. The fireplace does work and you can use it. Through here is your bedroom, walk-in closet, and en suite."

I follow her, my mouth still hanging open as I take in my new living quarters. I can see why she called them that instead of just a *room*. This place looks like one of those insane Parisian hotels that cost a fortune for one night.

"Oh my God, there's a balcony." I rush over to the beautiful glass French doors at the far side of the bedroom. "May I?" I ask as I reach for the handle.

Miss Perry offers me an unamused nod and I place a hand on each door, opening them both at the same time and dramatically stepping out onto the balcony. I giggle quietly as I take in the scene before me. I feel like I'm living in a fairy tale. I had no idea that places like this actually existed.

"It's perfect. I'll take it," I say jokingly as I step back through the doors. Miss Perry doesn't bat an eye at my joke. She simply turns and walks back toward the hallway.

"I've left an iPad on the coffee table here. It's connected to the internet and yours to use while you're employed here. You'll see everyone's schedule on there, including Eleanor's." She speaks rapidly as if she's said this all a hundred times.

"You'll also see the daily meal schedule and selection from the chef and you can communicate with him directly for any dietary or allergy restrictions you may have."

I nod along.

"There's also a folder there with all of the paperwork I need you to fill out immediately. Tax and insurance information, a background check form, a drug test, and any emergency contacts you may have."

She continues with her speech. "Tomorrow is Sunday which is always your day off and Eleanor is currently at her grandmother's house until this evening so you are free to get settled, fill out the paperwork, and familiarize yourself with the house and the grounds."

"Will you be showing me around?" I say, following after her as she starts walking down the hall.

"Absolutely not," she says with a hint of laughter. "I have a full-time job. There's an interactive map on the iPad. Use it to show yourself around."

I round the corner just as Phil is exiting the elevator with some of my bags.

"Oh, thank you, sir. Let me," I say, reaching to grab them, but he refuses.

"Not at all, miss; it's my job."

I follow him as he walks the bags into my room.

"I can grab the others, honestly." I feel bad. I've never once had someone wait on me hand and foot. Hell, I've always been too poor to even use a valet or a bellhop at a hotel.

"Not necessary, ma'am."

"Margot," I say, reaching my hand out toward him. He smiles and shakes it.

"Phil." He turns and leaves, assuring me he'll be right back with the rest of my belongings.

I spend the next hour unpacking what little items I have and filling out the paperwork Miss Perry mentioned before I grab my phone and FaceTime Shelly.

"Holy shit, this looks like that place from that movie you love, *Pride and Prejudice*!"

"Uh, you mean the classic novel?" I laugh and Shelly rolls her eyes.

"Seriously, what does this guy do for work again?" I pan around the parlor before flipping the camera back to me.

"And now for my favorite part," I say as I walk into the bedroom and flip the camera back so she can see the open French doors and balcony.

"Does he need a dog? I can bark. Seriously, that place looks unreal!"

"I know and check out this bathroom!" I spin around and run into the bathroom that is also bigger than my entire studio apartment.

The floor and walls are all a gorgeous marble. The dual sinks and massive window-sized mirror hanging above them are simple but elegant. The stand-alone soaker tub looks like you could sink the *Titanic* in it.

"You need to invite me over," she says as I back up to get the entire bedroom into the camera shot. "Whoa, you could have an orgy with like ten people in that bed."

I laugh as I take one more step backward and slam into something warm and hard. I drop the phone and stumble to pick it up, turning around to see Mr. Hayes standing in the doorway to my bedroom.

"Oh," I yelp as I fumble with the phone. I can hear Shelly asking me what the hell is going on. "I'll call you back," I say quickly before hanging up.

"Mr. Hayes, I'm so sorry. I didn't see you there." I can feel heat creeping up my cheeks and I don't understand why I'm such a bumbling mess every time I see this man.

"No apologies necessary. I know I'm encroaching on your private space. I can assure you I don't and won't make a habit of invading your quarters, but I simply wanted to stop in and officially welcome you."

He stands with his hands in the pockets of his gray dress pants, causing them to be pulled taut across his crotch.

Don't look, don't look, don't look! I repeat the phrase over and over in my head.

He has a matching vest that's fitted over his baby-blue dress shirt that has two buttons undone. I see a hint of dark hair at the base of his throat, peppering his tanned skin. I swallow, my mouth feeling like I just chewed on a cotton ball.

"Thank you. It was no intrusion at all. This is your house, after all. I, uh, I filled out most of the paperwork for Miss Perry and I was about to finish that up."

He nods his head as he glances briefly around the room before settling his gaze back on me. His dark eyes focus on mine, making me feel uneasy, I can't help but look away. I glance back in time to see his eyes drop down to my bare feet before slowly making their way up my body and my belly flip-flops.

Suddenly, I feel completely vulnerable. I curl my toes into the carpet, wishing I could disappear. Something about the way Graham Hayes looks at me without saying a word is scarier than standing naked in the middle of Times Square.

"Well, I'll leave you to finish your tasks then," he says as he turns to walk back to the parlor door.

I can't help it; my eyes drop down and take in his magnificent ass. He's got the perfect amount of perky projection—not that I'm an expert on the subject of the male form. God knows my experience ranges from a fumbling virgin freshman year of college to an entitled two-hump-chump that never got me over the finish line... not even once. Suddenly the desire to fall to my knees and bite it erupts in me, and I blush in embarrassment.

I bet Mr. Graham Hayes knows exactly how to make a woman tremble under his touch.

"Oh, and Miss Silver." He turns back to face me, slowly pulling his hand out of his pocket and rubbing his chin with an almost unde-tectable wink. "Let's keep the orgies to a minimum."

4

GRAHAM

I shut the door softly behind me as I exit Margot's quarters.

I had to bite my cheek to keep from chuckling at the way her eyes bugged out of her head when I mentioned orgies. Technically, she mentioned them first.

I had to stop myself from reaching out a hand to steady her when she ran into me. Clumsy little thing. But memories from the way her soft skin felt in my hand the night we first met came flooding back to me.

Only one woman over the years ever had such an impact on me with such a minor touch and that was my late wife, Meredith.

The two women are nothing alike as far as I can tell. Meredith was outspoken and driven, I guess what you'd call an *alpha* female. She wasn't meek or timid in the slightest. She could command a room with just her presence. She was my equal and I was drawn to that.

She challenged me.

Called me out on my bullshit.

From what I've gathered in our short interactions, Miss Silver is the exact opposite. Timid, perhaps a bit naive or innocent.

The kind of woman I have no business wanting to defile. And yet, from the moment I first met her, something has slowly started stirring in me. A desire to have her at my mercy, completely helpless against every filthy fucking thing I want to do to her.

An image of Margot stretched out on my bed, naked, arms and legs tied to the four posts, sends a pang of desire straight to my cock.

Would she beg me? Would she willingly give herself to me?

I bet she'd be fun to tease, I think to myself as I run my hand over my rough five-o'clock shadow. I close my eyes and pinch the bridge of my nose, trying to force images of sweet little Miss Silver begging for release from my mind.

I walk down to the end of the hallway where a large bay window sits, giving an expansive view of the backyard.

I never intended on making this estate my home. It was my late grandfather's house and while Meredith and I never had any use for this much space, she absolutely fell in love with the house when I showed it to her years ago. My mother insisted Meredith and I take it. My father had passed two years before we were married, and my mother couldn't bear to live here alone without him. She moved into a smaller place a few miles away and we moved in here.

I, on the other hand, now can't imagine parting with the house knowing how much it meant to Meredith.

"Sir, can I help you with something?"

The breathy sound of Miss Perry's voice interrupts my thoughts and I turn to face her, offering up a small smile.

"No, just—thinking. How was your vacation?"

I walk to where she's standing and we both turn to head down the main staircase.

"It was nice. Spent some quality time with my sister, sunning ourselves lazily on the beaches of St. Tropez and sipping a few too many fruity cocktails." Her voice is breathy and I know she's putting it on.

"Sounds relaxing."

"Oh, it was. You would love it there." She reaches out and touches my arm softly. "We ended up spending some time on a yacht owned by the Felton brothers. You know them, right? Teddy and Martin?"

Teddy? I know what she's trying to do and I'm not interested.

Nobody besides maybe his mother or whoever he's currently sleeping with calls Theo Felton *Teddy*.

"Yes, I'm very familiar with the Felton brothers," I say as I open the fridge and grab a bottle of water.

"Well, they spoke very highly of you. We certainly had a fabulous time with them and they invited us to join them on their next trip to the Amalfi Coast. I told them I would need at least six months to recover from this last trip and to make sure I have time to work off all those delicious cocktails. Can't be losing my figure before another vacation."

She giggles and it's like nails on a chalkboard. I'm not a total asshole. It's not that I hate Fiona. It's that I can't understand why she insists on using this flirty tone and her attempts to make me jealous.

I very stupidly and drunkenly made the mistake of taking her to bed—*once* a very long time ago. It was shortly after Meredith had passed and I was a wreck. I was lost and lonely and confused and after a few too many glasses of whatever I was even drinking, she found me in my study, and well, the rest is history.

After that night, though, I made it abundantly clear that it was a mistake and I wished her to stay working for me. She agreed and said she completely understood that considering my circumstances, I practiced poor judgment and it meant nothing more than that.

"I'm sure you have nothing to worry about, Miss Perry, and I'm sure the Felton brothers will provide magnificent company on your future vacation. I'll be in my office for the remainder of the evening." I check my watch. "Eleanor will be home from my mother's in a few hours. I've already informed Miss Silver."

I can see a look of disappointment on her face that I didn't take the bait and say something about the Felton brothers or her partying with them. I give her a nod and grab my bottle of water and head back to my office.

I sit down in my desk chair, my eyes landing on Margot's resume. I pick it up and read it for probably the fifth time. It doesn't reveal anything new, but then a thought occurs to me.

Where was she living previously?

I turn to my laptop and type her name into the White Pages website where her address is listed. I search the address and find it's a small apartment building on the west side of the city. There's a phone number listed. I pick up my phone and dial it and it begins to ring.

I'm not sure what I am planning to accomplish with this call. I guess I'm curious if she broke her lease and how much it was. I want to make sure that's covered. I can't imagine a public school teacher makes enough to cover that kind of expense.

"This is Charlie Zelinski," a raspy voice says abruptly on the other end of the line.

"Charlie, this is Graham Hayes. I'm calling about a previous tenant of yours. Margot Silver."

"Yeah, what about her? She's still gonna pay me, right?" And there's my answer.

"Well, that's why I'm calling. She's my live-in nanny now so it's my fault that she had to vacate her apartment early. I'm calling to settle any debt she might have with you."

"Well, ain't you a knight in shining armor. She still had five months on the lease and her monthly rent was thirteen hundred dollars, so that's"—he pauses while he does the calculations—"sixty-five hundred dollars."

Not surprised he's trying to take me for a fool.

"Now, Charlie, we both know that a tenant can break a lease in Chicago and the standard buyout is two to three months' rent."

Sixty-five hundred dollars is nothing to me, but I also can't stand someone who would take advantage of a young woman like that.

He hesitates on the line, his heavy breathing audible. "Fine, three months in full."

"Deal. I'll send my driver over with certified check." I hang up the phone before he argues with me, demanding more which I'm sure he would have done once I said something about having a driver.

I turn back to my computer and sift through a few emails when I see one that instantly makes my blood pressure skyrocket.

Warren Dorsey. A fellow billionaire, albeit a shady motherfucker who nobody in my circle trusts. He's always looking for some tit-for-tat bullshit favors.

I open the email and see that the entire email consists only of what he's written in the subject line: *We need to talk.*

He's gruff and has zero tact. He prides himself on being ruthless and downright cruel to anybody who would dare to compete against him. He got his start in the tech world during the dot com boom and then leveraged his earnings into *acquiring* other failing businesses that couldn't keep up in the market. What he does isn't necessarily illegal but it's unethical, and everyone knows he uses his power and wealth to keep a few elected officials in his pocket.

I let out a deep sigh and pick up the phone to give him a call.

"Graham, my boy." He sounds loud in the receiver. I can tell he has his signature cigar in his mouth. When women talk about a sleazy slimeball, Warren is who they're talking about.

"Mr. Dorsey," I reply.

"Oh, come on now, we're not that formal. Call me Warren."

"Warren. What can I help you with?"

I hear his lips smack around his cigar. "We've got a situation, Graham. We both know that the Felton brothers are twisted little shits."

They're not. They're just thirty-year-old twin brothers that have their dad's expense account at their fingertips and more drive and ambition to expand their family empire than anyone else I've ever met. They're fair and ethical and they've never had a single scandal to their name. Warren's just worried they're coming after his piece of the pie.

"They need to be knocked down a couple rungs in my opinion," he continues.

"So what's the problem they've created for you this time?" I try to humor him. For as much as I can't stand the sniveling dick weasel, he's not an enemy I want if I can help it.

"They've been sweet-talking Tech Titan Industries into a merger. They both know that I've been in bed with Tech Titan for the better part of two years. Sweet-talking those pussies and stroking their G-spot just right so I can buy them out."

I cringe. Everything that comes out of this fucker's mouth is offensive or just plain disgusting.

"And where do I come into this?" I ask.

I can tell he's smiling on the other end of the phone. "I need you to go in there and throw your weight around a little. Maybe convince Tech Titan that merging with the Felton twats will be a mistake. One that they'll regret, if you know what I'm saying?"

"You mean shake them down? Threaten them? Warren, I'm not doing your dirty work for you. I still have a business and reputation to uphold. I'm not a mobster with cronies who walks into global companies and threatens a hostile takeover."

He laughs maniacally and I pull the phone away from my ear.

"Calm down, boy. I don't mean threaten them. I'm talking about a civil sit-down. I'm putting a dinner meeting together with a few of the board members at Tech Titan and I'd appreciate if you were there. Hell, just seeing you at that dinner bodes very well in my favor."

I inhale and let it out slowly, closing my eyes. "And what's in this for me?" I ask the dreaded question.

"I'll make you part owner. Twenty-five percent of the shares."

"I thought it was twenty percent?" I say, reminding him of his last offer.

The last thing I want is to be in bed with Warren Dorsey, but I have to be very careful how I handle a proposition like this. If I refuse and he loses the deal, he'll make sure he comes after me and my next business venture. I've seen him do it to a few others. It's like watching a wildebeest fight for its life on the Serengeti. Slow and agonizing but it always ends in a bloody death.

"I'll consider it, Warren," I say. "Let me know when you plan on setting up the dinner."

"Thanks, boy," he says loudly. I don't know if he tries to be insulting with everything he says. He might have fifteen years on me, but he's not old enough to be my father. Calling me *boy* is his way of letting me know he's got more power, money, and balls than me.

I work through a few other emails, then look at my upcoming schedule and chew through a contract negotiation that's been in the works for several months.

By the time I'm done, it's almost five o'clock and Eleanor should be home any minute. I walk over to my wet bar and pour myself a glass of bourbon, savoring the bitter flavor that numbs my tongue.

I open my office door and walk down the hallway to where I hear laughter and talking. The sounds of Eleanor's high-pitched giggle echo through the entryway. It sends a pain straight to my heart when I think about the fact that it's a sound that Meredith never got to experience.

I lean against the doorway, out of sight from my mother, Eleanor, and Miss Silver as they talk. It appears that Margot has instantly charmed my mother, which isn't an easy task. She's a lovely woman but she can be a bit guarded, especially around people who are raising her granddaughter.

"Oh, you teach music? That's wonderful! I tried to get my Graham to stick with the piano when he was younger, but you can't talk a bull-headed teenager into anything, trust me."

Margot giggles and touches my mom's elbow.

"Oh, I've had a few teenage boys as students who insisted playing an instrument or taking voice lessons was so uncool until I told them that girls love a man who can sing or play an instrument and suddenly they wanted two or three lessons a week."

I grip the glass in my hand tighter. I bet those boys wanted a lot more than music lessons from Miss Silver. If I had to guess, that's why they wanted more lessons. To impress her.

I watch as Eleanor dances around the ladies' feet.

"Look, look what I can do!" she says as she twirls around on one foot for only a few seconds before losing her balance.

"Yay! You look like such a beautiful little ballerina!" Margot says as she and my mother clap and cheer, causing Eleanor to burst into a big smile and pretend to bow.

"I had a wonderful time with you today, sweetheart. Give grandma a hug and kiss." My mother leans down as Eleanor runs to her to oblige her request. "Now, you go listen to Miss Margot and be a good girl. Wash up for dinner."

My mother stands and places a hand on Margot's arm. "It was lovely to meet you, dear. I can't wait for you to bring Eleanor over to the house so we can have some tea and continue to get to know one another."

Margot smiles at her, pulls her in for a warm hug, and reciprocates the desire to get to know my mother better.

I'm not sure how I feel about this, I think to myself as Margot steps back from her embrace and reaches out a hand to Eleanor.

"I'm going to go say hello to my son before heading home. You ladies have a lovely evening."

Margot and Eleanor wave goodbye to my mother as they walk past me to go upstairs. Neither of them notice me, but I can't ignore the way Margot's legs look in her tight jeans. I drag my eyes lazily up them to where they meet her plump ass. I chew my bottom lip as an image of her bent over my desk swims through my brain.

"I don't think that's a good idea," my mother says, startling me out of my trance.

"I don't know what you mean." I sip my bourbon and turn to face my mother.

"She's a lovely young lady, and Eleanor already is very fond of her. Don't screw it up, Graham." My mother gives me her best stern look, the one that says she means business. It was the same look that kept me in line through my youth.

"Wouldn't dream of it, Mother."

She gives me a quick hug and a peck on the cheek before asking me how I'm doing. I answer quickly because I know a quarter of the time, this line of questioning from her ends up with, *are you dating? Have you met anyone? You need to get back out there.* All of which I have no interest in talking about.

"Sir, will you be joining Miss Silver and Eleanor for dinner?" Fiona interrupts us.

"I'll eat later," I say, finishing the rest of my drink as my mother scowls at me.

Fiona nods and walks away, her heels clicking behind her.

"Go eat with your family. That little girl is growing up fast and you're missing out on so much."

I'm not in the mood.

"Mother, always a pleasure to see you." I give her a big smile and she releases an audible sigh.

"I mean it, I like this nanny. She's good for Eleanor. Try to remember that next time you stare at her like she's something to eat." She raises her eyebrow at me before straightening her back and turning to walk to the front door where her driver is waiting for her.

Miss Silver isn't just something to eat; she's a mouthwatering morsel that I want to devour. I look down at my empty tumbler and head back to my office for another.

If I'm going to resist temptation, I'll need something else to tantalize my taste buds.

5

MARGOT

"Is Daddy coming?" Eleanor takes a bite of her pasta as we eat dinner at the large kitchen table.

I glance over my shoulder at Miss Perry who looks like she's preparing a plate on the kitchen island.

"Uh, Miss Perry?"

She doesn't bother looking up from her task when she answers. "Does it look like he's coming?"

I snap my head around at her curt remark and turn my body to face her. "There's no need to be rude to a child, Miss Perry. She was simply asking a question."

The spoon in her hand clatters loudly back into the dish as she lifts her eyes to meet my gaze.

"I wasn't being rude, Miss Silver." She spits my name out like it's bitter. "Mr. Hayes will be eating later, as he always does. Eleanor knows this and knows not to bother him. She's been told this several times." She looks down her long, thin nose at Eleanor as she says the words.

"I'm sorry, sweetie." I reach out a hand and hold Eleanor's in mine as her bottom lip quivers. I'm not sure if it's in response to Miss

37

Perry's condescending tone or the fact that her daddy isn't going to eat dinner with us.

"How about after dinner we play on the piano? I can teach you how to play 'Mary had a Little Lamb.' How does that sound?"

Eleanor nods and her pouty lip turns upward into a smile as she shovels another bite of pasta into her mouth, red sauce gathering at the corners.

"Mr. Hayes prefers silence in the evenings," Miss Perry says as she picks up her plate and stares at me. "Perhaps you can play the piano another day." She spins on her heel and walks out of the kitchen.

"Don't listen to her." I nudge Eleanor's shoulder. "She's just grumpy she wasn't invited to play with us."

Eleanor giggles and we both go back to eating our dinner. After we finish, I clear our plates and walk over to the massive freezer.

"Let's see what we can find for dessert." I glance around and find several pints of ice cream in the door. I hear the scrape of Eleanor's chair on the floor as she jumps down and runs over to look at the ice cream flavors with me.

"Cookie dough!" she shouts as I read off the flavors to her. "No, cookies and cream!" She's overwhelmed with excitement, her little eyes shifting back and forth as I see her try to make up her mind. It's adorable.

"How about a little of both?" I grab the pints and look through the cabinets till we find some small sundae dishes.

"You know what would really make this great?" Eleanor shrugs. "Whipped cream," I whisper and her eyes light up.

"And sprinkles!" She claps.

"And sprinkles."

I scoop us both up a small portion and top them with the whipped cream and sprinkles. We sit back down at the table and enjoy our ice cream as Eleanor tells me all about her dream pet kitten.

"And she's white and fluffy and has a cute little pink bow." She licks the whipped cream off her spoon that has run down her fingers. "And she says EEYOW!" She mimics the meowing of a cat.

"She sounds absolutely perfect. What would you name her?"

She scrunches up her face like she's thinking through a math problem, taking the question very seriously.

"Um, maybe muffin or cupcake."

"Have you ever had a pet before?" She shakes her head and it makes me sad for her. I grew up with a few different pets over the years, a dog named Rascal that we had for twelve years and two cats. Guppy and Walter both lived well into their mid-to-late teen years.

We finish up our sundaes and place our dishes in the sink before washing our hands and making our way to the sitting room where the grand piano is situated.

I still haven't walked around this entire house yet. It'll probably take me a week or two just to explore all the rooms. The sitting room, as Mr. Hayes called it, is to the right of the grand atrium of the house. It doubles as a library, with large built-in shelves filled with books that I have every intention of exploring at a later date.

There's a fireplace so large I could walk into it in the front, center of the room along with several couches and chairs.

I pull out the bench on the piano and take a seat, Eleanor climbing up to sit next to me.

I start with some general lessons. "This is called a piano key, and this is middle C." I point to the key and tap it a few times.

"Now you do it," I say. She touches it softly. "You can press down harder," I say and she does. A smile spreads across her face at the sound it makes.

"Miss Bridgette wouldn't let me play the piano. She said Miss Perry said it's not for kids."

Miss Bridgette must be the nanny that worked here previously. I'm confused at her comment. Why would Miss Perry insist on not touching the piano when the ad clearly stated they wanted someone with musical experience? Miss Perry is starting to sound and seem a bit like an uptight woman who doesn't care for children at all.

"Well, that's just nonsense. Pianos are for everyone."

Eleanor and I spend a few moments tapping around on the piano before she tells me to play her a song. We start with "Mary had a Little Lamb," both of us singing along to it a few times before I start in with "Baby Shark."

Eleanor laughs and belts the song at the top of her lungs, pretending to play along with me as she hits a few keys.

"Miss Silver, if you could please keep it down!"

Miss Perry's shrill voice startles us both as we remove our hands from the piano keys.

"Mr. Hayes is working in his office just down this hall and that racket is absolutely distracting."

She stands with her hand on her hip, the other pin-straight at her side.

"Apologies, Miss Perry." I smile sweetly at her. "Eleanor and I will be heading upstairs momentarily to get her bath and play in her room for a bit before bed. Give Mr. Hayes my apologies?"

She nods and walks away without another word, leaving Eleanor and me in a fit of giggles.

After her bath, I help Eleanor dress for bed and brush her teeth. She shows me her favorite stuffed animals and explains how she got each one, what their name is, and on what days of the week she sleeps with each one. I can remember doing this same thing, insisting that no stuffed animal be left behind because I didn't want to hurt their feelings if I didn't sleep with one of them.

I tuck her into bed and read her the book she picked out.

"Is Daddy mad at you?" she asks as I place the book back onto the shelf.

"I don't think so." I furrow my brows, confused as to what she's referring to.

"Cuz we were loud on the piano," she says and I walk back over to her bed.

"Oh no, sweetheart. I'm sure he wasn't mad at all. Miss Perry just didn't like the noise is all." I brush her hair out of her eyes.

"When Daddy is mad at me, he kisses me on the forehead to tell me sorry."

"That's very sweet of him. That's what mommies and daddies do."

"Do they kiss each other when they're mad?"

I nod, a little worried with the territory these questions are heading into. "Mm-hmm, mommies and daddies kiss each other to say sorry too. Does your daddy come tell you good night?" I ask quickly, hoping to change the subject.

"No." She shakes her head and squeezes her stuffed doll, her eyes getting heavy.

"Good night, Eleanor." I lean down and kiss her forehead. "I'm just down the hall if you need anything, okay?"

She nods her head and closes her eyes. I stand and exit the room, closing the door softly behind me.

The fact that Mr. Hayes doesn't say good night to his daughter bothers me. I can tell there's distance there, like he's avoiding her for some reason.

It's not my business but maybe if I pop into his office and tell him that Eleanor is down for the night, it will prompt him to go upstairs and tell her good night. At least I can plant the seed and hope that eventually he'll take the hint.

I make my way back downstairs and turn the corner to walk down the long hallway to where Miss Perry mentioned his office was located.

I take a few steps and then stop, looking into a giant mirror hanging on the wall. I pat down a few flyaway hairs and give my cheeks a little pinch to bring some life into my otherwise pale face. My makeup is simple, as usual. Just some tinted moisturizer, bronzer on my cheekbones and eyelids that never seems to actually bronze my face, mascara, and well-worn-off gloss.

I pull the loose ponytail out of my hair and bend over to fluff my hair a little. When I lift my head back up, my strawberry-blond curls are fluffed up, giving me a bit more of a mature look rather than the freckle-faced teenager most people assume I am.

My stomach fizzles a little at the thought that I'm suddenly very aware of my appearance when I know I'm going to be in Mr. Hayes' presence.

We all care what we look like. It's totally normal, I think, trying to convince myself that's all it is and not the beginnings of a crush. Because *that* would be a big mistake.

I continue walking down the hallway. Suddenly I can hear muffled voices and I realize that this must be his office. I'm about to raise my hand to knock when I hear my name hissed by who I know is Miss Perry.

I know I shouldn't, but I lean my head a little closer to the door, my ear almost pressed against it.

"Miss Silver doesn't like taking direction, sir. I told her not to be banging on the piano at this time of night and she took Eleanor and their sticky ice cream fingers and did it anyway!"

I don't hear a response from him, so I lean a little closer and hold my breath.

"Sir, did you hear me?"

"Yes, Miss Perry. I heard you and I don't care if Miss Silver and Eleanor play the piano. I want her to learn music."

Relief washes over me when I hear his response.

"But, sir, that was Meredith's piano."

My breath catches in my throat. I had no idea about that fact.

"She just picked it out. She never touched it, didn't even know how to play," he responds, sounding very uninterested in her argument.

I hear a change of tone in Miss Perry's voice, going from shrill to syrupy sweet.

"I'm sorry, sir. Did I do something wrong? I feel like you're incredibly tense and I will absolutely make sure that the right person is hired for the nanny position this week."

"Margot is perfectly adequate, Miss Perry. I don't know why you took so long in the first place to hire someone."

"Margot?" I hear the surprise in her voice, and I can only assume it's because he called me by my first name, something he hasn't done in front of me.

"Yes, Miss Silver." I can hear the agitation growing in his voice. "Now if you please, Miss Perry. I have some work I need to finish up before my work trip next week."

"But Mr. Ha—"

"Enough!" I hear him bark and it causes me to jump back. "Miss Silver is the new nanny. She is more than adequate and until she proves otherwise, I don't want to hear another word about it."

I can hear my heart thumping in my chest. I turn and sprint down the hall back toward the parlor before Miss Perry can open the door. I hear her heels clicking at a rapid pace. I peek my head around the door and see her stomping up the stairs, hands balled into fists.

I giggle to myself at her petulant display and go back to looking over the books on the shelves. I'm reading over the names when suddenly the thought hits me that Miss Perry *likes* Mr. Hayes.

Is that why she didn't call me back? Is she jealous of another woman in the house?

I shrug at the thought and run my fingertips over the spines of the books. I pull one from the shelf. *The Two Magics: The Turn of the Screw* and *Covering End* by Henry James. Two of my favorite books.

I open the cover. "Holy shit!" I say as I close it cautiously and put it back on the shelf.

"Something startle you?"

I jump and clutch my chest. Mr. Hayes is standing in the doorway eyeing me.

"Did you know that's a first edition?" I say, thumbing toward the book I just put back on the shelf.

"I'm aware," he says, and I feel a little silly asking him that. Of course he knows. It's his house, his books.

"It doesn't bother me if you handle them or read them. That's what they're there for." He shoves his hands deep into his pockets and I realize that he's still in his dress pants, oxfords, and vest. Even his thick black hair is still perfectly in place.

Does he ever just throw on sweats and chill?

The image of him in gray sweats causes my cheeks to flame and I turn my attention back to the shelf, praying he doesn't notice.

"Miss Silver, I have a business trip coming up on Monday. I'll be gone for a few days, but you have my contact information and so does

Miss Perry. Also, my mother is close by should you need any assistance with Eleanor."

He turns before I can say anything and walks out. I let out a sigh of relief. But just as quickly he's back.

"Oh, and Miss Perry mentioned she still needs your paperwork so if you could finish that and give it back to her tonight."

"Yes, it's done. I meant to give it to her before dinner and forgot."

He nods but this time he doesn't walk away. He just stands there and I'm unsure what else to say so I go back to looking at the books.

"You like to read?" I look back at him.

"Not particularly." His tone is flat, uninviting.

I see a copy of *The Phantom of the Opera* on the shelf above my head. I stand on my tiptoes, extending my arm as I reach for it but it's just a little too far out of my grasp. I fall back on my heels and suddenly, I feel Mr. Hayes' presence right behind me.

I can feel the warmth of his chest inches from my back as he extends his arm and grabs the book, bringing it down to my hands. The movement causes his cologne to waft in the air. It smells rich and warm and causes my belly to tingle.

"Thank you." My voice sounds breathy, like it doesn't belong to me. I spin around but he's already walking back to the door.

"Have you ever re—"

"Good night, Miss Silver," he cuts me off and exits the room, walking back down the hall toward his office.

I feel light-headed and dizzy and suddenly I realize I've been holding my breath. I exhale a shaky breath and clutch the book to my chest before walking out of the parlor and sprinting up the stairs to my bedroom.

I place the book on my nightstand and grab the papers I need to give to Miss Perry. Her room is a few doors down from mine so I walk over and knock softly on her door.

"Miss Perry, I have the paperwork you need from me."

The door opens and she greets me with a fake smile, holding her hand out toward me. I place the papers in her hands, and she goes to shut the door, but I put my hand up to stop her.

"I'm sorry but I have a quick question." I can see by the scowl on her face she's already annoyed with me.

"Eleanor has been talking a lot about getting a cat. I asked her if she ever had a pet and she said no."

"And?" Miss Perry says, not seeing where I'm going with this.

"Well, I didn't know if Mr. Hayes would be open to it. I know the posting said 'no animals' but I assume that meant he didn't want the new nanny bringing along pets, but do you think he'd be okay with Eleanor getting a kitten? I would absolutely make sure she took care of it. I'd teach her and help her."

Miss Perry's scowl morphs into a big smile that reaches all the way up to her eyes. It reminds me of that scene in the cartoon version of *How the Grinch Stole Christmas* when he gets the idea to dress up as Santa and rob Whoville of all the presents.

"You know, I think he would absolutely adore a kitten." Her voice has morphed into that overly sweet tone that I heard her speaking in earlier behind closed doors. "I'll make sure I tell him but if I were you, I would absolutely go adopt a kitten for little Eleanor. Mr. Hayes will be very happy she has something to occupy her time. He's actually a huge animal lover himself."

"Oh, wow! I'm actually shocked, I thought for sure you'd say it's a bad idea. I'll double-check with hi—"

She darts her hand out and places it on mine. "No, no, don't trouble yourself, sweetie. Honestly, he does whatever I tell him so it's probably best I'm the one who mentions it. I'll be sure to tell him tomorrow morning before his trip so you and Eleanor can pick one out this coming week." She gives my hand a squeeze, then she winks.

"Okay." I shrug. "Sounds great! And thanks so much. I super appreciate your help on this. Have a good night."

"Good night, dear." She smiles and it seems genuine, then she softly closes the door.

Maybe I misread her and we just got off on the wrong foot. I'm glad to see she seems to be taking the talk Mr. Hayes had with her earlier to heart.

I head back to my room and run a warm bath and light a candle to settle in and read a few chapters of *The Phantom of the Opera* but every few sentences, my mind drifts back to the feeling of Mr. Hayes standing so close to my body, and that warm fluttery feeling settles in my belly.

6

GRAHAM

I take the rest of my bourbon in hand and trudge up the stairs toward my bedroom. It's late, nearing midnight, and I'm the last one still up. The rest of the house is dark and silent.

I step onto the landing of the second floor, hesitating momentarily. I glance down the long hallway, swirling the remaining liquid in my tumbler.

My bedroom is on the third floor of the house. Originally, Meredith and I used the room that Margot is now living in. In fact, the other night when I stepped in there and startled her was the first time I'd been in there since Meredith died.

Against my better judgment, I take a right and walk down the hallway until I'm standing in front of Margot's door. I have no idea what I'm doing. I take a sip of the liquor, bringing my free hand to rest on the doorframe. I lean my head forward till it's resting against the door.

I don't hear anything coming from inside the room which is good. If she were to open her door right now, she'd probably scream and think I was a fucking creep. In her imaginary defense, I am.

I wonder if she's fast asleep. I also wonder what she sleeps in. Silk? A matching pajama set? Maybe just an oversized shirt and nothing else. I feel myself growing hard at the images my brain is conjuring. I let my hand fall from the doorframe to the handle before realizing what I'm doing and I step back like it burned me.

Anger surges through me. Anger at myself for wanting her so badly. Misguided anger at her for tempting me just by simply existing in my presence.

I don't know what power this woman has over me or why it was such an all-consuming and instant infatuation with her. I know better. This is gross and unprofessional. She's young and naïve; she trusts me not to invade her space and cross her boundaries.

I walk back down the hallway, making my way up to the third floor to my bedroom.

"I need a cold shower."

The next morning I wake early to pack my overnight bags for my trip this morning. I double-check the time. My private plane departs in an hour. I grab my bags and head downstairs where my driver Phil is waiting to take them to the car.

"Good morning, sir." Phil gives me a nod as he takes the bags.

I walk to the kitchen and grab an espresso, downing the shot and chasing it with a bottle of water.

"Good morning, Mr. Hayes!"

Margot's chipper voice surprises me and I turn around to give her a nod before walking back toward the front door.

"Oh, sir, sorry to bother you, but I was wondering about something?"

I let out an exaggerated exhale as she follows behind me. I'm already running late and the last thing I need or want is a slew of questions.

"Yes?"

"Would it be okay for me to drive Eleanor in my own car? The reason I ask is because I saw there's this really cool exhibit happening at the children's museum and I thought she would absolutely love it."

"Miss Silver."

"Oh, and what about the zoo? I know some people are really

against zoos and I wasn't sure if that would scare her or if she's allergic to—"

"Miss Silver." I say the words loudly this time and she stops mid-sentence with a small jump. "I told you previously to consult Miss Perry on these matters. I'm late."

The words come out harsher than I mean them, and I see her countenance fall.

"I'm sorry. That was harsh. Yes, you can drive her and take her to both of those places. That being said, please ask Miss Perry to give you the book that has all of the information you need regarding Eleanor. Read it thoroughly and double-check it before asking more questions."

I step forward and reach for the door.

"Sir, are you going to call Eleanor while you're away on business?"

I give her a questioning look.

"She'll miss you. She already asks about you when you're at the office all day. Just thought it might be nice for her to hear your voice while you're gone." She folds her hands together as they hang in front of her.

"Why don't you let me worry about that."

I open the door just as Phil steps up onto the porch. "Sir," he says, motioning toward his watch.

"Aren't you going to tell her goodbye?" I grip the door handle tightly, flashing Phil an apologetic smile before turning back and stepping inside. Margot smiles at me as I walk past her and take the stairs two at a time till I'm at Eleanor's door.

I knock softly and open it to find her sitting on the floor with a pile of construction paper and markers.

"Eleanor, I'm leaving for a work trip. I'll be gone for a few days."

"I know, Daddy. Miss Margot told me."

I crouch down to where she's coloring and tilt her chin up to look at me. I study her big blue eyes as they dart back and forth. She looks so much like her mother.

"Give me a hug goodbye," I say as I fall onto my knees and open my arms. She stands up and walks into my arms, wrapping her arms around my neck as I hold her tightly against me. I close my eyes briefly as I savor the moment before planting a kiss on her forehead and standing back up.

"Be good for Miss Silver and Miss Perry, sweetheart. I love you."

"Love you too, Daddy," she says as she goes back to coloring.

I make my way back downstairs and think I've dodged a bullet when I don't see Margot anywhere. I'm about to shut the door behind me when I feel resistance and hear her voice again. I can't help but roll my eyes.

What is with this annoying woman?

"Oh, one more thing, sir." She's handing me a piece of paper with scribbles on it. "It's a card from Eleanor. She drew it earlier this morning and wanted to make sure you took it with you so you wouldn't forget her."

I take the paper and nod at Margot.

"Have a safe trip." She smiles.

I finally slide into the back seat of the car and make my way to the airfield.

"She's something else, isn't she." Phil laughs, interrupting my thoughts as I stare at the picture Eleanor made me.

I shake my head. "She really is. A little annoying," I mutter, and he laughs even harder.

"It's nice having some young energy around the house. Earlier this morning she saw me outside and came over to make small talk. Asked me about fifteen questions about this car. Said she'd never heard of a Maybach before."

"What was she doing out that early?"

"Out for a run I believe, sir."

Silence falls between us as I imagine her running the grounds, her tempting little body wrapped in spandex.

"She's young, sir. I'm sure she's just enthusiastic about her new job, and if I may speak freely?" I mumble my approval and he continues. "She's probably intimidated by you."

My eyes snap to his in the rearview mirror. "Intimidated?" I arch an eyebrow because he didn't see how she just demanded I say goodbye to my own daughter and then proceeded to school me on how I should call her while I'm away. She's not wrong but I'm not exactly used to be being brought to task by the hired help.

"Yes, sir. She said as much in our brief chat this morning."

I lean back, letting the thought marinate in my brain for the rest of the drive. I like the idea of her being intimidated by me. I want her to be scared. I want her to keep her distance and stop trying to make small talk and get to know me. Not because I'm just a grumpy asshole but because for as much as I want to snap at her, to tell her to mind her business and keep her distance from me, I also crave her. I don't trust myself to keep my distance from her. I feel like I'm a ticking time bomb and it's only a matter of time before I give in and do or say something stupid.

I land in New York, then check into my hotel and head out to meet with my clients. We spend the afternoon in meetings at their headquarters in Manhattan and by the time I return to my room, it's after nine p.m. Eleanor will have been asleep for hours at this point. I feel terrible but I promise myself that I'll make time to call her tomorrow.

I'm exhausted. I order room service and work for another two hours before calling it a night and falling asleep in front of the television.

The next morning, it's the same thing all over again. My first meeting starts at eight a.m., but I get up a few hours early to catch up on work before I head into the office.

I decide to hit the streets for a morning run, inspired by Margot's run yesterday. I've always made it a point to keep myself in shape. I'm naturally lean and tall, but I make sure to stay on top of a healthy diet and regular exercise. I finish a five-mile run in Central Park, then grab a cup of coffee from a cart on my way back to the hotel. I promise myself that I'll make time to call Eleanor tonight before the day gets away from me.

* * *

I CHECK my phone as we arrive at the restaurant. It's already pushing seven p.m. here in New York, which is six p.m. back home. Eleanor will have eaten dinner by now and is probably playing before she takes her bath and gets ready for bed. Guilt eats at me when I realize I've fucked up again. I finish my old-fashioned and slide the glass across the bar.

"Expecting a call?" Jerry, one of the guys, nudges me as I slide my phone back into my pocket. "Got a lady waiting for you back at the hotel?" He laughs hysterically, his large round belly bouncing as his already glowing cheeks redden even more.

He's had at least four drinks to my one and from the looks of it, he's probably a functioning alcoholic.

"My daughter back home." I smile. "I kind of told my nanny that I'd be better at telling my daughter good night." I didn't actually tell Margot that, but that's what my intentions were.

"The nanny," he says again before nudging me and laughing even harder as a few of the other men join in.

"Well, don't hold back. Let's see a picture of her!" another one adds.

"Is she young?"

Instantly, I have to tell myself not to haul off and punch this sleazeball right in the fucking mouth. Instead, I just motion to the bartender for a second old-fashioned. I'd planned on stopping at one, but if I have to sit through another few hours with these idiots, I'm going to need some liquid assistance.

"Gentlemen, I'd prefer to leave my private life private. Looks like our table is ready." I motion toward the hostess who is approaching us.

"Hey, sweetheart. Are you on the menu?" Jerry asks the young woman as she gestures toward our table.

I can tell by the look on her face she's used to this kind of bullshit from drunken assholes.

"My apologies," I say to her as I flash a sympathetic smile. "I'll tighten his leash."

By the time I've left the restaurant, I've had three drinks and it's just after ten p.m., which means it's nine p.m. at home and I've missed my chance to call Eleanor. I pour myself a little more bourbon when I get back to my room. I loosen my tie and pull it over my head, tossing it and my vest onto the chair and kicking off my shoes.

I'm not quite drunk but I'm certainly tipsy. The normal care I take with my clothes seems less important as I open the balcony door and take a seat on one of the lounge chairs. The city lights flicker like diamonds against the night sky. From this height, it feels eerily quiet in Manhattan. There are just a few dull sirens and a horn honking in the distance.

I pull my phone out of my pocket and flick through my contacts till I pull up Margot's number. I hit dial and wait for her to pick up.

"Hello?" She sounds confused.

"Miss Silver." My voice sounds deeper than usual, the effect of the alcohol and talking all night I assume.

"Everything okay, sir?"

Sir. Such an innocent little word that when spoken by her sends all sorts of thoughts racing through my brain.

"No. I fucked up." The bourbon has clearly lowered my inhibitions.

"Oh?"

"I meant to call Eleanor, but time got away from me."

"I understand. Did you want me to wake her up?"

"No, that's not necessary," I say, unsure where this conversation is going or why I even called this late when I damn well knew my daughter was already asleep. From her questioning tone, it's clear Margot is wondering the same thing.

"Did she have a good day?"

"She did. She drew you another picture for your office and we went to the children's museum which she loved. It really wore her out though." She giggles and I can picture her plump pink lips curling up into that beautiful smile.

"That's good. Did *you* have a good day?" The other end of the line is silent. "Miss Silver?"

"Yes, yes, I did. Thank you for asking. Did you?"

"It was fine."

I know we're both thinking the same thing right now—why the fuck are we on this call? But I can't bring myself to hang up just yet.

"How'd your meetings go?" I picture her lying back in her bed, one hand behind her head as she stares at the ceiling and talks to me. I adjust myself in my chair, leaning back and kicking my feet up on the other chair on the balcony as I take another sip of my liquor.

"They went well. It's a proposal for an acquisition that's been in the works for the better part of a year. Seems like things are moving forward and contracts will be ready soon."

"Wow, a year? Sounds so official and—honestly, a bit frustrating."

I can't help but laugh. "You're not wrong. These kinds of deals can take years. This one is actually moving quite quickly. It just requires a lot of ego stroking and hand-holding with these men so they feel special and comfortable."

I don't know why I'm sharing so much with her. Maybe I'm lonelier than I realize or perhaps it's the fact that nobody asks me how my day or meetings go… ever. At least not since Meredith. It feels good to share, even if it's just out of obligation since I'm keeping her on the phone.

"Sounds like you need a woman involved. We're good at getting things done pretty quickly and efficiently."

"Maybe next time I have a negotiation I'll bring you along. You can be my liaison. Whip these men in shape."

"Well, now that sounds like fun, whipping a man." She laughs.

I'm tempted, *very* tempted to make a comment about whipping or spanking or hell, even asking her what she's wearing and completely throwing her off guard. It's on the tip of my tongue but I swallow it down instead.

"On that note, I should be getting to bed. Have an early flight."

"Of course. I'm glad your meetings went well, Mr. Hayes. Sleep well."

"Good night, Miss Silver," I say and disconnect the call. I drop the phone onto the table beside me, leaning my head back and closing my eyes.

Images of Margot lying in her bed permeate my thoughts. I

imagine her bare legs on the white sheets, her braless tits beneath the thin material of a t-shirt, her hard nipples poking through. I feel myself growing stiff beneath my pants and I slide my hand down to undo my belt and zipper.

I know I shouldn't, but the temptation is too great. I slip my hand beneath my boxer briefs and fist my now rigid cock in my hand. I pump my hand up and down my shaft, my lips parting as I imagine sliding her panties down her creamy thighs.

I hear my breathing grow ragged as I continue to pleasure myself. My chest burns as I pump harder, faster, my impending orgasm growing so fast I can barely hold off. I reach down and lift my shirt just in time as I spill myself directly onto my stomach.

I look down at the mess, cock still in hand, and shame takes over. I stand up quickly and remove my shirt, pants, and underwear like they're to blame before jumping into the shower to clean myself off and tell myself that I'll never let that happen again.

I wake the next morning feeling well rested and in a good mood considering how disgusted I felt with myself last night. Between the release and the nice chat I had with Margot, I find myself surprisingly chipper.

I'm not usually in a bad mood, but it's fair to say that my reputation isn't that I'm an overly cheerful guy. I'm not ruthless or unfair. I'm a great boss, a loyal companion and friend, and I'm a pretty big stickler for ethics when it comes to business. I just prefer to keep to myself. Even before Meredith died, I wasn't going out of my way to be social. I prefer a quiet evening at home or the solace of my own company in my office where I can think undisturbed.

The flight home is smooth and quick. Phil is there to greet me on the tarmac, taking my luggage and getting us quickly on the road back to the house.

We're only a few minutes from the house when I receive a text from Warren Dorsey.

Warren: *Graham, the dinner meeting with Tech Titans is set for next Thursday. Morton's at 7 p.m. Be there.*

My good mood is instantly gone. Who the *fuck* does he think he is?

I told him I'd *consider* a meeting between him and Tech Titans, not that I was absolutely getting involved in this mess he created. I don't respond to the text; I'll deal with it later. I shove my phone back into my pocket as we pull up the driveway.

I take a few deep breaths, not wanting to drag my work life into my home life. I open the door and step inside with my bags, dropping them at the front door as I step inside. I'm instantly hit with an offensive smell.

"What the hell?"

I wrinkle my nose and glance around but nothing seems out of the ordinary. That's when I take the step off the front door landing, my foot sliding out from beneath me, and a brown streak follows it across the floor.

"What the fuck is that?" I catch myself on the corner of the wall and turn around to see a small pile of what looks like animal shit on my custom Italian marble floor.

"Miss Silver!"

7

MARGOT

"She loves it!" Eleanor squeals as her new kitten Muffin chases the ribbon across the floor. The small bell on her pink collar jingles as she jumps and tumbles across her lap.

"Are you excited to show your daddy?"

"Yes. I hope he loves her as much as I do," she says, distracted by the kitten jumping across her lap.

I was hesitant to let her adopt a kitten even after speaking to Miss Perry, but then yesterday afternoon, Miss Perry showed up with a kitten and adoption papers. I was shocked and told her as much, but she said that Mr. Hayes was fully on board and when she stopped by the shelter and saw this little furry angel, she couldn't risk her being adopted out from under her nose so she pulled the trigger.

Clearly, she's never had a pet before because she brought home *only* the kitten, no food or necessary care items. It was no worry though. I took Eleanor out to the pet store and we picked up all the necessary things along with way too many toys and a few little outfits she insisted we buy.

We set up a litter box in Eleanor's bathroom and I talked her through how to scoop the litter, which is thankfully flushable, how much and how often to feed Muffin, and a few other housekeeping items regarding cats. I don't expect her to take care of her on her own at all; I'll be there to make sure she gets fed every day, her litter scooped, and the occasional nail trim.

Our playtime is interrupted when I hear Mr. Hayes scream my name from downstairs. I bolt upright and Eleanor looks at me with a concerned expression.

"Stay here. I'll be right back," I say with a cheerful smile, hoping she doesn't get worried about her father's temperament. I scramble down the hall and bound down the stairs.

"Everything okay, Mr. Hayes?"

"Does it fucking look like it?" He spits the words out, not even bothering to look up at me as Miss Perry hands him a paper towel. I watch as he wipes the bottom of his shoe off and that's when I notice the brown streak across the floor.

"Oh goodness," I say as I run the rest of the way down the stairs and toward the kitchen.

"Stay here," he says through gritted teeth, and I stop in my tracks, slowly spinning around to face him.

"What is that?" He points to the now smashed pile.

"Umm, cat poop?" I don't mean for it to sound like a question, but it does.

"And why the hell is it in my house when we don't have a cat?"

My eyes dart from his to Miss Perry and I'm thoroughly confused.

"Uh, we do have a cat now. Muffin, the kitten we adopted for Eleanor?"

I can see rage settle over his face, and I think he's about to explode like a volcano.

"What?"

"Miss Perry said—"

"This isn't about Miss Perry. This is about you allowing my daughter to adopt a cat when I don't recall ever having that conversation with you."

I glance nervously back at Miss Perry who has quickly ducked out of the entryway and out of sight. *That bitch set me up.* I shake my head when the realization hits me. I should have known she switched from hating me to being warm way too quickly and way too easily.

"Well?" He gestures angrily, his hair flopping.

"I'm sorry, sir. I had a complete lack of judgment and I'm terribly sorry. It won't happen again."

"You can bet your ass it won't happen again, and you can take the fucking cat back to wherever it came from!"

I open my mouth to respond but it's too late; Eleanor heard him. I turn when I hear a cry and see her standing at the top of the stairs holding her kitten.

"Daddy, no! I love Muffin." Tears stream down her face as I run up the stairs to embrace her.

"Now look what you did," Mr. Hayes snaps as he removes his shoes and picks them up, holding them with his fingertips like they're going to bite him. "There goes eight hundred dollars down the drain."

"Sir, please." I scramble, trying to comfort Eleanor who is sobbing while Mr. Hayes starts to storm down the hall to his office.

"Do—we—have—to get rid—" Eleanor struggles to say the words, her breath hitching in her chest as she sniffs and hiccups.

"No, no, sweetie. I'll fix this. I promise," I say, hugging her as I hear Mr. Hayes yell at me once more before slamming his office door.

"Clean up that mess, Miss Silver!"

I take a very confused Muffin from Eleanor's trembling hands and walk her back upstairs to her room.

"It's okay, sweetie. I'm going to talk to your dad and get everything fixed. You just sit tight here with little miss Muffin, okay? Can you give her lots of attention for a few minutes while I go clean up and talk to your dad?"

Eleanor smiles, wiping away a few stray tears with the back of her hand, and nods before lunging into my arms to give me the tightest little hug that makes my heart feel like it's about to explode.

I head back downstairs and clean up the mess in the entryway before walking confidently down the hall toward Mr. Hayes' office.

The door is ajar and as I approach, of course, Miss Perry is already running to the rescue, nursing Mr. Hayes' temper tantrum and probably telling him that she thought the cat was a terrible idea and told me as much.

"Yes, I completely agree with you, sir. I'm on your side on this," she says as she picks at a piece of lint on his shoulder before following it up by smoothing the material down. I watch momentarily, noticing the way she looks at him, her eyes traveling down his body and back up... Her demeanor and tone completely change when she's speaking to him. Her body is so close to his.

"Thank you, Miss Perry. I have some things here I need to finish up."

"Of course." She smiles sweetly at him. "If you need anything at all, don't hesitate." She touches his elbow, her hand lingering a little too long.

I knock softly on the door and open it a little wider as Miss Perry makes her way out of his office, her smile falling the moment she sees me, instantly replaced by a thin, hard line.

"I'm not in the mood, Miss Silver," Mr. Hayes snaps at me and I hear a slight chuckle from Fiona as she scurries down the hall.

"I don't care, sir. We need to talk." I cross my arms over my chest, trying to summon the courage I'm pretending to have. His head snaps up and he looks at me, probably surprised at my boldness.

"Your daughter loves that kitten more than life and I don't think it's fair to force her to give it up when it wasn't her mistake."

"Frankly, I don't give a damn what your opinion is on the matter, Miss Silver, and you should think twice before you barge in here and start telling me how to be a parent."

"That's rich," I scoff and I know I shouldn't but now I'm angry.

"Excuse me?" His eyes narrow. "If you have something to say, just say it."

"Alright. I don't think you spend enough time with Eleanor. She's only five years old and she craves time with her dad. She needs it, sir."

"Let me guess, you learned this in one of your *how to be a parent* classes in college? Maybe a child psychology class? I'll let you in on a secret. Being a parent is so much more than a textbook or theory, Miss Silver. I wouldn't expect *you* to understand that."

I've clearly struck a nerve with him but against my better judgment, I don't shut up; I keep going. "Well, then I feel like you would know that a child who has lost one parent, needs more attention from the other parent. You can't just avoid her, Mr. Hayes!"

"You're on thin ice, lady!" he shouts, pointing a finger at me. "Now, you listen to me."

"No, you listen." I don't know what's come over me. I know I have no right to speak to him like this and I'm about two seconds away from losing my job, but it kills me to see him pulling away from this little girl.

"That little girl *needs* you. She asks me every day what you're doing, when you'll be home, if you're eating dinner with us." Tears prick my eyes but I continue on. "She just wants more time with you, sir. And if you doubt my ability to care for a child, then frankly"—I hesitate before taking in a deep breath—"I don't know why you hired me then."

He's leaning forward on his desk, his hands balled into fists that are smashed down on the surface. He stares at me, his chest rising and falling rapidly. The silence between us is deafening. Finally, I see the anger leave his face as he slowly sinks down in his chair and looks out the large window to his left.

"I'm sorry," he finally says and relief washes over me. "You're right. She can keep the kitten but"—he points his finger again—"you're responsible. You make sure she keeps up with it and that it's taken care of and no more messes in the halls."

"Yes, sir, absolutely." I raise my hand like I'm taking an oath and I don't know why.

"One other thing. Miss Perry mentioned that while I was gone, Eleanor was banging on pots and pans and running around the house, causing a ruckus."

I bite my tongue. *God, this woman! What does she have against me?* I open my mouth to speak, but he raises his hand.

"I know she exaggerates and Eleanor is only five. If she's not breaking or damaging things, I don't care, but Miss Perry is very important to this household so please do your best to just stay out of her hair."

I nod my head and now I'm left wondering just *how* important she is to the household. *Is there something going on between them?* Maybe the flirting I see from her isn't so one-sided like I thought it was. I have no idea what their history is and frankly it's none of my business. Still, I feel a tinge of jealousy welling up in my chest at the thought of him holding her.

"I will. I'm sorry for raising my voice. I shouldn't have done that, and I apologize again for going behind your back with the cat thing. And I'll do my best to stay out of Miss Perry's way. Wouldn't want to force her to be the victim any more than she already is."

Damn. I almost kept my smart mouth shut. I flinch, fully expecting another tongue-lashing from Mr. Uptight but instead he breaks out in a roar of laughter, his head falling back and everything. It's a relief, not only that I didn't get my head bitten off but also seeing him relaxed... and laughing. It makes me laugh in return.

"You're not wrong there," he mutters. "Thank you, Miss Silver." He smiles politely and gestures toward the door. I take the hint and exit, closing the door softly behind me as little butterflies dance in my tummy at the realization that I made Mr. Hayes laugh.

* * *

I CAN'T SLEEP.

I roll over and look at the alarm clock on my bedside table. It's 2:14 a.m. I've been tossing and turning for most of the night, my mind replaying this afternoon with Mr. Hayes. Well, more like replaying the conversation we had on the phone the night before and then him laughing this afternoon.

I tried to imagine the situation when he called me. He sounded calm, tired maybe. His voice was deeper and raspier than usual. I was confused when I saw his name pop up on my phone, knowing it was well past Eleanor's bedtime. I enjoyed the brief moments that we talked, though, like we were just two friends catching up.

I huff, tossing the covers off and giving up on actually getting any sleep. I stretch my arms overhead and decide that maybe a snack will help me reset. I stand up and put on my slippers, questioning if I should also grab some pants but ultimately decide against it. My oversized t-shirt is long enough it covers halfway down my thighs and it's the middle of the night, so nobody will see me.

I open the door and glance down the hall before walking out of my room and down the stairs to the kitchen. I open the pantry door and don't bother turning on the light. There's enough glow from the moon hitting the kitchen windows that I can make out what's in front of me.

I spy a Cheez-It box and pop it open, reaching my hand inside, grabbing a handful, and shoving them into my mouth. I turn to exit the pantry and find a small dish to pour some in when a shadowy figure crosses the doorway, and then the light flicks on, blinding me.

I shield my eyes, my mouth dropping open just as a scream is about to erupt from my throat. But before I can make a peep, Mr. Hayes' strong arms are enveloping me as his hand clamps down over my mouth.

"It's just me," he whispers against my cheek, his warm breath fanning across my face. Suddenly I realize he's shirtless. The heat from his bare chest pressed against my body sends my senses into overdrive. I feel my heartbeat double in pace as I slowly swallow down the mouthful of crackers and he removes his hand.

He steps back. Instantly, I miss the connection.

"You okay?" he asks, running his hand through his mussed hair, a curl flopping down partly over one eye.

Oh my God. My ovaries feel like they just exploded as I take in a shirtless Graham Hayes, complete with low-slung pajama bottoms that expose the deep *V* cut and dark trail of hair that disappears beneath his waistband. I know I'm staring but I can't help it.

His defined chest is peppered with dark hair. I love hair on a man's chest. His body has the muscular, lean look of an athlete without being overly bulky like a gym bro.

Dammit, now I know exactly what's beneath those bespoke suits and pressed shirts.

"Yes, you just scared me." I place my hand on my chest, willing my heart to calm down.

"Sorry about that. Couldn't sleep either?" he asks, leaning against the doorjamb so I'm trapped in this tiny room with him. I nod my head.

Dammit, a house this big and the pantry couldn't be double this size? I feel like I'm being interrogated, a bright light in my eyes.

He drags his own eyes down my body now, agonizingly slow. He reaches his hand up to his face, running his finger along his bottom lip as he studies me, and I'd give anything to know what's behind those dark eyes right now.

He pushes himself off from the doorway and takes a step toward me. For some reason, I take a step backward. He notices and steps closer. I too step back again. We repeat this little dance till my back hits the shelves and I drop the box of crackers at my feet.

He stands centimeters apart from me, towering over me as he looks down. Slowly he reaches up his hooked finger, resting it just beneath my chin as he tips it upward.

"Why are you scared of me?" he finally says, barely above a whisper. I don't dare speak—I don't even blink or breathe.

He removes his finger from my chin, slowly dragging it down my neck as he wraps his fingers around the base of my throat.

"So delicate," he says, but I don't think he realizes he's saying the words out loud. I don't know what to do with my hands. My arms hang at my sides like dead fish.

I feel his other hand now as he slowly drags his fingertips up my bare thigh. My breath catches and I'm afraid it will ruin the moment, but he doesn't stop. I don't know what he's doing but frankly I'm not about to refuse.

He grabs the hem of my shirt, lifting it just high enough to reveal my pale-pink panties. His eyes drop from where his hand rests around my throat to the top of my legs. His tongue darts out when he sees my panties and I can see his Adam's apple bob in his throat as he swallows.

He fists my shirt in his hand, closing his eyes tightly like he's in pain as his forehead gently rests against mine for a brief second.

"Fuck—the things I would do to you."

He mutters the words just as he releases my shirt and throat and steps back, looking at me like I've somehow just burned him. He runs both hands through his hair and my eyes fall down to just below his waist where I see the outline of his growing manhood. I dart my eyes back upward, but he turns and walks out of the pantry without another word.

I slowly sink down to the floor, my mouth hanging open in confusion and shock as I absentmindedly grab the crackers and shove another handful into my mouth.

"What was that?" I whisper the words to myself as I try to make sense of what just happened.

I feel giddy, turned on, sexy—all of it. Instantly, I regret not making a move. What would he have done if I had reached out and touched him? If I'd reached up onto my tippy-toes and kissed him?

I put the box away and quietly make my way back up to my room, throwing myself on my bed as I lie back and let my mind fantasize how that interaction would have ended if things had gone further.

I slip my fingers into my panties and feel wetness already soaking through them just from the few seconds of that interaction.

This man just might completely and utterly destroy me.

8

GRAHAM

I should have kissed her.

No. I shouldn't have touched her. Shouldn't have even looked at her.

And what the hell was I thinking muttering those thoughts out loud. At least I didn't actually let slip what was running through my head—images of dropping to my knees and burying my face in her sweet, wet pussy.

I've spent the better part of the last two days replaying that little moment in the pantry over and over again in my head. I made sure the next morning I was gone to the office downtown long before Margot was awake and I made sure when I came home, I shut myself in my office and tiptoed around my own damn house like a coward just to avoid her.

What the hell was I thinking?

Clearly, I wasn't, but in that moment, I felt completely helpless and defenseless against my own desires to reach out and feel her. It's like every little crumb of interaction between us fuels this burning desire in me to take her, to claim her.

I stare out the window of my high-rise office. The cars below me look like toys, the people scurrying through the streets of Chicago like ants.

I know that if I don't get a handle on this craving, I'm going to snap and do something that will fuck everything up. Despite how much she might annoy me and despite now having a cat in my house because of her, I can't risk losing her as a nanny. She's good for Eleanor. Bridgette, the last nanny, was efficient, but she didn't have the connection that Margot has. When I watch Margot with Eleanor, it's like what I imagined it would have been like seeing her own mother with her.

I shove my hands in my pockets, lost in thought when I hear the buzzer on the intercom.

"Mr. Hayes, there's a Mr. Dorsey on the line for you."

I turn and walk back to my desk. "Thank you, Olivia," I say into the intercom before picking up the receiver.

"Warren."

"Haven't heard from you, Graham. You avoiding me?" The raspy voice of Warren Dorsey instantly puts me in a bad mood. If I really were Bruce Wayne, Warren Dorsey would be the super villain in our version of *Batman.*

"Just busy, Warren. You know how business can be." Not many—or really anyone for that matter—can intimidate me or make me uneasy, except Warren Dorsey. We're both powerful men with more money than most, but unlike him, I'm not willing to wield my power and funds for evil. This man has no qualms whatsoever about destroying someone, even me.

"Thought you might be backing out of our dinner on Thursday."

"Well, I never actually agreed to go to dinner if you recall. I said I'd consider it. I have to admit, your demanding text message made me bristle a little at the idea of actually attending." The line is silent for a moment.

"Fine, thirty percent shares," he says.

I grip the phone in my hand tightly. *Fuck.* I shouldn't even consider being in bed with a man like Dorsey but I've been wanting to diversify my portfolio and expand my empire. Walking away from an opportunity like this is the kind of business decision that could haunt you.

"I'll be there," I say, even against my better judgment.

"That's my boy." The phrase turns my stomach. "Oh and we changed it from Morton's here to in Manhattan on their turf. Figure it makes 'em think they've got a leg up on their own turf."

And with that, the line goes dead. I hit the intercom button and summon my assistant, Olivia.

"Yes, Mr. Hayes?" She walks through the double doors of my office, iPad in hand.

"I need you to call the airfield and make sure my plan is set to fly to Manhattan Thursday morning, returning Friday morning. Also, arrange my usual penthouse suite and car."

"Absolutely, sir." She taps on the iPad.

"That will b—" I'm about to dismiss her when the sound of Eleanor's high-pitched laugh interrupts me.

I stand up and peer over Olivia's shoulder down the hallway to see Eleanor and Margot hand in hand, walking toward my office.

"Knock, knock," Margot says as they enter.

"Oh, hi, sweetheart. Do you remember me?" Olivia crouches down in front of Eleanor. "My goodness, it's been nearly two years since I've seen you." Eleanor looks up at Margot, gripping her hand.

"Eleanor, say hello," Margot says to her and Eleanor gives her a big smile and a wave.

"Hi!"

"Miss Silver?" I try to keep my composure as Olivia and Eleanor chat. I glance down at Olivia, giving her a stern look that she understands.

"Why don't we go out to my desk. You can tell me all about your new kitten and I can show you pictures of my puppy. How does that sound?"

"Okay," Eleanor says, placing a hand-drawn picture on my desk before grabbing Olivia's hand and following her out of my office.

"I'm sorry, sir. I didn't think it would be a big deal for us to stop by.

We were downtown to go to the aquarium and Eleanor mentioned that she forgot to give you that drawing for your office."

"This is a place of business, Miss Silver, and I really don't understand why I have to explain to you that it's no place for children." I place my fingertips on the surface of my desk as I lean forward, enunciating my words.

"She just wanted t—"

"No. Don't blame Eleanor here."

"I'm not *blaming* her!" Miss Silver straightens her back, that red blush creeping up her delicious neck again. "I'm simply telling you why we stopped by, but clearly it's unwelcome so we'll just be going!" She turns on her heel and I lunge around the desk to grab her arm.

"Daddy, be nice!" Eleanor appears in the doorway, her hands on her hips and a scowl on her face. "You have to say sorry."

I stare at her, letting out an exasperated sigh before turning my attention back to Margot. I give her a forced smile. "My apologies, Miss Silver."

She nods and opens her mouth to speak, but Eleanor interjects again. "Now kiss her." I snap my attention back to Margot whose face is a bright, glowing red.

I walk over to Eleanor and crouch down in front of her, placing my hands on her arms. "Now, sweetheart, why would you say that?"

"Miss Margot said that when Daddy and Mommy fight, they kiss to say sorry."

I slowly turn my head to look at Miss Silver. Her hands are now cupping her flaming cheeks. She's staring straight ahead.

"Well, while that is true, Eleanor, and I am *your* daddy"—I choose my words carefully—"Miss Silver is your nanny, not your mommy, and that wouldn't be appropriate for me to kiss her." I glance sideways to look at Margot, but she's still refusing to look at me.

"Okay, sweetie. I think we should let your dad get back to work," Margot says as she turns and puts her hands on Eleanor's shoulders to usher her out of the office. Eleanor walks through the double doors, but I reach out and grab Margot's hand, jerking her backward a little more forcefully than necessary. She stumbles a little but rights herself.

I get my face close to hers. "We'll finish this conversation at home."

"Damn, who was that?" Garrett, my CFO, whistles as he steps into my office, his eyes trailing Margot as she walks down the hall toward the elevator.

"Nobody," I mutter, not looking up from my computer.

"Well, is nobody available? I'd like to sink my tee—"

"What do you want, Garrett?" I snap.

He eyes me suspiciously for a brief second before placing a stack of documents on my desk. "This quarter's financials," he says, followed by a snicker.

I grab the papers and look up at him. *Why is he still standing here?*

"Something else?" I ask, leaning back in my chair as I pretend to read the report. It's no use; my brain is solely focused on Margot.

"Nobody, huh? Sounds like you might have a little crush." I drop the report and look up at him. He raises his hands and gives a look of *it's none of my business* before walking out of my office.

"Go home to your fiancée," I say after him and he just waves.

I keep staring at the clock for the rest of the day, counting down the minutes and seconds before I'll be in her presence again. I know I overreact toward her. I wasn't actually mad that she brought Eleanor by my office. It was because seeing Margot, knowing I can't have her pisses me off more than anything.

By the time five thirty p.m. rolls around, I'm beyond amped. I feel *frazzled*, A word I rarely use and a feeling I hate.

I *detest* not feeling like I'm in control.

I join Eleanor and Margot for dinner. Eleanor does most of the talking. I watch Margot out of the corner of my eye as she pushes her green beans around her plate like she knows something is coming. I wait until they finish eating dinner before saying anything.

"Miss Silver," I say to her as she ushers Eleanor out of the kitchen. "When you're done with Eleanor's bath, could you please meet me in my office to finish our discussion?"

"Yes, sir," she replies with a small smile before exiting the room.

"In trouble again, I see?" I didn't realize Miss Perry was behind me. She has a knack for just appearing out of the blue and it's annoying.

"Nothing you need to worry about." I shut it down before she starts to pry and I can see the disappointed look on her face.

I retire to my office, sipping a glass of bourbon. Later I hear Miss Silver's telltale knock on my door.

"Come in, please. Have a seat." She sits down gingerly, her fingers knotted together in her lap.

"I wanted to first apologize for reacting poorly this afternoon. I certainly didn't mean to upset Eleanor or you for that matter. I was taken off guard. But I also feel like we need to finish the discussion we were having earlier."

I interlace my fingers and place my hands on top of my desk as she continues to sit up pin-straight.

"I want to make it clear that I appreciate what you do for Eleanor, how involved you are, and how much you care for her. But we both need to make sure that we are crystal clear with her about your role in the house." She stares at me and I elaborate to make sure there's no misunderstanding. "Miss Silver, I don't want her confused, thinking that you are her mother."

"I can assure you, sir, I will not confuse her and it was certainly never my intention to do so. I'll make sure she understands."

"Good," I say, standing. She follows suit.

She nods her head and then turns to leave but stops and spins back around to face me.

"If I can point out, sir, I think there is a little confusion on Eleanor's part but it's not regarding me."

I furrow my brows. "Meaning?"

"Well…" She takes a step closer to my desk and glances over her shoulder quickly before continuing. "The other day Eleanor noticed Miss Perry fixing your tie in the entryway and you two were having a private conversation. She and I were just walking by and later she asked me if Miss Perry was going to be her new mommy."

I sit back down and rub my eyes. *What the fuck?*

"I didn't know how to respond to her because I don't know the nature of your relationship with Miss Perry and it's none of my bu—"

"She's the house manager." I emphasize the words. "Nothing more,

Miss Silver, I can assure you." My tone is sterner than it needs to be but it's because I don't want there to be any confusion about that matter between Margot and me.

"Yes, sir," she says.

Every time the word sir slips past her lips it sends my cock into overdrive. *One of these days I'll have her saying that on her knees in front of me.*

"I'll talk with Eleanor about it," I say just as I hear her shout for me. "Daddy!"

We both stand. "Oh, she was hoping you could come tuck her in tonight."

"Seems like Daddy is being summoned," I say and step to exit the office. "Good night, Miss Silver."

"Good night, daddy," she replies, and it instantly stops me in my tracks. I feel my blood pressure spike through the roof and my balls tighten.

I don't know if she meant to tease me, but I'd venture a guess that a naïve woman like her has no idea what that sounds like to me. I slowly turn back around to face her. I walk toward her slowly, one step in front of the other till I'm staring down on her, our bodies almost touching.

My breathing is shallow; I can see my chest almost touch hers with every inhale. I can smell her, like a delicious bouquet of flowers that I want to defile in the most vile ways.

I have no idea what I'm doing.

I don't know what to say.

She is staring at me, unblinking, like she's also trying to read my mind, to figure out what I'm about to do.

If she only knew the thoughts I was having… again. She'd probably run for the hills if I told her I wanted to see her bound and gagged as I fucked her mercilessly.

I dig my fingernails into my palms, willing myself not to touch her.

Finally, I lean my head down till my lips are barely brushing her ear and I say in a calm but strangled voice, "Don't call me *that* again unless you're willing to be punished."

9

MARGOT

I can hear my heartbeat in my ears.

It sounds like rushing water. It feels like my heart is about to beat out of my chest.

I watch as Mr. Hayes walks out of his office calmly like he didn't just say the most delicious and cryptic statement to me.

I wait a moment till I know he's most likely upstairs in Eleanor's room before I dart out of his office and run up the stairs and down the hall to my room. I shut my door and lean against it.

"Oh my God." I giggle before running and launching myself onto my bed.

I lie back, closing my eyes and replaying his words from tonight and the other night in the pantry over and over in my head. I fantasize about him losing control. I reach down and unbutton my jeans, sliding my hand into my panties. Wetness is already pooling. I pull my fingers out and see they're coated in my desire.

Suddenly the realization that while this is exciting, tempting, and so deliciously naughty—the possibility of an illicit affair with my boss —it could also end in disaster. Instantly, questions pop up in my brain one after the other.

What happens after? Does he fire me? Get bored with me? Does he do this with every nanny?

That last question has my stomach in knots but I push them out. I slide my jeans and panties down my thighs and close my eyes, images of Mr. Hayes' face between my thighs taking over as I pleasure myself.

It only takes me a few moments before my back is arching off the bed and a thin sheen of sweat breaks out across my skin. My legs tremble as I bite my lip, trying not to say his name over and over as I come.

* * *

IT'S A BEAUTIFUL SUNDAY MORNING, my day off. My phone buzzes with a text from Shelly letting me know she's on her way to the coffee shop. I tap out a reply and hit send as I grab my keys and wallet and make my way downstairs.

Me: *Leaving now. See you in thirty.*

After I arrive and we settle at a table with our food, Shelly says, "So how are things going over at Wayne Manor? I need to come see that place." Shelly takes a bite of her donut, glaze clinging to her lips as she rolls her eyes back in her head. "Oh God, that's good."

"You and that donut seem to be on an intimate level." I laugh. "Speaking of, how are things with your new plan? Karter with a *K* still trying to weasel his way back into your panties?"

"Ugh. I swear it's like the moment men know that you're happy without them and you've made the decision to focus on yourself, they send you a text. It's like there's a fuck-boy beacon that goes off, sending a signal straight to their little shrimp dick the *moment* we are happy."

"Sooo, I take that as a yes?" She nods her head. "And did you let him?"

She avoids my gaze, instead taking another bite of her donut before hanging her head.

"You did! Shelly."

"I knoooow, but I was lonely. And even though he's an asshole, the dick is... okay."

I shake my head and swallow down my bite of donut. "It's just familiar dick; that's why it seems okay. Okay dick isn't worth feeling like shit after; that's only reserved for spectacular, firework, life-changing, back-breaking dick. The kind that leaves your head swimming for days."

She raises a curious eyebrow at me. "Are you experiencing this kind of dick or something?"

"No." I quickly shake my head but I can feel myself blushing. *Shit.*

"Spill," she demands, placing both hands on the table and leaning forward.

"There's nothing to spill."

"Is it him? Bruce Wayne?"

I wave my hand like her suggestion is insane and stuff an entire half of a donut into my mouth just to avoid answering.

"Oh my God. I was kidding, but it *is*, isn't it? You're sleeping with your boss?" Her hand darts to cover her mouth and she gasps loudly like I just told her I know where a body is buried.

"Calm down." I reach over and pull her hand from her mouth. "First of all, no, I am not sleeping with him, and second, that was a bit of an overreaction." I take a sip of my coffee. "But—"

"Oh my God, there's a but!" I give her another look that says calm the hell down because people are staring and she looks around before letting out a long breath. "Sorry, carry on."

"Okay, so he's very intimidating and moody, pretty sullen. Honestly, most of the time, it feels like he's annoyed with me. I'm either screwing up by adopting a kitten or—"

"What?"

I shake my head. "Story for another time. Or it feels like he's annoyed with the amount of questions I ask him regarding Eleanor, his daughter, or when I try to make small talk. I have caught him looking at me before."

"Looking as in?"

"Like I'm an actual human, a woman. A little lingering side-eye action."

"Ohhh," she squeals.

"So anyway, the other night I couldn't sleep so I went to get a snack in the pantry and he had the same idea I guess because he scared me, and then he put his hand over my mouth to stop me from screaming and then—" I raise my hands for emphasis. "He put his hand on my throat and lifted up the edge of my shirt, revealing my underwear."

Shelly's mouth drops open.

"But here's where it gets good. He said to me, and I quote"—I lean forward, whispering the words for emphasis—"*The things I would do to you.*"

"The things I would do to you?" Shelly flings herself back in her chair like she's fainting. "Holy shit, that is hot. That's the kind of hot where he doesn't even need to elaborate. He's that confident of an alpha. Oh my God, I need a minute." She fans her face dramatically as I laugh.

"There's more… Last night I called him daddy, not in a sexual way. I was referring to his daughter calling for him, and he threatened to punish me if I said it again."

Shelly's jaw is glued to the floor at this point.

"I'm not sure what he meant by that."

"What he meant by that was he wants to spank you or do some *Fifty Shades* shit to you! Holy shit, woman. You are living out all of our fantasies right now. Working for a brooding billionaire that wants you so bad he's losing grip?"

I can't help but laugh at how dramatic she's being, but I also wonder if she's right. Is that why he seems frustrated with me half the time?

"Doesn't matter though. I've decided it's just a fun little flirty fantasy and nothing more."

"You're kidding me, right? Hold up. Let me see a picture of this guy."

I grab my phone and Google his name, pulling up an image of him from the company website, then I hand it to her.

"Goddamn! You're insane. Like actually certifiable, if you say no to this man." She whistles before clicking through several more photos of him. "Oh, come to mama."

I reach out and grab the phone from her, an image of him shirtless on a yacht taking up the entire screen. I let my eyes linger.

Maybe she is right. I'd be crazy to pass up on an opportunity for one night with him, right?

"Did I mention he was shirtless in the pantry and had on *very* thin pajama bottoms?"

"And?"

"Anaconda, possibly a python."

We both howl with laughter as she pretends to wrangle an imaginary snake.

"How's the coffee shop job going?"

"Same." She shrugs. "Terry wanted to make me the manager, but eh, I don't want the responsibility."

"Shell, that's great. Why not take it? I'm sure it's a lot more money."

"Because I'll get comfortable. I've been looking at different art programs, thinking I'll go back and finish my bachelor's. Is it crazy to think I might want to be a teacher?"

"Uh, hello, I'm a teacher! I think that's amazing! Speaking of teachers, I wanted to ask you if you'd be interested in my teacher friend Hank? He's the phys ed teacher where I used to teach. He's tall, athletic, super cute, and charming."

She eyes me suspiciously. "And why haven't you dated him?"

"We're just friends, never had that kind of interest or spark. Besides, I don't think he's really *my type*."

"Your type meaning cute, charming, and tall?"

"Uh, more like not my type because he's my age." I laugh. I've always had a thing for older men and clearly, my current crush on Mr. Hayes just reiterates that.

"I dunno, Margot." She takes a sip of her coffee. "I'm not looking for anything serious."

"Well, I have no idea if he is either. I haven't said anything to him, but I know that he's fun and super outgoing. Might just be a fun friend or f-buddy or something. Plus, he could take your mind off Karter."

I grab my phone again and pull up his Instagram account before handing it to her. "Here, check him out."

She mulls it over, running her finger around the rim of her water glass as she scrolls through a few photos. "What the hell; it can't hurt."

I spend the rest of the morning and most of the afternoon with Shelly. We window shop, walk through the city, and end up having an early dinner at my favorite bistro that I used to live near.

"Oh, while we're over here, I need to stop in at my old apartment and pay the landlord. Since I'm not breaking my lease, I'm just going to have to suck it up and pay the rent for the next five months."

We get to the building and I duck inside. "Hi, Mr. Zelenski. I'm just stopping by to pay rent." I reach into my purse and pull out my wallet.

"Already paid but I'll be happy to accept it twice," he says, laughing heartily.

"Already paid? I don't understand."

"Dunno." He shrugs. "Some hotshot guy called and paid it all off."

I'm confused. "Oh, okay." I turn to leave, but then ask, "Did he say who he was?"

"A Mr. Hayes or Halls. Sorry, kid. I don't really remember."

I tell him goodbye and walk back out of the building.

"So, that was weird," I say, walking back over to Shelly. "He said Mr. Hayes paid off my entire lease already."

I'm not sure what to make of Mr. Hayes' extremely generous gesture. I guess I'm wondering why he did it and how he even knew that I had a lease I had to pay off. Also, why wouldn't he mention it to me?

I say goodbye to Shelly, promising her I'll give her contact information to Hank, then I head back to the suburbs to pick up Eleanor from her grandma's house.

"It's really so kind of you to pick her up on your day off. I have no problem driving her over," Mrs. Hayes says to me as I step inside her beautiful home.

"Not a problem at all, Mrs. Hayes. I was on my way back from the city anyway."

"Please," she says, reaching out and touching my shoulder. "Call me Margaret."

I make my way farther inside, taking my shoes off and placing my purse next to them.

"Why don't you come have a cup of tea with me. Eleanor is finishing up her movie. She's watching *Moana* for probably the fifteenth time."

I follow her to the kitchen where I help her assemble the tea tray, complete with a fine china teapot, saucers, and glasses that I'm sure cost more than my car. She grabs a few different types of cookies, cream, and sugar cubes.

"Wow, this is so fancy. I feel like I'm having tea with the queen."

"You're too sweet. Here, come sit. Let's get to know one another."

I glance around the room that looks similar to Mr. Hayes' sitting room, only smaller. I'm nervous holding liquid while sitting on the crushed red velvet love seat that also happens to be sitting over what I assume is a real Persian rug.

"Your house is stunning, Mrs. Ha—Margaret," I correct myself. "Did you decorate yourself?"

"Oh no, darling. I hired a designer. I don't have an eye for that sort of thing." She picks out a few cookies, placing them on a plate and handing it to me. "So, do you have anyone special in your life?"

I shake my head no, chewing the bite of cookie in my mouth.

"Really? That's a shame. Such a beautiful, young thing like yourself."

"I dated someone in college pretty seriously and it didn't end well so I'm just taking time to focus on myself." It's a lie. That was the reason why I didn't date for the first year after college, but I've been out for three years now. It's just been a total dry spell on my part because of a complete lack of trying.

"Graham is very impressed with you, you know?" I choke on the cookie I just popped into my mouth.

"Um, no, I didn't know that. Did he—did he say that?" I try not to stumble over my words, fearing she'll see right through my childish crush. I will my cheeks not to turn pink, but I can feel the heat already setting in.

"He did. He said that Eleanor is absolutely enamored with you and that she's coming along on the piano." She lifts her tea to her lips, her pinky finger extended perfectly.

"She's a little natural on the piano. So far we've learned hand placement, middle C, and she's even gotten pretty good at 'Row, Row, Row Your Boat' and 'Mary Had a Little Lamb.' I don't even have to remind her to practice."

"She needs a mother in her life," she says, taking me completely off guard. "If only my son would realize that and stop wasting his time with silly women only after his money."

That makes my stomach knot. I haven't seen any women at the house besides Miss Perry and me, but that doesn't mean much. I'm sure if he was dating someone, he'd most likely not share that information with me or bring her around the house. I want to ask her what she means, but I know it would seem rude to intrude on something so personal. Instead, I just sip my tea, hoping she elaborates on her own. And to my surprise, she does.

"I told him that last woman was a gold digger through and through. I appreciate that he doesn't bring women home in front of Eleanor, but I don't feel like it's much better taking them to work functions and charity events so they're photographed on his arm like a trophy." She wrinkles her nose and I'm suddenly curious about who these women are.

I make a mental note to look through the Google images that came up earlier today. I was completely distracted by the one of him shirtless on the yacht and I didn't even notice the others.

"Miss Margot!" My thoughts are interrupted when Eleanor comes waltzing into the room.

"Hi, sweetheart. I was just talking with your grandma. How was your movie?"

"Good," she says, already distracted by the cookies on the tray.

I spend another thirty minutes chatting with Margaret as Eleanor eats her cookies and cleans up her toys. The conversation never ventures back to Graham and instead she asks me about my teaching career and where my love of music came from.

We say goodbye and I drive the short distance home. Eleanor already had dinner and her bath at her grandma's house. I walk her upstairs and help her change into her pajamas before reading her a short story and tucking her in for the night. It's still my day off but I enjoy these little moments with Eleanor, and her grandma is right; she needs a mother figure in her life.

I walk back to my room, exhausted after my day out with Shelly. My mind is being pulled in two directions. I'm still wondering when Mr. Hayes paid off my lease and why, but mostly, I wonder who these women are that his mother spoke about.

I lie across my bed on my stomach as I open my phone and go back to the image search results from earlier. I scroll down a few rows. Most of the images are professional headshots for magazine interviews or internet articles, but then I see one. He's in a tux, a beautiful, willowy brunette on his arm. He's whispering something in her ear and there's a megawatt smile spread across her face.

I keep scrolling. There's another picture of him exiting a restaurant with a leggy blonde on his arm this time. Both women look manufactured, like they're perfectly designed fembots meant to make the rest of us average women feel awful about ourselves.

"Do people actually look like this?" I say to myself as I zoom in on the photo. I toss the phone to the side, deciding it's enough torture for the night.

But truthfully, it's the reminder I needed that this isn't a fairy tale where the sexy, rich billionaire falls head over heels for the average help. This is reality and I'm just a convenient fantasy for a man who is probably still mourning the loss of his wife. I'm sure if I disappeared tomorrow, he'd probably never think twice about me again.

10

GRAHAM

I drag my thumb across the gold embossed lettering of the invitation in my hand, flipping it over for the sixth time. It's for an upcoming charity event this weekend that I still have yet to RSVP to.

Normally I'm not this indecisive on things like this, but this one is different. It's for a charity that raises funds for underprivileged and inner-city schools, to enhance and develop their music and fine arts programs.

My issue is I want to invite Margot. Not only would she be an amazing asset at an event like this, educating fellow billionaires on the importance of these kinds of programs, but I also think she might enjoy it. And I'd be lying if I wouldn't admit that the thought of having Margot on my arm all night has my heart in overdrive.

I can't get the look of her face from the other night out of my head. I also can't get the feel of her soft skin where I touched her slender neck off my fingertips.

That fucking neck.

It's an obsession at this point. It was one of the first things I noticed about her. It's so slender and delicate, I feel like I could wrap my fingers around it completely with barely any effort.

I've had so many fantasies of clutching her tightly while I bury myself inside her. Of dragging my tongue over her tempting skin. Of pressing my lips to that little dip where her throat meets her collarbone.

I reach down and adjust myself. Just the mere thought of her name floating around my head gets me hard.

I wish I had the balls to kiss her. The way her full, pouty lips beg me to taste them is driving me absolutely insane, but I told myself I wouldn't. It feels too intimate, too—

"Mr. Hayes." The voice of my assistant interrupts my daydream.

"Yes, Olivia?"

"Your eleven o'clock is here."

"Thank you. Send him in."

I sit up and straighten my tie, tossing the invitation to the side.

It's nearly seven p.m. by the time I make it home. I'm overly exhausted and it's only Monday.

I peer in the kitchen to see Miss Perry fixing herself a plate for dinner.

"Fiona." I say her name and she jumps, but her scowl is instantly replaced by a grin so big she looks like the Cheshire cat.

"Oh, Graham, you startled me." I cringe at the way she says my name. She never calls me Graham and actually, I never call her Fiona —no idea why I did just now.

"Apologies, Miss Perry," I say, hoping it establishes some formality again. "I have to fly to New York on Thursday morning. I'll be back Friday but just wanted to give you a heads-up."

She places her plate on the counter and opens her mouth to speak, but I just give her a nod and then turn and exit the kitchen. I'm really not in the mood for whatever she's wanting to complain to me about or her attempts to get me to *talk.*

I make my way upstairs, the sound of soft giggles coming from Eleanor's room. I stop outside the door, my hand poised to knock, but I listen for a brief moment as I hear her and Margot playing. It instantly sends a warm feeling to my chest followed by a bout of panic.

Lusting after Miss Silver are feelings I can deal with, feelings I can manage. But feeling *this*—whatever this is—is something I'm not ready to face.

I knock softly before opening the door.

"Daddy!" Eleanor shouts as she scrambles to her feet and charges at me. I reach out my arms as she hurls herself into them and hoist her up in the air where she wraps her tiny body around me.

"Hello, sweetheart." I plant a kiss on her forehead.

"We are playing with my ponies," she says.

"I can see that." There must be at least fifteen different horses and ponies scattered about, all with different types of colored manes and some even with diamonds on their hooves.

"We watched *My Little Pony* today so naturally, she had to introduce me to all of hers." Margot stands, adjusting her shorts that have ridden very far up her thighs.

I have to tell myself to avert my eyes and not make her uncomfortable but it's damn near impossible.

"I wanted to let you both know that I unfortunately have to attend a meeting in New York on Thursday so I'll be gone, but only for a day."

"Can we come?" Eleanor says. "Pleeeeease, Daddyyyyy." She wraps her arms around me even tighter as she begs.

"Not this time, sweetie, but someday I promise we'll go there when you're a little older and it won't be when I'm working so we'll get to spend the entire trip doing everything you want to do. Deal?"

She scrunches up her face like she's thinking about it and finally says, "Deal!" Then she climbs down and returns her focus to her ponies.

* * *

I SWIRL the last remaining ounces of my bourbon in my tumbler as Warren Dorsey drunkenly tells Mark Powers of Tech Titans his obviously bullshit deep sea fishing story.

"I shit you not, that sucker was damn near fifteen hundred pounds!" he shouts as the other men at the table eat up the story.

Normally I can suffer through work dinners just fine. I understand that it takes a certain level of babysitting and hand-holding in this world to get what you want, but tonight, all I can think about is Margot.

I guess that's not an entirely new problem for me considering she's been living rent free in my mind since the moment I met her.

I feel my phone buzz in my pocket and I slip it out, seeing a text from her. I slide open the message and see a picture of Eleanor on my screen. Her big toothy grin has a pink paint smudge next to it across her cheek and she's holding a half-finished picture in her hands.

Margot: *Eleanor insisted on sending you a picture of her current masterpiece she's painting for your office. It's not done yet.*

I smile and send her a message back asking how things are going at home.

"Getting some sexy pictures from a hot date, I hope?" Warren's words are slurred and his jowly face is glowing red.

"Afraid not. Just a picture of my daughter from my nanny." I regret mentioning her the moment the words leave my mouth because with a group of disgusting hyenas like these fools, the word *nanny* instantly solicits unwanted remarks.

"Nanny, huh?" Warren says as he elbows Mark. "She come with privileges?" Both men burst into laughter.

"No. Margot is an extremely smart and talented educator. A music teacher actually and my daughter absolutely adores her." I shut it down quickly, reminding myself that flying across the table and smashing a glass in Warren's face isn't the answer here.

"Margot?" Warren asks with a hook in his brow, his expression morphing into seriousness.

"Yes, Margot," I repeat, not liking the way he's asking.

My phone buzzes again and I excuse myself from the table to read the message.

Margot: *Things are great. Eleanor's music comprehension is coming along so well, she is learning to read music already. You might have a prodigy on your hands. :)*

Me: *All thanks to you.*

My stomach flutters, the liquid courage from the two glasses of bourbon I had to make it through dinner coursing through my veins. I'm about to do something stupid, like asking her to send me a picture of her when I see the bubbles appear on the screen to indicate she's typing. A few seconds later, a picture of her pops up on my screen and I do a double take to check if I actually did send her a text asking for one, but I didn't.

Margot: *Sorry. Eleanor insisted she send a photo of me with my painting as well. Look for it in the art museum soon.*

I smile at her self-deprecating joke but I'm lost in her eyes. Her beautiful, big green eyes that are sparkling through the picture. Her hair is swept in a messy bun atop her head, a few strawberry tendrils hanging down, clinging to her neck. Her smile reaches up to the crinkles of her eyes and she too has a slight smudge of light-blue paint on her cheek.

"Fucking adorable," I mutter to myself as I type out a response.

Me: *Now that picture is a masterpiece I'd hang in my office. The art museum can have your painting. ;)*

I just sent her a flirty text with a winking smiley face. *Who the fuck am I?*

I feel my stomach do a small flip as I wait for her response.

Margot: *Eleanor misses you. We hope your meeting goes well.*

I'm a little annoyed she didn't respond to my comment; I want to keep the flirty feeling going.

Me: *I miss her too and thank you both for the well wishes.*

I slide my phone back into my pocket and I'm about to head back to the table when I type out another message.

Me: *Do YOU miss me?*

I can see the three dancing little dots appear again as she appears to be typing out a response but just as quickly, they disappear. I stand there at the bar, staring at my phone for another minute before heading back to the table to excuse myself.

"Gentlemen, I feel like we had a very successful meeting here tonight. I'll be in touch in the coming weeks, but I have an early flight and should head back to my hotel."

The men stand and shake my hand, and I go outside and hail a cab, not in the mood to wait for an Uber. I check my phone a few more times but there's no response from Margot.

The drive back to the hotel is quick. I pay the fare and decide to give her a call.

"Hello?" Her voice sounds cautious and a bit timid.

"Hello, Miss Silver. I wanted to call and wish Eleanor a good night if I could?"

"Of course, let me put her on."

"Hi, Daddy. I, uh, I painted a picture for your office, and Miss Margot made one too."

I smile at the excitement in my little angel's voice. "I heard, sweetie. I can't wait to see the finished picture and hang it in my office."

She tells me in great detail about her day, how much she loves playing the piano, and all the new things Muffin is doing.

"Muffin, say eeyow!" she says a few times and I can hear the cat's bell jingling on the other end. I also hear Margot giggle as she instructs Eleanor to be careful with the kitten.

"Let me talk to Miss Silver now, sweetie. Be a good girl and get ready for bed, okay?"

"Okay," she says sadly. "I love you, Daddy."

"I love you too, sweetheart. Good night."

I wait momentarily for Margot to pick up the phone again.

"Hello, sir?" she says cheerily.

"Eleanor getting ready for bed?" I ask, loosening my tie as I kick off my shoes and lean back on the bed.

"Yes, she's brushing her teeth currently."

It's silent for a moment but I can't hold back from asking her what I asked earlier.

"You didn't answer my question earlier," I say, and I can hear my voice drop a few octaves. Most likely a result of the alcohol, talking a lot today, and the general mood I'm in.

"Wh—uh, what question is that?" Her voice wavers a bit, her escalating pitch telling me she knows exactly what question I'm referring to.

"Do *you* miss me?"

I can hear her breath coming out in soft puffs. "Of course, sir. We both miss you around the house."

More silence.

"I should really get in the bathroom and help Eleanor."

She's not playing my game.

I laugh, rubbing my eyes. The exhaustion is clearly getting to me.

"Have a good night, Miss Silver," I say before hanging up.

I flip back over to my email and type out a message to my assistant, Olivia.

Olivia,
Please respond to the invitation for the Chicago Music and Fine Arts event
this weekend. I'll be attending with a plus one.
-Graham

"MISS SILVER, can I have a moment of your time?" She glances up from the book in her hands, her legs curled comfortably beneath her as she sips a mug of tea in the sitting room.

I nod toward my office as I walk back down the hallway and wait for her to enter.

"Sir?" she says as she stands in front of my desk. I motion for her to take a seat and she does.

"I have a charity event this weekend—tomorrow night actually. It's a benefit for music and fine art education programs in inner-city and underfunded schools." I see her eyebrows raise. I stand up and nervously walk to the window.

"I was hoping you would accompany me to the event."

"Me? Uh, I don't really have anything—is it fancy?"

"It is, black tie, but that's not an issue if you do say yes." I sit back down behind my desk as she perches on the very edge of her seat.

88

"There's a woman, Marsha Brixton over at Saks. She's already been informed and she will help you pick out a dress and shoes, whatever you need. Phil will take you tomorrow morning and Eleanor will already be at her grandmother's so you don't need to worry about that."

I can see her trying to process all this information.

"You would be a great asset at an event like this. I really think it would make a difference for these out-of-touch billionaires to speak to an educator, someone who works with these kids and can tell them how important these programs are."

I lean back in my chair and she nods her head slowly before smiling.

"That's very generous of you to invite me and to have enough faith in me to convince the elite rich that this cause is worthy of their money."

"So you'll come?"

"Yes, yes, I will," she says with a smile.

"Great. I've also arranged for you to stop by Cartier. They'll have jewelry you can borrow. Don't worry, I'm not buying; it'll just be on loan for the evening."

"Oh, wow, that's scary," she says, bringing her hand up to her chest.

"Thank you for agreeing to attend, Miss Silver, and my apologies for the short notice. We'll leave here tomorrow evening at five p.m."

I'M NOT GOING to say that I counted down the minutes and hours till I was able to knock on Miss Silver's door and see what she picked out to wear tonight, but it's the only thing I've managed to focus on for the last twenty-four hours.

Eleanor is spending the night at my mother's house so I won't have to worry about getting Margot home at a reasonable hour to tuck her in.

I stop in front of one of the large mirrors in the hallway and double-check my bow tie is on straight and my cuff links aren't askew.

I knock on Margot's door at the same moment she pulls it open.

"Oh! Am I late? I'm sorry. I was just heading downstairs to meet you."

I step back, trying not to be obvious about checking her out. The dress she chose is breathtaking. It's a crimson strapless gown that tastefully accentuates her décolletage and slender collarbones. The silken material glides over her narrow waist and slight curve of her hip. I have to stop myself from reaching out and running a hand along her sexy silhouette.

"Not at all. I'm here to pick you up for our date."

"It's a date?" She grips her small clutch in her hand as she squeaks the words out and I chuckle.

I lean in, brushing a soft curl off her shoulder. "I asked you to attend with me, didn't I?"

She nods and I offer my arm. She stares at me, blinking.

"Thought you might need some assistance going down the stairs."

She glances down at her feet that are wrapped in delicate braids of gold and diamonds. Her towering heels are probably something she's not used to walking in.

"Yeah." She giggles as she gingerly takes my arm, her fingers ever so softly gripping my bicep.

We descend the steps and walk to the front door that is already opened, Phil waiting for us with the car running.

I place my hand at the small of her back as I help her into the back seat of the sedan before sliding in next to her.

"I'm nervous," she says as the car pulls away from the house and down the long driveway.

"You'll be fine. Trust me, in that dress, with your knowledge, you'll have them all eating out of the palm of your hand." I give her a wink and I see her shoulders drop a little in relief.

She turns to stare out the window on our drive into the city and I can't take my eyes off her. I don't even care if she catches me. She's absolutely stunning.

"You're staring," she says just above a whisper without looking at me.

"Does it bother you?"

"No," she replies, then turns to look at me. "Why are you staring?"

I'm surprised at her confidence; I think she is too.

I smirk and turn my attention to fidget with my cuff link, something I do when I'm nervous.

"It's our first date, Miss Silver, and I'd like to remain a gentleman this evening so if you don't mind, I'll keep that answer to myself."

11

MARGOT

I feel like I'm about ten seconds away from melting into a puddle of complete gooey feels in the back of this car.

For as much as I love the banter and tension that seems to have built between us over the last few weeks, I can't quite put my finger on his intentions. One minute he seems like he's seconds away from losing control and ripping my clothes off, the next he's stoic and wants to remain professional.

I'll admit, I'm completely out of my league here. Images of those beautiful women who usually adorn his arms come flooding back and suddenly I feel too warm. I crack the window, hoping some fresh air will blow the thoughts right out of my head.

I want Mr. Hayes to want me. God knows I crave him, but I also kind of feel like I wouldn't have a clue what to do with him if I got him. A man like him knows not only what he's doing in the bedroom, but I'm sure he expects his partners to know what they're doing too.

I'm not a virgin. I've been with three guys, only two I went all the way with, but I'm not experienced by any stretch of the imagination. Just having Mr. Hayes place his hand around my neck was more exciting than all of my sexual experiences combined—and then some.

I can feel his eyes still burning into me as I watch the city lights dance around us while Phil navigates traffic.

"Something on your mind?" His melodic voice interrupts my thoughts.

Yeah, your hands around my neck, touching my waist, my lower back.

I smile. "No, I'm just excited for the evening. Thanks again for inviting me. I feel a bit—" I look down at the dress that cost more than my rent and lightly touch the gold and diamond rope necklace on my neck. I made the associate hide the tag so I wouldn't know how much it cost when she put it on me. "Out of my element is all."

"I understand. These people can be… intimidating. Most of them are just full of shit like the rest of us, pretending they have it together when they're full of anxiety and have issues just like us."

"Just like us. Right." I nod, reminding myself that I'm not like Mr. Hayes or any of them. I'm the hired help.

"Well, they might not have financial issues, but I can tell you they're not as *together* as they'd like to seem." He leans forward as the car slows to a stop in front of the Chicago Art Institute. I glance out the window. A red carpet leads up the stairs, right between the two giant lions that adorn the entrance.

"Listen," he says, reaching out and taking my hand. I glance down to where we're joined and his skin feels like it's burning through my own. "Don't be scared of these people. You're more genuine and real than most of them. It's good for them to hear about where their money is going, and I say this not to be derogatory so please don't take it that way, but from a *normal* person. Not someone who's so far removed from reality because their world is money."

"I thought they were just like us," I say, his fingers still holding mine.

He drops his gaze to our hands as he runs his thumb softly over the skin on the back of my hand.

"They're like us in the sense that they're scared too. Money can buy a lot of things, including power, but it can't buy goodness or genuineness. It can bring you all sorts of opportunity, but it can also leave you very… lonely."

93

A look of sadness darts across his face and it feels strange for us to be having this intimate moment in the hustle of downtown Chicago where people are piling out of cars and horns are blaring.

"Sir?" Phil says as he opens the back door, snapping Mr. Hayes' attention back to where we are.

"Time to go." He plasters on a big smile and steps out of the car, extending his arm to assist me.

I feel like a baby deer on wobbly legs or perhaps cattle being led to the slaughter. I'm so out of my element here. I have a moment of panic when we step through the entrance and into the great hall. I don't know what I was expecting but it wasn't this. There are dozens and dozens of people milling about. A band plays in the corner as white coat waiters pass out hors d'oeuvres and flutes of champagne.

"Graham! Pleasure to see you." A short balding man approaches Mr. Hayes with an outstretched hand.

"Walt, pleasure's mine," Mr. Hayes says curtly before turning to me. "And this is Miss Silver. She is a music educator. Dedicated her life to bringing music and the arts to children."

"Good evening, sir. Pleasure," I say, extending my hand before second-guessing if I should curtsy. I've never been to anything this fancy in my life, and I realize there's probably a standard of etiquette here that I am completely unaware of. That scene from *Pretty Woman* flashes through my brain where she's trying to count the tongs on the forks to determine which one to use.

"Relax," Mr. Hayes whispers in my ear as he attempts to release his hand from my iron grip. I let go, not even realizing I was still clinging to him.

After a few more introductions, I'm feeling a little more confident in myself when I see people perk up at the mention of my background and education. Not to mention, the glass of champagne I downed in the coat closet a few moments ago. I nurse a second glass, talking joyously with three others about the need for funding and importance of teaching music and the arts to young people. It feels wonderful to be surrounded by people with such means that could make a huge impact on something so important to me.

"So, Margot, tell us. Is a beautiful young woman like yourself single? Some of us have eligible sons." Miss Weatherby, a woman probably around my mother's age, nudges me gently as the others around us laugh.

"Seriously, my David could use a bright young woman like yourself to keep him on the straight and narrow." Mr. Shaw, a fellow member of the billionaire's club like Mr. Hayes, shakes his head and rolls his eyes in exasperation. "Helluva kid though," he says to me as if that will somehow make taking on being the mother to a problem child in his early thirties less toxic.

I can feel myself blush as everyone stares at me, waiting for me to answer. I glance to my right and see Mr. Hayes staring at me as well. I lift the flute of champagne to my lips and take a small sip, about to answer when he steps forward and puts his hand on my elbow.

"I think Miss Silver needs a moment to catch her breath and grab something to eat." He smiles.

Thank you, I mouth to him as he ushers me away from the vultures lurking.

"Guess I forgot to mention that these things are also treated a bit like a matchmaking game. Most of the time they're just looking for someone to take over being a parent for their man-child that has a 'social' drinking problem and mainlines cocaine and opiates like they're candy."

"That sounds lovely." Shock settles over my face. "And you're friends with all these people?"

"No, it's purely business."

We both pick up a fresh drink from the bar and make our way to a private area with a view of the city.

"So what do you normally do at these things?" I swirl the stir stick around my drink.

"Pretty much the same thing. Socialize. Try to get these schmucks to give up their money."

I laugh and his eyes dart to mine.

"Who is your normal date?" He takes a long sip of his drink as if he's contemplating what to share or maybe how to say it.

"I wouldn't say I have a *normal* date. Nobody that I bring regularly. Most of the time it's just me. I've taken a few different women over the years, nobody of importance. Why do you ask?"

I shrug. "Just curious, I guess, what a real date with Graham Hayes looks like."

"A *real* date? As in this"—he motions between us—"isn't a *real* date?"

"Well, I guess it's a date of sorts but like you mentioned previously, my expertise and education lent to the subject matter of tonight's event." I'm trying to sound coy, hell, maybe I'm even flirting with him to try and bait him to tell me it was more than that.

"And what constitutes a *real* date to you, Miss Silver?"

I tilt my head off to the side, contemplating his question.

"I wouldn't say there's a list or specific formula for a date but oftentimes, or at least in my limited experience, there's dinner, drinks, dancing… definitely flirting."

He nods, taking another sip. "Limited experience?" he asks, staring out the window.

"I'm only twenty-six, Mr. Hayes. I haven't really had that many interested parties." I laugh.

"I noticed you didn't answer their question earlier, about if you were single."

"I was about to, but you stepped in and whisked me away."

He places his drink down on the windowsill and turns to face me, taking a few steps closer until he has to look down on me.

"And what would your answer have been?"

"Yes, I'm single."

"So, we didn't have dinner here but there were hors d'oeuvres and we both have drinks and I think that"—he points to the middle of the room where a few couples have begun dancing—"is dancing."

I look over my shoulder. "And your point is?"

He takes the drink from my hand and places it next to his before linking his fingers through mine and leading me out onto the floor. He snakes his arm around my waist, pulling me closer to him while his other hand is still holding mine.

"That we've had drinks, some food, and now dancing."

I feel like my heart is about to pound through my chest. I'm worried he'll feel it against his. He leans his head down, placing his lips at my ear.

"I'd say that's a pretty damn real date."

We sway to the music, his feet gliding across the floor as he takes me with him. I had no idea I knew how to dance. I don't actually; it's more like he's guiding me and I'm following along. I close my eyes briefly, the warmth of his body pressing against me so tightly. I can smell his cologne. It's doing all sorts of things to my lower belly. A heavy pressure is building and I can't seem to control it.

"Relax." He says that word to me again as he drags the hand that's on my waist up my back till it rests at the base of my neck. His fingers pinch me softly before rubbing small circles into my skin. A tingle runs from where he's touching me all the way down my spine.

"I'm trying. I just never danced with my boss in front of people before at an event with billionaires and elected officials." I let out a shaky laugh.

"Mmm, I guess I am your boss, aren't I?" The way he says it sounds so naughty and forbidden.

The song ends and we stop moving but he doesn't disconnect from my body. I look up at him slowly. His eyes feel like they're staring into my soul. I lick my lips instinctively and his eyes drop from mine to my lips as my tongue drags across them.

We're so close. It feels like time is standing still and every fiber of my being is silently begging him to kiss me. Kiss me, kiss me, my brain says over and over again as I hold my breath.

"Mind if I cut in?" A stranger's voice breaks the spell and Mr. Hayes steps back, breaking our connection as the moment evaporates.

"Fuck off, Garrett," Mr. Hayes says as he turns my body away from the man.

He ushers me through the crowd of people, giving quick handshakes and acknowledging a few people here and there as we walk toward the exit.

"Are we leaving?" I ask, confused.

"Yes."

"Who was that guy?" I glance over my shoulder, but he's already lost in the crowd.

"My CFO." His tone is clipped.

"You just told your CFO to—"

"Yes. Trust me. His intentions weren't good and I wouldn't trust him to touch you with a fifty-foot pole."

We walk quickly down the stairs as Phil is already waiting with the car, the back door open.

The drive home is silent.

"Did I do something wrong?" I ask as the car pulls to a stop and we exit, making our way back inside the house.

He's practically dragging me up the stairs and I stumble, my heel getting caught on the carpet. He reaches out his arms to catch me, helping me right myself on the landing.

"No," he whispers, tucking a piece of hair behind my ear.

"Well, if this were a normal date, I'd ask if you wanted to come inside for a drink, but this is your house and we're already inside." I glance around. The house is totally dark as I walk toward my quarters. "And it seems late."

"And I'm your boss." He repeated my observation from earlier and I realize that was the pivotal point in the evening that snapped him back to reality before he dragged me back home.

"Yes, and there's that," I say nervously. "Hey, thanks again for bringing me tonight. I feel like I was able to share a lot of valuable knowledge with important people that can make a difference. I just hope it helped."

He follows me to my door. I turn, my back against it, and grab the handle just as he reaches his hand out to grab my chin. He steps even closer.

"I would say yes."

"To what?" I ask, knowing full well what he meant. I just want to hear him say it.

"To coming inside for a drink."

I swallow as I realize what he's saying.

"Put your hands against the door."

I don't reply, just obey, placing the palms of my hands flat against the door behind me as he bends down a little to grab for my dress with one hand as the other makes its way around my throat again.

"Don't move them from the door."

He lifts my dress, his hand sliding down the front of my panties. His other tightens around my throat as he drags the pad of his thumb across the dip at the base.

"Don't say a word."

His face is centimeters from mine, his lips so close I could tip my head up and kiss him, but I don't.

He slides his finger up my slit once, then twice. Moisture was already gathering long before he touched me. He presses his finger against me, sliding inside just an inch, and I gasp. He releases the finger, sliding it out and then all the way back in as a long, low moan tumbles from my lips.

He repeats the process over and over until he brings a second finger to join the first and his thumb begins to circle my clit.

I'm panting, tiny little moans escaping my lips each time he thrusts his fingers back inside me. I close my eyes, trying to grab at the wooden door behind me as he crooks his fingers and thrusts harder and faster.

I lean my face forward, attempting to capture his lips, but he presses his hand against my throat so my head rests against the door, stopping me.

My legs are shaking.

My breath is jagged and uneven.

I close my eyes.

"Look at me." The words sound gravelly and deep like he's gritting his teeth. He tightens his grip on my throat as I begin to tremble, my orgasm so close. He doesn't say anything else, just watches me intently as I tremble and quiver at what he's doing to me.

I'm trying to be silent but it's no use. I press my palms hard against the door as he slams his fingers into me over and over, his hot breath coming out in puffs against my lips as his eyes bore into mine.

I'm done. I fall apart, my body clenching around his fingers as my knees let go and I fall against him. It's silent, just the sounds of our labored breathing echoing around us.

Slowly he pulls his fingers from me before hooking them in my panties and sliding them down my legs completely. He leans down, helping me out of them before fisting them in his hand. He uses them to wipe between my legs, cleaning off his fingers in the process and then sliding them into his pocket.

He reaches around me, his hand on the door handle as he gently opens it.

"Good night, Margot."

I stand in utter disbelief, still unsure if that really just happened, but the tingling sensation running through my body and the feeling of delicious relief confirms that it did. He doesn't say another word, just walks down the hall to the stairs leading up to the third floor.

A smile breaks across my face as I turn toward my doorway when I see a shadowy figure in the moonlight. I think I'm seeing things, but then it moves and I see Miss Perry emerge from the darkness.

"Be careful." Her icy words startle me. "This isn't the first time we've had to hire a new nanny."

12

GRAHAM

That was stupid but I don't regret it.

I finger her lace panties in my pocket, pulling them out and bringing them to my nose to inhale her scent.

"Fuuuuck," I groan as I reach down and adjust my hardening cock.

I wanted to lick every drop of her sweet nectar from my fingers when I pulled them from her, but I knew if I did, I would have ripped that dress off her and fucked her right there on the floor within an inch of her life.

I close my eyes, reaching down to undo my belt and slide the zipper down my trousers. I reach inside my boxer briefs and grip myself. I stroke myself once, then twice, feeling my release already building.

I walk to my bathroom, removing the rest of my clothes along the way, but keeping her soaked panties in my hand.

I'm a sick fuck, I think to myself as I bring them to my nose again and inhale the scent as I return my attention back to my throbbing cock.

I'm not gentle. I stroke myself roughly as I grip her panties. It feels like I'm fighting a losing battle as I try to shut out the voice in my head that says to stop.

I don't stop. Instead, I tease myself, bringing myself to the brink of an orgasm a few times before finally losing all control and grunting loudly as I spill my release into the sink. I stare at myself in the mirror; a thick layer of sweat beads on my forehead, and the veins in my neck bulge at the exertion.

After a long shower, I lie in bed, staring at the ceiling, promising myself that tomorrow I'll be a better man.

* * *

"Good morning, sir." Miss Perry's chipper voice instantly annoys me. "To what do we owe the pleasure of having you join us for breakfast?"

I pour myself a cup of coffee and reach for one of the muffins on the table.

"Good morning," I say as I pull out a chair next to Eleanor. Margot's eyes catch mine briefly before she looks away, a faint hint of pink blossoming on her cheeks.

"I have to go into the city this morning after I drop Eleanor off at her grandmother's. I just thought it might be nice to eat breakfast with her," I reply to Miss Perry.

"Yay! Breakfast with Daddy!" Eleanor says around a mouthful of blueberry pancakes.

"It's your day off, Miss Silver. You don't need to get her ready for the day."

"It's no worry. It's part of my routine and I love spending time with her," she says softly as she clutches her glass of orange juice like it's about to run away.

"Any plans for the day?" I ask her.

She looks up at me and then over at Miss Perry like there's something going on I'm not aware of.

"Uh, yeah, actually. I'm meeting a friend at a coffee shop around eleven and we're just going to spend the afternoon together."

"In the city?"

She nods her head. "Yes, over off of Madison near Racine."

"Why don't I take you? I have to drop Eleanor off at my mother's soon and I'm heading downtown anyway."

"Oh, no, that's not necessary. I'm heading to the west loop so..." She trails off.

"So it's on my way into my office, then." I smile. "It's a deal. We'll leave here in twenty," I say as I stand and check my watch. I walk out before she can respond.

* * *

"We'll take the Range Rover," I say as I hit the button to unlock it.

Margot helps Eleanor into her car seat as I take her bag and place it in the back seat along with Muffin in her carrier who is letting me know she's not very happy about it.

"Why does the damn cat have to go with her?" I mutter, climbing behind the wheel.

"Grammy likes Muffin," Eleanor says with a whiny tinge to her voice. She hates any time I speak poorly about her kitten. As much as I hate to admit it, the damn thing is starting to grow on me.

"I think daddy does too," Margot says under her breath with a chuckle.

"What makes you say that?"

She snaps her head up from buckling her seat belt, clearly not realizing I'd heard her.

"I saw her sneak into your office the other day and she didn't come out for over an hour." She smiles. "And then I heard you ask Miss Perry for a lint roller."

I shake my head as she and Eleanor giggle.

After we drop off Eleanor, the ride to the city is quiet. Margot stares out the window, lost in thought again.

"Hey," she says, pulling her head away from the window and turning to face me. "I've been meaning to ask you something and I completely forgot about it. I stopped by my old apartment to pay my rent, and my landlord said *you* called and paid my entire lease off?"

I nod.

"You really didn't need to do that, Mr. Hayes."

"I did. One of the requirements of this job was to be a live-in nanny and that required you to move out of your current residence. It's only right I pay it off."

"Well, I appreciate it very much so thank you."

"No thanks necessary. It's simply a contract negotiation and it was pocket change."

I see her nod and turn back to the window. I feel bad. I purposely made it sound cold and not like it was something I did out of the goodness of my heart. I'm deflecting. Wanting to push her away after what happened between us last night.

"You're welcome... Margot." I say her name for only the second time and a smile spreads lazily across her lips. Something about saying her name just makes things all too real, but I like it.

I pull the SUV into a parking garage near the coffee shop she mentioned and put it in park. I point to the clock; it's only twenty minutes past ten.

"We're early, so do you mind if I walk in with you and grab a coffee myself?"

"Only if I can buy it for you for driving me."

"Deal."

We exit the vehicle and make our way out of the parking garage and onto the sidewalk. I instinctively place my hand at the small of her back as we walk the two blocks to the shop. It's a trendy place with exposed brick walls and brass light fixtures with Edison bulbs. A young hipster with a handlebar mustache and a bright-orange beanie welcomes us.

"You don't come to coffee shops much, do you?" Margot asks as I stare over the menu of items I don't even recognize.

"No. I'm a black coffee man. The darker the roast the better."

She giggles and touches my chest softly, a small gesture that instantly makes me want to reach out and pull her to me.

"Don't worry. I'll help you out." She steps up to the counter and orders.

"I'll have a grande dirty chai tea latte with oat milk and he'll have a grande Americano."

"That was English?" I ask and she laughs again.

"Oh, come on, you're not that old. Starbucks was around when you were my age."

The mention of age is one of those immediate dampers on any good thoughts I have about me and her.

"Wasn't a coffee drinker back then," I say as we move over to the waiting area for our drinks.

I find myself standing a little behind her; my hands instinctively come out to rest on her waist. It feels oddly natural and I feel her slightly relax her back against my chest.

They call our order out and we step up and grab our drinks.

"I still have thirty minutes. Do you want to sit with me for a bit?" She motions toward a small table in the corner and I follow her. Just before we get to it, I see a love seat that's open and grab her hand, steering her toward it instead.

I want to be close to her, to feel her against me. I take a seat and pull her down next to me, our bodies touching from shoulder to knee.

We sit in silence for a moment, both of us savoring our coffee before I feel her turn a little in the seat to face me.

"So is this the part where you give me a talk and tell me last night was a mistake?"

I let out a single, throaty chuckle, turning to look at her.

"I probably should but no." I reach out, taking a piece of her hair between my thumb and forefinger. "Is that what you wanted me to do? Apologize? Tell you that I have no business messing around with a woman young enough to be my daughter?"

"Your *daughter*? You're not that old."

"I'm forty-two, sweetheart. Technically, I could have fathered a child at sixteen." I raise my eyebrows and she just rolls her eyes.

"Is that what we're doing? Messing around?" she asks.

I let the curl in my fingers fall to her shoulders and move my hand to cup her cheek, running my thumb across her lip. The tip of her pink tongue darts out and makes contact with the skin of my thumb and I inhale a sharp breath.

Fucking little tease.

"You know exactly what you do to me, don't you?" Her eyes are big, focused on mine, and she doesn't say anything. "You look like such an innocent little thing, but I bet if I put my cock to these lips, you'd know exactly what to do."

I've lost all sense of control. My blood pressure is probably off the charts right now and I'm close to crushing this cup of coffee in my hand.

"Margot?"

A man's voice interrupts us and she jumps back, breaking our contact.

"Hank!" she replies leaping off the love seat and running up to the man with arms outstretched.

This is her friend?

I'm instantly annoyed. Not only because he just ruined the moment but because who the fuck is this big oaf and why didn't she mention she was hanging out with a man?

"It's so good to see you," she says as he releases her. She turns back to me.

"Mr. Hayes, this is Hank Byers, my friend from teaching. He's the PE teacher at my old school."

Hank juts his hand out to me enthusiastically, his blond hair flopping with the movement.

"Hank, this is my boss, Mr. Graham Hayes."

She says it so cheerfully but the word *boss* feels like ice running through my veins. No, we've never said we're anything more than that, but literally fifteen seconds ago I was talking about having my cock in her mouth and her eyes were so heavy-lidded with lust I was sure I could talk her into a blow job back in my SUV with zero effort.

"Nice to meet you, Hank." I smile before turning my attention back to Margot. "Thank you for the coffee, Miss Silver. I'll see you back at the house."

And with that, like a puppy with my tail between my legs, I drag myself and my damaged ego across the coffee shop and out the door. I glance back through the pane glass windows to see if she's looking after me, but she's not. She's already smiling at something Hank is saying, her hand resting on his bicep as her head falls back in laughter.

That's exactly the reminder I need that whatever feelings I thought might be brewing between her and I are one-sided.

* * *

I BURY myself in work over the next week. I go into the office early. I stay late. I do any and everything I can to avoid Margot and when I do have to interact with her, I keep it brief and to the point.

I don't try to analyze my actions. I know damn well why I'm punishing her like this.

I hear a soft knock on my home office door. I don't bother saying anything. I know it's Margot by the way she knocks. Still, she walks softly into the room until she's standing in front of my desk.

"Can I help you?" I say, not even looking up from the report I've been pouring over for the last hour.

"Just wanted to check in and see how things were going? I haven't really seen you around much lately." She takes a seat in the chair across from me.

I can hear the trepidation in her voice which tells me she's either clearly picked up on my mood and the distance I've put between us or she's feeling unease about letting me down easy with *Hank*.

What a stupid jock name, I think to myself. It's childish and downright petty, making fun of a man's name in my own head, but I'm in no mood to talk sense into myself or be rational.

Is this what rejection feels like?

"Been busy," I mutter as I pick up another stack of papers to appear busier than I actually am.

"Yeah, I noticed." She stands, shoving her hands into the back pockets of her jeans and walks over to the bay of windows that overlook the pool.

"Is there something you need, Miss Silver?"

Her head snaps toward me. "So I'm Miss Silver again?"

I lean back in my chair. I'm aware of the point she's trying to make but I play like I'm not.

"Haven't you always been?"

She nods, her tone instantly changing to mirror my own. "I'm going to take Eleanor swimming after her nap." She continues looking out the window. "But yes, I do need something. The contract wasn't clear on if I work every Saturday, and since I've worked most since being brought on, I wanted to let you know that I have plans this Saturday so I can't work."

"Great," I say, turning my attention back to my desk. "Let Miss Perry know and make sure you close my door on your way out."

Without another word, she does exactly that.

A short while later I'm still buried in reports, but my concentration is interrupted by the sound of Eleanor squealing, followed by a splash.

I stand from my desk and walk over to the windows, looking down at the pool where she and Margot are playing. At least Eleanor is playing. She has her floaties on her arms as she splashes around the shallow end. I watch her, pure joy radiating off her as she runs and jumps into the water.

My gaze drifts to where Margot is stretched out on one of the deck chairs, a little two-piece stretched tightly over her taut body. I feel my mouth water as I drag my eyes up her legs, to the juncture of her thighs where I had my fingers buried not too long ago.

I love the slight swell of her hips just before the drastic dip of her tiny waist. Her perky tits look positively delicious wrapped in the emerald-green spandex material. I squint, the outline of her hard nipples just visible. I'd give anything to suck one into my mouth, biting down as I plump the other breast in my hand.

I look down at my crotch, my erection tenting my pants. I should feel ashamed but I don't. I want to pull my cock out and get myself off but not with Eleanor running around outside.

I lift my eyes once more to look at her, only she's staring right back up at me. She pulls her sunglasses down briefly, revealing her eyes before turning over so that I have a clear view of her half-naked ass.

Is she teasing me?

I crack my neck and walk back over to my desk. If she thinks she can flirt with me and then act like it meant nothing to her the moment Hank pops back into her life, she's got another thing coming.

13

MARGOT

Something is clearly going on with Graham.

He's made it more than clear that our flirty, innuendo-laden moments are something he regrets, and frankly, I don't have the energy to play his little game of hard to get or *figure out what's wrong with me.*

I'm chalking it up to our meeting with Hank. There's nothing going on between me and him, but I'm not going to let him throw a tantrum about it and then run to make him feel better. If he has questions about me and Hank, he can ask me like an adult.

I don't actually have plans for this Saturday night but I wanted an excuse to talk to Graham, to see if he'd gotten out of his funk, and I am in serious need of some me time. As much as I love spending as much time as I do with Eleanor, I could use a spa day or even just a junk food and Netflix night in my room or at Shell's.

I adjust myself in the deck chair, already aware of his presence in the second-story window. I pull my glasses down, letting him know I can see him before making a show of turning over. I flip, arching my back a little extra, sending my ass sky high before settling onto my stomach to cheer Eleanor on in her attempt to nail the perfect cannonball.

"Eight point five!" I say as she emerges from the water. "I think your last splash was a teensy bit bigger."

My phone chirps and I pick it up from the table and see a text from Shelly.

Shelly: *Hey! Thanks again for setting me up with Hank. He's so hot! Having our second date tonight.*

I smile, excited that they hit it off. God knows she's been in serious need of a man who will treat her right.

Me: *Yay! Told you he was fine. So, second date, huh? Things are going well, I take it?*

Shelly: *Yeah. We had a great time on our first date. Had drinks but then they turned into dinner and then that turned into second drinks and then dancing.*

Me: *So did you guys...?*

Shelly: *No... weirdly. He was so nice and genuine, and we had such a nice time that I didn't want to just jump right into that. I felt like I wanted to spend more time with him first.*

Me: *Oh my God. Awwwww, you like him; that's why!*

I send several heart emojis and the silly smiley face that looks like hearts are floating around it.

Shelly: *Eww, no, gross. Don't ruin it. It was our first date. Relax. We just had fun and we're having fun again tonight. Who knows, it might happen tonight.*

Me: *Where are you guys going tonight?*

Shelly: *One of those fancy dinner cruises on Lake Michigan. Some dude handed us a flyer with a coupon when we were walking around yesterday, and we both realized we've lived here our entire lives and never gone on one.*

Me: *That's so romantic. Look at you two making memories already.*

I know she hates when I try to make things romantic or bring emotions into her dating life, but I can't help it; I want them to fall in love.

Shelly: *Again, gross feelings. Eww, no. It's just dinner on a boat.*

She follows it up with several of the flipping off emojis and it makes me laugh.

Me: *Whatever you say. I hope you guys have a great time. Keep me posted!*

I put my phone down and spend the next hour in the pool with Eleanor.

"Hey, how about we make some cookies?" I say to her as I dry her off.

She claps her hands and jumps up and down. "Yes, cookies!"

After we dry off and get dressed, I tie her apron around her and place a chair next to me against the counter so she can help.

"Okay, two eggs," I say, holding out my hand.

"Two eggs," she says, reaching into the carton. "One." She places it in my hand as she reaches for a second, "Tw—" It slips out of her hand and rolls across the counter before splatting on the floor.

She looks over at me, her eyes huge like she's worried she's in trouble, but I laugh to let her know it's okay.

"What the hell is this mess?"

Mr. Hayes walks into the kitchen, his eyes immediately going to the broken egg on the floor and the random splotches of flour everywhere.

"We're baking cookies," I say with a smile.

"Yeah, Daddy. Chocolate chip ones."

"Make sure you thoroughly clean this up when you're done," he mutters before turning and walking back out of the room.

"Why's Daddy mad?" Eleanor's lower lip pokes out and her chin quivers.

"Here," I say, picking her up from the chair and setting her on the floor. I grab a handful of paper towels. "You clean that up really quick while I go talk to your daddy, okay? I'll be right back."

I step out and chase after Mr. Hayes down the hall.

"Sir," I say, and he slows down to turn toward me. "I'm not sure what's going on or why you've suddenly decided to aim all of your anger and vitriol toward me, but I can take it. She, on the other hand" —I point down the hall toward the kitchen—"doesn't understand. She's been asking about where you are all week and why you're in such a bad mood."

I see his jaw tick. "Excuse me?" he says, taking a step toward me.

I straighten my back and stand my ground. He's not going to intimidate me about this.

"You heard me. She doesn't deserve for you to take out whatever immature feelings you have going on in there. You're being childish." I cross my arms over my chest and jut my chin out to show that I'm serious.

He takes another step toward me, then another. I tell myself to stand strong, but I falter, stepping back to keep some distance between us when my back hits the wall. He places his hands flat against the wall on either side of my head. He leans his head down, tilting it so his lips are near mine.

"You've got a mighty bold tongue on you, Miss Silver. Someone should teach you a lesson on how to control it."

"Are you offering?" I don't know what compels me to keep running my mouth, but a sudden wave of courage takes over. I drop my arms to my sides, his presence completely overtaking me.

He lets out that low, throaty rumble of a laugh and it makes me feel all sorts of tingly sensations between my thighs. He steps closer, pressing his body against mine as he grabs my wrists in a flash and pins them above my head, his hardness pressing against my lower belly.

I gasp, his movements so quick they hardly register.

"I don't think you could *handle*"—he pushes his hips into me harder, his manhood growing harder by the second—"a lesson from me."

I try not to let it show but I'm absolutely trembling with need for this man. I want to tell him to go fuck himself but instead I rise up on my tippy-toes. "Or maybe you're all talk," I whisper in his ear.

"Why do you insist on teasing me?" He presses his nose against mine. "Or defying me."

Suddenly, he drops my hands and takes several steps back. His eyes are glassy, his breath shallow as his chest rises and falls. And just like nothing happened, he turns and walks back down the hall to his office, slamming the door behind him.

* * *

I FLOP BACK on my bed. It's only eight thirty p.m. on a Thursday. Eleanor is down for the night and I'm still trying to come up with plans for Saturday night.

I grab my phone and send a text to Shelly to see if she'll be available.

Me: *Hey, so how'd the date go? Want to hang on Saturday night?*

She doesn't respond right away so I start looking through Netflix to add things to my list in case she's busy.

I click through a few romantic comedies, adding one about a guy who sounds perfect on paper but from the synopsis sounds like he's a fraud.

I also add *Schitt's Creek* back to my list even though I've seen it at least three times. I mean, can you ever really have too much Dan Levy?

Moments later Shelly texts back.

Shelly: *Date went well. Sorry, just got busy with work. Which brings me to Saturday. I'm working a double Saturday and Sunday. Sorry! Rain check.*

I toss the phone on my bed and step into my bathroom.

"Guess it's a self-care night in."

I contemplate a bath when my phone rings. I rush to flip it over, seeing Hank's name on the screen.

"Hey, how's it going?"

"Hey," he says, sounding a little off.

"I just texted Shell. She said she had a great time on your dates."

"Yeah." He hesitates. "They were great."

"What's wrong? You sound weird." I furrow my brows even though I know he can't see me.

"Well, that's why I was calling you actually. I know this is probably super weird, but uh, would you want to grab a drink this Saturday? I kind of wanted to talk to you about Shelly, maybe pick your brain."

"Yeah, for sure," I say, a bit concerned. "Everything okay?" Now I'm worried that Shelly might be way more into him than he is into her. That's always the shittiest position to be in.

"Yeah, yeah, I just wanted to ask you some things about her, not in a talk behind her back or get information kind of way, but since you're her good friend, I just thought it would make sense to get your input and it's easier talking in person than text. I would explain it all right now but I'm actually about to ump a softball game."

"Yeah, sure. I totally understand. How about Jillian's over in your neighborhood at seven?"

"Perfect," he says, "And thanks, Margot. You're the best."

I hang up, glad I have plans for Saturday finally, but a little worried about what's going on with Hank and Shelly, or rather, more confused.

I spend most of Friday preoccupied with what Hank needs to talk to me about. I was tempted to text Shelly and double-check if something happened, but I figured I should wait to hear what Hank has to say first.

Eleanor will be home for lunch soon from her ballet class. I assemble a plate for her when Miss Perry comes barging into the kitchen.

"Mr. Hayes needs you to work Saturday," she says, not even looking at me.

"I already told him I have plans and can't work Saturday."

"Well, you need to cancel them," she snips.

"Why does he need me to work?" I ask suspiciously.

"I don't think that's really any of *your* business." She talks down to me like she's not part of the same staff I am. Like somehow, she's better than the rest of us.

I toss the fork in my hand onto the counter. "He working from home today?" I ask, not waiting for an answer as I march my ass down to his office.

I don't bother knocking this time. I open the door and slam it behind me. He looks up at me, a surprised expression on his face that quickly morphs into annoyance. I don't wait for him to scold me for not knocking.

"I told you I had plans Saturday and I can't work. Funny how you've never once demanded I work a Saturday before, but this *one* time I tell you I have plans, you decide, nah, screw her plans; she needs to work."

"Believe what you want, Miss Silver, but it was purely coincidental. I have a work event in the city this Saturday, and I simply can't miss it."

"So cancel it then," I say with a giant fake smile, flailing my hands in the air.

He stares at me, his eyes narrowing. "I cannot leave Eleanor with Miss Perry all day and all night and my mother has a bridge tournament. Last time I checked, I pay *you* to be the nanny so you will work this Saturday."

"Or what?" I say, attempting to call his bluff. "You fire me? Then that puts you in an even bigger situation because then you won't have anyone to watch her Saturday or Monday or Tuesday." I list off the days of the week on my fingers and I can see he's not amused.

"Can you please find someone to watch her, then?"

I exhale, feeling a bit like an ass since he's not lashing back out at me like I expected him to. "I'll watch her during the day, but I need to leave here for the city by five thirty p.m. at the latest. That's three hours; Miss Perry can handle it. Eleanor just needs help getting ready for bed, but she'll entertain herself with the iPad, her toys, a movie. Trust me, she doesn't want to engage Miss Perry any more than the rest of us."

I see him contemplating my offer. "Deal," he says and I turn to leave.

"Where are you going?"

"Eleanor will be home any minute. I need to finish her lunch."

"Saturday," he says, picking up a document and looking it over as he waits for me to answer.

I know I shouldn't. I tell myself not to goad the man, but the opportunity is right there in front of me, begging for me to take it.

"I have a date," I say matter-of-factly.

I actually see the red slowly creep up his neck, and yeah, it gives me a lot of pleasure.

"Make sure you write down where you'll be. I'll need to know in case of an emergency and I or Miss Perry needs to reach you."

"Why would you need *me* in case of an emergency? Wouldn't you be the person to reach out to in case of an emergency or maybe emergency personnel? Besides, you have my cell and so does Miss Perry."

His lips tighten and I can see his patience is wearing thin.

"Fine," I say, walking over to his desk and grabbing a Post-it Note and a pen. "Jillian's bar on Wabash." I write down the name and street and toss it onto his desk before leaving his office without another word.

* * *

"So LET me get this straight, the dates were perfect. You guys had an instant connection and crazy chemistry? She's the one who told you she wanted to see you again, and then she ghosted you?" I take a drink of my martini as Hank nods along to what I'm saying.

"She didn't fully ghost me. I'm not blocked or anything, but she's been super short with me, takes forever to respond, and keeps blowing off any of the dates I suggest to hang out again."

My phone buzzes in my purse for the third time since I've sat down with Hank only twenty minutes ago.

"Sorry, let me check this." I roll my eyes and glance down to see Mr. Hayes' name on the screen.

Graham: *Where are her favorite pj's? She refuses to wear the Cinderella ones.*

I type back a furious response to his third *where is this* question for the night. Turns out, his work event was canceled at the last minute so he stayed home with Eleanor.

Me: *Third drawer on the right. Please ask Eleanor these questions. I'm busy. She knows where everything is. Good night.*

"The boss. Anyway." I roll my eyes as I gesture toward my phone before placing it facedown on the bar. "Have you straight-up asked her what's going on?"

He shrugs. "In so many words. She said she's just busy with work and it's nothing personal, but it feels off."

I finish my martini and motion for a second from the bartender while I think over what Hank just said. My phone vibrates again.

Graham: *She said Muffin needs her nightly treat. What treats? Where?*

I contemplate what Hank is saying to me as I type out a rushed response.

Me: *Pantry, bottom shelf in the bin that says CAT STUFF. These aren't emergencies. Stop texting me. Good night.*

I see Hank's eyes drop to my phone. "So what's up with that guy anyway? You guys sleep together or something?"

I choke on my drink as I shake my head no.

"No, he's just not used to watching his own daughter on his own." I shrug, hoping that's the end of the conversation.

"Seems like you two were pretty close when I showed up at the coffee shop."

Shit. I hoped he hadn't noticed that.

I shrug. "I dunno. It's complicated, I guess. He's too scared to even kiss me and I can't imagine getting involved with your boss is ever a good idea."

He shakes his head and laughs. "I imagine not."

"How'd you guys end things on your last date?" I ask, changing the subject.

"We, uh…" He smiles as he looks down at his feet. "She stayed over."

"Ohhhh." I wriggle my eyebrows at him.

"Yeah, it was—amazing. I told her that it was the best I'd ever had, and she said the same. We stayed up all night talking and… ya know. The next morning I made her pancakes and she told me she wanted to see me again. We agreed, and then she left for work. We were texting back and forth very regularly that day and the next, and then I told her that I could see myself falling for her an—"

"Whoa, whoa, wait. That's it, Hank." He looks at me, confused. "You scared her." I reach out and grab his hand. "Shelly is wonderful and driven, but she's also kind of wild. Not in a *Girls Gone Wild* kind of way, but in a *she's young and wants to have fun* kind of way. I'm not saying there's no hope for you guys; please don't think that. But maybe she just needs to take things slower. She's been screwed over a few too many times."

The bartender hands me my second martini and I take a sip. I rarely drink and especially now that I'm a live-in nanny in the suburbs, I never get a chance to go out so the thought of tossing a few back and letting loose has my name written all over it.

My phone buzzes again, then again and again. I flip it over, look down at the screen, and see there's three more texts from Graham and two missed calls. I put it on airplane mode and toss it back in my purse.

"Dammit," he says, hanging his head. "I feel like an idiot."

"Don't, honestly. I should have told you that. I just didn't expect you both to jump in with both feet like that. I thought you would hit it off and just hook up and maybe have a little fling."

"Maybe I should just be honest with her. I'll tell her there's no need to rush things, but I like her and I'm not going anywhere."

"Maybe." I shrug. "I think you guys will be fine. I think she's just scared, but I promise if she says anything to me, I'll talk you up a lot, reminding her she's running away from a good thing." That makes him laugh. "And I'll keep you in the loop. Don't want you wasting your time or getting hurt."

"Thanks, Margot. You're always the best, you know that?" He nudges my shoulder as he finishes his beer. "You know, a few of the teachers at work always asked why we never dated."

"Yeah, I've gotten that question too." I laugh.

"Is it weird that for as awesome as you are, I only ever saw you like a sister?" He cringes a little when he says it, like he's scared he's going to hurt my feelings.

"Oh God, no. I feel the same way! I think you're amazing, but yeah, you're like my brother." We both laugh and go back to reminiscing about teaching together. He fills me in on the current gossip going around, including the rumor that the current administrator is dating the volleyball coach, and while they think they're being sneaky, everyone knows about them.

It's great catching up, but it makes me miss teaching. I haven't allowed myself to go down that rabbit hole since I got fired and became a nanny. For one, I can't imagine leaving Eleanor behind, and two, I don't want to be apart from Graham either.

Two hours later I've finished my third martini and I'm moving and grooving on the dance floor with Hank when suddenly I hear my name being shouted and someone pushing Hank away from me.

I spin around to see Graham, anger radiating off him as he grabs Hank's arm and leads him off the dance floor.

14

GRAHAM

"Hey, man! Whoa, what's going on?"

Hank holds his hands up and stumbles backward as I fist the front of his shirt.

"The fuck you think you're doing?" I spit. A few people are watching us, but I don't care.

"We're just having a good time, man. Who are you again?"

He looks at me, squinting like he remembers meeting me but can't place me.

"Oh, you're her boss. Shit, I thought it was her night off?"

He's clearly confused and probably a touch inebriated. I release his shirt and look back. Margot waves at us before returning to the bar.

"Why'd you let her get so intoxicated, hmm? What's your fucking angle?" I'm still up in his face and he's still trying to back away from me.

"We're just friends, I swear. I didn't try to get her drunk; we're just letting loose."

I step back. He seems genuinely confused and like he's telling the truth.

"Go close out your tab and head home. Your date with Margot is over." I run my hands through my hair, exasperated that I'm standing here. I told myself not to get involved in her private life, especially on her day off, but I couldn't shake the thought of her going home with another man.

"It's not a date—never mind," he mutters as he walks past me and back over to where Margot is sitting.

Not a date?

I follow behind him. I can see the angry expression on Margot's face as I get closer to where she's sitting on the barstool. Her dress has ridden up a little, exposing her thigh. It's a simple black dress with a small slit on one side.

"What the hell is going on? Why are you here?" she snaps the moment I approach.

I reach down and grab the hem of her dress, pulling it down roughly, causing her to slip on the stool. She slaps my hand away.

"Hey, Margot, I'm heading home. I had a great time," Hank says.

"What? It's barely even ten; why are you leaving? Don't leave because of him; he's *leaving*," she snaps, looking over at me, her eyes a little glassy from the alcohol.

"It's okay, really. I've got a game tomorrow morning. I'll be in touch." He gives her a half hug, half pat on the back, clearly not wanting to further upset me, then takes off.

I turn to Margot, her eyes narrowed on mine. She points her finger in my chest.

"What the f—"

"Get your shit; we're leaving," I say, cutting her off.

"No. No, it's my night off and I'm having fun. I'm not leaving." She grips the edge of the stool and stomps her feet down on the lower rung.

We stare at each other for a moment.

"Why are you here?" she asks a little calmer this time.

"It was late. You were clearly ignoring my texts, and I don't trust Hank."

I don't mince words and I'm not going to pretend I'm here for any other reason.

She smiles.

"What?"

"You were jealous."

"Not even close," I lie as I pull the stool next to her a little closer before taking a seat.

"Whatever. But that was rude. Hank is a good guy and he's a friend. *Just* a friend."

"Then why'd you tell me you were on a date with him?" I motion to the bartender and he leans in to take my order. "Bourbon, McKenna, neat."

She just shrugs. "Looks like you wanted to make me jealous."

"He's dating my friend. They're having some issues and I was just offering some advice since I set them up."

I reach for her untouched glass of water and bring it to her hands. "Drink," I command.

"You know, you—"

"Drink it. All of it now. I won't say it again." This time she obeys. When she's done, I hand it to the bartender to refill as he places my bourbon down.

I can feel her looking at me out of the corner of my eye. She's spun her barstool to face me, her knees pushing against my thigh.

"Still wearing a tie, I see?" I watch as she places one hand on my thigh while reaching across me with her other hand to grab my tie. She leans closer, flipping it over to reveal the red, green, and gold logo.

"Gucci, of course." She slips it through her fingers before letting it fall back down against my chest, her hand still resting on my thigh.

I like her a little tipsy. She's not drunk; she just had enough that her inhibitions are clearly down... not that I would take advantage of that. I drag my eyes away from where her hand is burning through my pants to her exposed thigh. She crosses her leg, her dress riding up a little further. I swallow, my mouth salivating at the thought of dragging my tongue up her skin.

"See something you like?" She's watching me. *Fuck it.* I don't care if I'm being obvious. I let my gaze linger before slowly letting my eyes drift to hers.

I glance at my watch. "We should get home; it's late."

"I told you I'm not ready to leave. I'm off tomorrow so I can sleep in. Besides, you haven't finished your drink yet."

It feels a bit awkward between us, the air thick with innuendo, but for the first time in my life, I don't have a fucking clue what to say to break the tension.

"Hank asked me if we've slept together."

That'll do it. I swallow down the bourbon in my mouth, savoring the burn. I don't say anything; I just turn my head to look at her.

"I told him no, you were too scared to even kiss me."

Well, fuck me.

"Why are you scared to kiss me?" She takes the tumbler from my hands, her fingers softly grazing mine. She brings it to her lips and takes a drink, her eyes never leaving mine.

"I practice discretion, Margot."

"Oh, I'm Margot again. And that's not an answer to my question." She leans forward. "Graham."

The way she says my name sends a lightning bolt straight to my cock. That's the first time I've heard her say it and fuck me, I want to hear her moaning it, screaming it as I destroy her tight little pussy.

"Let's play a game."

"A game?" I arch an eyebrow.

"It's a drinking game we played in college. Called truth or drink or truth or shot."

"You're only having water." I motion to the still-full second glass in front of her.

"We'll do the shot version." She motions to the bartender and orders us each a shot of 1800 Tequila. "Here are the rules. We each have five questions we can ask the other person. You have to answer truthfully, or you can skip one question but you have to take a shot."

The strap on her dress slowly slides off her shoulder. I stare at it, distracted.

"So we have to answer at least four questions?"

She nods as the shots are placed down in front of us. I'm sure I'm going to regret this, but what the hell.

"Let's play," I say, reaching out to gently pull the strap back up her shoulder. Her head turns to watch me, her pupils dilating. I let my fingers linger a little longer than necessary. We're sitting face-to-face, my thighs spread and her legs somewhat between mine.

"Oh, and one other thing. Do you have a coin to flip?"

I reach into my pocket and pull out a quarter.

"We either play the sweet or spicy way. Heads it's sweet, tails it's spicy."

"Spicy? Sweet?" I'm thoroughly confused.

"Sweet meaning normal questions." She leans in as she says the next part like it's a secret she doesn't want anyone to hear. "Spicy meaning... *dirty* questions."

She flips the quarter and covers it with her hand as it lands.

Please let it be sweet. I don't think I could handle any more temptation.

"Tails... spicy." She giggles.

I let out an audible exhale; I have no idea what I'm getting myself into.

"I'll go first," she says as she chews her bottom lip, her eyes gazing off like she's trying to conjure up a good question. "Oh, got it, are you more of an ass man or boob guy?"

I chuckle because her eyes grow big like she's asking me something so naughty and devious, but yet she worded it so innocently.

"Both. Can't say I prefer one over the other."

"That's such a cop-out answer." She rolls her eyes.

I'm tempted to play it safe, but I decide to test her limits a little, push the boundaries.

"What can I say? I want to have my cake and eat it too. They're both fun to play with, touch, pinch, bite." I can see her breath quicken. "I love a good hand or mouthful of both at one time. And I like to fuck both of them."

Her mouth falls open and she lets out a little gasp. I take a sip of my bourbon, pretending to remain unbothered when the truth is, I'm thinking about fucking her in the ass right now.

"My turn." I smile, looking her dead in the eyes. "Have you ever been fucked in the ass, Margot?"

"No," she says, her cheeks fully pink.

"Hmm, shame."

She grabs for her water, taking several mouthfuls. "Have you ever had a threesome?"

"No. Doesn't appeal to me." I sip my drink. "Has a man ever made you squirt?"

She adjusts herself in her seat as she shakes her head no. *More water drinking.*

"If you're uncomfortable, we can stop the game." I reach out and place my hand on her exposed thigh. Her eyes drop down to watch as I draw lazy circles on her skin.

"No, I'm not uncomfortable. I'm just not used to hearing those words from *you.*"

"Trust me, sweetheart, I'm keeping it tame." I slide my hand between her thighs, letting it rest on the inside of one of her legs.

"Have you ever made a girl—squirt?"

"Yes." I squeeze her thigh and I feel her pull them together, trying to get more. "Have you ever fucked Hank?"

"No!" she responds quickly. "I promise, there's nothing there."

"Have you ever—"

She looks off in the distance again, thinking of a question. My eyes fall to her tits, begging to be handled, sucked, kissed—probably a full C if I had to guess.

"Oh, what did you mean when you said *don't call me that again unless you want to be punished?*"

I think back on the moment. I remember it clearly. I'm tempted to take the shot, not because I'm ashamed of the answer, but because I'm not sure she's ready to hear those thoughts. I don't want to scare her off.

I lean in, brushing her hair back as I snake my hand around the back of her neck. "I'll try to keep this brief and as nice as possible... but I like control in all aspects of my life. I'm sure that's pretty evident. And you are sweet and young and innocent." I run my hand up her throat.

"I'm not a virgin," she whispers.

"No, I know that. I mean, you're innocent." We're so close, both on the edge of our stools. I can feel people's eyes on us but I don't care. "When I mentioned fucking your ass and your tits a moment ago, you blushed. Now I know you haven't had a cock in your ass before, but I'd guess by your reaction that you've never had a man"—I drag my hand down until my finger slips between her breasts—"fuck these tits either, marking you with his cum."

She squeezes her thighs tightly around my hand that's still resting between them. She swallows and shakes her head no, confirming my suspicions.

"Now, when you called me *daddy* in my office that night"—I put my fingers around her throat and lean in closely—"it made me want to defile you and punish you in all sorts of filthy ways. If you want to call me daddy, then I'm going to punish you. I'll take every fucking liberty I want with your petite little body, and when you tell me you can't take me fucking you any longer, I'll flip you on your belly and use your ass. Does that answer your question?"

Her lips are parted, her breath heavy. I know if I dragged my hand up just a little higher I'd feel her panties sopping wet too.

"Your turn." I wink, releasing her body and drinking down the rest of my bourbon.

"You go," she croaks the words out, stumbling for her water.

"This is my last question, I guess..." I think for a moment. "Are you fucking anyone?"

"No." Her answer is quick.

She steps down from her seat, coming to stand right between my thighs.

"Have you pictured me naked?" She absentmindedly runs her hands up my thighs as she leans into me. I don't think she's even aware how fucking tightly wound I am right now. The liquor has clearly relaxed her.

I laugh as she reaches for my tie again. "You can always take a shot if you don't want to answer."

"What's your next question? Maybe I'll keep my shot for the last question."

"That's cheating."

"Yes, I've pictured you naked." I glance down her body. "Doing it right now."

"Why haven't you kissed me?" Her voice is breathy as she leans in again, her hands back on my upper thighs this time, clearly unaware how close she is to touching *me*.

"That your final question?" I take a sip of her water.

She nods her head yes as she drags her teeth over her bottom lip.

"Sweetheart, you've got about three seconds before you feel me against your leg." I glance down at her hands on my thighs but it's already too late. My cock throbs with need as it threatens to rip through my pants.

She looks up at me before releasing my thighs. "Stop avoiding my question or take the shot." She points with a nod of her chin to where it sits on the bar.

"I don't like tequila," I say as I reach out, grabbing her behind the neck and pulling her to me forcefully.

I press my lips to hers but she's too stunned to move. I lean back a few inches, my mouth hovering over hers. "Open your mouth for me, sweetheart." She obeys and I kiss her again. This time I don't hold back.

I sweep my tongue into her mouth, once, twice, three times. Each time I go deeper. I don't let myself linger though. I know if I don't break the kiss now, I'll have her in the bathroom bent over the counter in about five seconds.

"Now, let's go home," I say, tossing a few bills on the bar and grabbing her hand to lead her out to the waiting car.

The night air has cooled. I pull Margot close to me as we exit the bar and slide into the back of the car. I can't tell if she's tired or starting to sober up, but she's dead silent. Worry creeps in and I wonder if I may have pushed her too far too quickly tonight.

But just as we pull into traffic she turns toward me, pulling her dress up and silently climbing into my lap to straddle me. I reach over, sliding the divider up so Phil doesn't feel uncomfortable.

"What are you doing?" I ask as she settles on my lap. Warmth radiates from between her thighs.

"Why do you like to grab my throat?"

I reach up and do it. "Because it's so delicate. It's one of the first things I noticed about you." I rub my thumb back and forth over her skin before leaning in and planting a soft kiss. "Your skin is so soft. I wanted to drag my tongue up it the moment I saw you."

"Ohhhh." Her moan is barely a whisper as I do just that, dragging my tongue up her neck to her earlobe.

"I knew if I kissed you, I was done. I wouldn't be able to resist you. That's why I gripped you so tight, trying to keep distance between us." I pepper her neck with kisses, my hands falling to her hips, gripping them tightly.

In a single moment, we go from teasing to frenzied touching and kissing. I wind my hand in her hair as I reach up and pull the strap and top of her dress down. She's not wearing a bra. Her tits bounce free, her rosy-pink nipples hardening in the cool air.

I lean forward as I pull her hair back, hard. She yelps a little as her head falls back, exposing her neck and tits to my mouth as I lavish each nipple with kisses. I swirl my tongue around the hard bud once, twice before sucking it into my mouth. I repeat the process on the other, my hand at her hip pushing her down against my rigid cock.

I lean back as she begins to grind against me. I lean forward again, this time biting down on her nipple till she yells in pain.

"I want to fuck you so hard I split you in two," I grunt.

She opens her eyes, her hands trembling as she reaches for my belt. She undoes it, going for my zipper next, but I dart my hand out to stop her.

"Not like this," I say. "I'm not going to fuck you tonight, baby; you've been drinking."

She stares at me blankly before moving to fix her dress and climb off me.

"I didn't say I wasn't going to make you come." I hook her waist and pull her back onto me. I reach up and pull her dress back down as

I grab both her tits in my hands, taking them in my mouth, one after the other.

I reach my hand between her thighs. This time I don't stop. I press my hand against her panties. "Just like I thought, you're fucking soaked." I rub my thumb over her. "I want to bury my face in your pussy but I'll save that for later."

She whimpers, *fucking whimpers*, driving me insane. "I want to see your cunt, baby." I yank her dress up forcefully before pulling her panties to the side. "Fuck me." I grind my teeth as I look down at her little pink slit, begging to be stuffed.

"Please," she begs as she paws at me.

"Oh, are you begging me?" I run my thumb up and down her slit a few times, her thighs beginning to quiver.

"Yes, please, please." She repeats her plea as I slide two fingers inside her.

I'm not gentle. I have no interest in being gentle with her tonight. I glance out the window; we're nearly home.

"We've got about four minutes before we're home, baby. Let's see if we can make you squirt."

"I—I don't know if I can," she pants.

I hook my fingers as I find that spot inside her, applying pressure on her lower belly with my other hand. I thrust my fingers inside her as her fingers dig into my biceps.

"You're certainly aroused enough," I groan as her juices drip down my fingers.

She's moaning so loud I know Phil can hear her but I don't give a shit. I work her over harder and faster, her walls clenching around me as I tease her clit. I clamp my teeth down around her nipple as an animalistic scream erupts from her throat and she clenches my fingers with her pussy.

Her body convulses as an orgasm rips through her. I look down, watching as she squirts all over my shirt. I continue fucking her with my fingers till she rides out the last waves of pleasure and the car comes to a stop in front of the house.

I slide my fingers from her, her body limp against mine. This time,

I let myself taste her. I bring my fingers to my mouth, the scent heavenly as I lick them clean.

I can feel the fingers on my other hand digging into her hip. She'll have a bruise, no doubt. The only thing I can focus on right now is getting her inside and as far away from me as possible before I completely ruin her in this back seat.

15

MARGOT

I feel like I'm floating above my body, watching myself as I fall against Graham's chest in exhaustion.

I feel him remove his fingers from me, bringing them to his mouth. His moan is guttural as his fingers dig into my hip so hard I have to hold back tears. I can feel him shaking beneath me. I think he's going to give in and take me when I hear the back door open and the overhead light comes on.

"Thanks, Phil," he says, wrapping his arms around me and holding me against him as he climbs out of the car.

I wrap my arms tightly around his neck, my lips resting against his skin. I can taste the saltiness of the sweat on his neck.

The house is completely dark and silent. It's probably after midnight at this point. I bury my face in him as he carries me up the stairs and down the hall to my room. He stops at my door, sliding my body down his slowly till he steadies me on my feet.

I look down at his shirt. *Oh my God, it's wet!* I feel my hand cover my eyes in embarrassment, but he grabs it and pulls it away from my face.

"Don't," he whispers before planting a soft kiss on my forehead.

He reaches behind me, opening the door and walking me just

inside. I keep walking through the sitting area until I reach the bedroom door, but he doesn't follow. I turn back around and look at him. He hesitates, then takes a few more steps toward me.

"You need sleep," he says as he reaches for the hem of my dress, dragging it slowly up my body and over my head. It falls to the floor and my hands involuntarily come up to cover my breasts.

"I need a shower," I say, glancing toward the bathroom.

He steps around me, walking into the bathroom and turning on the light. I hear the water turn on. He steps into the doorway, reaching his hand out toward me.

He pulls me into the bathroom, turning me to face the mirror as he stands behind me, his hands on my shoulders. He pulls my hair to the side, kissing my neck softly, then my shoulder. His fingertips glide down my arms till they rest on my waist. His eyes catch mine in the mirror as his fingers stop at where he was grabbing me in the car.

"I'm sorry," he whispers, rubbing the spot that's already beginning to welt and bruise. Goosebumps break out across my skin as my head lulls back against him. His hands circle my waist, sliding down over my belly before moving back up my body to cup my breasts.

"I won't join you in the shower; it's too tempting." He massages my breasts, wetness pooling again between my thighs.

"I want more." My voice is heavy with need.

"So do I, but it's late and you need sleep." He hooks his thumbs in my panties, lowering himself as he drags them down my thighs. I turn and look over my shoulder. His gaze is settled on my ass. He looks up at me, then leans in and plants a soft kiss to each cheek before standing back up.

I can feel his cock pressing against my crack. I press back against him and hear his sharp intake of breath. Before I can register it, he pulls his hand back and brings it down swiftly against my cheek.

"Ow!" I yelp and he clamps his hand over my mouth.

"Don't fucking tease me, Margot. I told you. Unless you want to be punished. If you think that hurt, then trust me, you'll be begging for mercy if I really work you over."

He stares at my eyes in the reflection of the mirror. "Do you understand me?"

I nod my head and he releases his hand from my mouth, dropping it back down to my throat. He squeezes it tight as he presses his body against mine, his mouth at my ear.

"Good. Now, be a good girl and take a shower and go to bed. And next time you think about playing with me, just remember tonight, okay? Remember all the places I'll take it out on you. I'm not interested in being teased by you anymore. Next time, I'll take it and I won't go easy on you."

And with that, he turns, leaving me alone in my room, completely and utterly ruined for any other man.

I SLEEP in well past my normal alarm. I made sure to turn it off last night since today is Sunday. I don't tend to sleep past nine a.m., even on the weekends, but my body was begging for a few extra hours today.

I stretch my arms overhead, arching my back. My body feels like I went to the gym, which I haven't done in about six months. I make a mental note to get back to working out, especially if things between Graham and I progress.

That thought brings an instant unease to my belly. The warning from Miss Perry the other night comes back to me.

I huff and pull the sheet over my head. I have no idea what kind of situation I'm getting myself into by going down this road with Graham, but my gut is telling me it won't end the way I want it to.

I sit up, my head slightly pounding, but it's not bad considering I forgot to take any Advil before bed. Thank goodness Graham forced me to drink several glasses of water.

I walk to the bathroom, flick on the light, and start the shower. I know I took one just twelve hours ago, but I need the water to wake me up. I pull my nightshirt over my head, and my mouth falls open when I catch a glimpse of my naked reflection.

"What the..."

I trail my fingers over the marks on my body.

A perfect teeth imprint on my right breast.

Another on my shoulder.

The bruised outline of Graham's fingertips on my hip.

It's exciting, exhilarating. I contemplate grabbing my phone and sending him a photo, but I decide against it. I'm not sure what kind of mood he's in today, if he woke up this morning regretting last night. It wouldn't surprise me, especially after how distant and cold he became after our date at the charity event.

"You're innocent..." His words from last night echo in my brain and I realize now what he meant. At the time I thought he assumed I'd never been with a man before, but *this* is what he was referring to. He's right. I've never been with a man who wanted me so unapologetically.

A man who isn't afraid to scare me.

A man who demands things from me I didn't even know I could give.

I step into the shower, letting the hot water ease my muscles.

After my shower I take the time to dry my hair, applying some makeup and making sure I pick out an outfit that will cover the bite marks and bruises. I settle for a pair of high-waisted jeans and a long-sleeved crop top.

My phone buzzes. I pick it up and see a message from Shelly.

Shelly: *Change of plans. I'm finishing my shift at noon. Tell me you're free so we can hang out.*

I smile, then I remember the conversation I had last night with Hank. *Shit. Hank!* I check my messages and see he texted me, asking me if I was okay and made it home safe.

Me: *Hey. Yeah, of course. Just got ready. I can be in the city in an hour.*

Shelly: *No need. I'll come out to the suburbs, see this fancy-schmancy place you're being held captive in... and maybe get a glimpse of the beast while I'm there. ;)*

I panic briefly. I don't think Mr. Hayes would mind me bringing a friend over, but I also know Shelly, and if she gets a chance, she'll say something inappropriate in front of him. Against my better judgment, I tell her to come over.

Me: *Okay, but PLEASE be on your best behavior... I know how you are.*

I send her the address, then open the message from Hank.

Me: *Hey, not even sure where to start. Yes, I made it home safely, but I was a little tipsy and slept it off this morning. I'm sorry about last night.*

Honestly, I don't remember what all happened, but I know that Mr. Hayes showed up and you left. Please don't hate me.

P.S. Shelly is coming over today. I'll see what I can find out.

I don't hear back from Hank. I'm not surprised. He's always busy on the weekend either playing baseball, umping it, or working for his uncle's painting business.

Shelly messages me back.

Shelly: *It's Sunday, Margot, the Lord's day... Of course I'll behave.*

I want to believe her, but her text is followed by the devil smiling emoji.

I give up.

I head downstairs to the kitchen in desperate need of coffee and carbs. I glance around. There's no sight of Mr. Hayes or Eleanor anywhere.

"They're not here." Miss Perry's nasal voice makes me jump.

"Where'd they head off to?" I ask, trying to sound nonchalant as I pick out which espresso pod I want.

"Mr. Hayes is playing golf and Eleanor is with her grandmother." I'm surprised she actually answered me instead of making some snooty remark.

"Are you having a nice day?" I give her a genuine smile as I wait for my coffee to brew. She's perched on the edge of a stool at the end of the island, sipping a cup of tea. Her legs are crossed at the ankles as she peers over slim glasses perched on the end of her nose. Her hair is pulled tight in a bun, her body adorned in a perfectly tailored lavender sheath dress and nude pumps.

Does she ever relax? Wear normal clothes?

She slowly turns her head to face me, like that girl in *The Exorcist.*

For a minute I'm actually worried she's about to spew hot green liquid at me.

"I was," she says, staring at me.

I'm tempted to ask her what changed, but I'm not dense. I know she's referring to before I woke up and made my presence known in the house. Instead, I just smile harder at her.

I add some cream and sugar to my coffee, then grab a croissant from the island before making my way to the exit.

"Oh, my friend Shelly is coming over shortly. We'll stay out of your way, but I just wanted to let you know in case you hear another voice coming from my room."

"Did Mr. Hayes okay that?" she calls after me.

"I didn't ask him. I didn't think I needed to since it's my day off."

"Miss Silver." I hate the way she says my name, dragging out the *S* sound for emphasis. "Whether you want to accept it or not, this isn't your home. This is the Hayes' home. You are a guest so please treat it accordingly."

There are so many things wrong with her statement, but I don't care enough to argue with her. I just give her a nod of understanding and make my way back to my room.

TWENTY MINUTES later Shelly is on my bed, already making me double over in laughter as she tells me about how two giant rats broke into the coffee shop yesterday and caused complete mayhem.

"So then Terry is freaking out because there's at least eight people in line for coffee and these two rats that are legit the size of a chihuahua go running across the floor through their legs and back through the kitchen!"

"Oh my God." Tears are pricking my eyes as Shelly acts out how people were jumping like pieces of popcorn to get out of their way.

"Needless to say, we got the rats out, *alive* mind you. I was not about to let him murder them in there." She shakes her head and takes the last bite of my leftover croissant. "These are amazing. We should sell them at the café."

"Niles, the chef, makes them fresh every weekend. I'm shocked I haven't gained ten pounds."

"You guys have a private chef here?" She rolls her eyes. "Oh, to be the one percent."

I gave her a quick tour of the house, at least the parts I felt comfortable showing, the parts I go into. I didn't show her the yard. I knew she'd want to go for a swim, and I can't exactly be in a swimsuit right now. Not with Graham's love bites marking my body.

"Well, this isn't my real life, you know. As Miss Perry likes to remind me, this isn't my home and I'm just the hired help." I let out a sigh, not wanting to admit my reality to myself. For as much as I know this thing with Graham is just a fling, probably a way for him to avoid dealing with the loss of his wife, a tiny little fairy-tale part of me still hopes that it could somehow turn into something more.

"So what's going on with you and Hank?" I finally ask and I see her mood instantly change.

Shit. Did something happen since last night?

She grabs a pillow and holds it over her face, muffling a dramatic scream. I reach over and pull it down, expecting to see her laughing, but instead, there are tears in her eyes.

"Shit. What happened, Shell?" I reach over and touch her knee.

"I think I'm in love with him," she finally says, burying her face in her hands as relief washes over me.

"What? That's wonderful, Shell. Why are you acting like this about it?" This was not at all what I was expecting her to say and I'm still just taken aback.

"Because, Margot, this wasn't supposed to happen. I was supposed to live this next year floating around the city, guy to guy, living out my craziest fantasies and kicking ass. Now I'm just some mopey, emotional loser who can't stop thinking about this guy and imagining marrying him and having his damn babies!" She flails her arm, tossing my pillow across the room in the process, and I burst into laughter.

"What's so funny? This isn't funny, Margot!" She slaps my leg, and it just spurs me on.

"I never thought I'd see the day when Shelly Prescott fell in love. Can I tell you something?"

She looks over at me. "What?" she says nervously.

"Don't be mad, but Hank reached out to me the other day. We met for drinks last night. He was terrified that you were ghosting him. He said you guys hit it off, the sex was great, blah, blah, blah, and you made plans for a third date, and then you got weird."

She hangs her head.

"He's not mad; he's crazy about you. He was worried that when he told you that he saw himself falling for you it scared you off… and I told him it probably did." I laugh.

"You're both right. It did scare me because I was having those thoughts myself, but I figured it was just the whole butterflies, honeymoon phase thing and he didn't feel the same way. We just connect, Margot," she says, drawing out the last syllable of my name. "Oh my God, it's so good. He makes me laugh and feel so relaxed and I can be myself. And the sex. Oh God, the seeeex!"

I clamp my hands over my ears. "I don't want to hear about it; he's like a brother to meeeee!" I sing and she pulls my hands down.

"So are you going to be mad?"

"Mad? About what?"

"That your two best friends are dating and like in love or whatever."

"Are you kidding me? I think it's amazing. At your wedding I'm taking full credit for this shit." We both laugh. "But seriously, all I care about is that you guys are happy. Well, I care more that you're happy first, then him, but yeah, it won't be weird. Just don't go making out and getting all handsy around me all the time." I wink at her, and she pulls me in for a hug.

"You're like the sister I never had, babe." She pulls back and looks at me. "Seriously, I love you so much."

"I know. I love you too, Shell."

We spend the rest of the afternoon together. We venture downstairs where Niles makes us custom-ordered wood-fired pizzas that are out of this world. Finally, Shelly leaves around four p.m. to head back to the city.

Graham still isn't home, and I can't decide if that's a good thing or not. I feel like if I were to see him, I'd be embarrassed. I don't regret what happened last night, but I was certainly the one that took things in the direction they went. Mostly, I'm worried he regrets it and is avoiding me.

Around six p.m., Eleanor returns home from her grandma's house, fed and bathed, with Muffin in tow.

"Look, look, look what I made Muffin," she says with excitement, holding Muffin up so I can see the friendship bracelet she has around her paw that matches the one on Eleanor's wrist.

"That is beautiful," I say as I take Muffin in my arms.

"I made you one too," she says, reaching into her tiny pocket and holding one out to me.

"Oh, thank you, sweetheart." I hold out my wrist so she can slide it over my hand.

We sit on the floor of her bedroom as she tells me everything she did at her grandma's house today.

"Do you like my daddy?" The question comes out of nowhere.

"Yes, of course I like your daddy. I also like you and your grandma and Phil," I say, hoping I'm not confusing her in what way I mean.

"Do you *love* my daddy?" She doesn't look up from brushing her doll's hair.

I don't know what to say here. I certainly don't want to confuse her. Mr. Hayes made it abundantly clear that he doesn't want her confused about my role in this family.

"Well, sweetie, I wouldn't say that, but he loves *you* very much." I try to steer the conversation in a different direction.

"I think Daddy loves you."

My heart feels like it just dropped into my ass.

"No, sweetie. Your daddy doesn't love me. Me and your daddy are friends and I love you very much."

"Are you and Daddy going to be kissing friends?"

Oh my God, what did she see? Panic grips me.

"Uh, why would you ask that, sweetie?"

She looks up at me and shrugs. "Cuz I—I want you to be together."

She says it so matter-of-factly it really concerns me. I feel like I've gone out of my way to never give her the impression that there's anything going on between her dad and me. And when things did happen between us, she wasn't even home.

"I think Daddy loves you. He talks about you all the time," she says dramatically.

"Daddy doesn't love me—he talks about me?" I'm intrigued.

"Mm-hmm." She keeps brushing her doll's hair. I reach out and put my hand over the doll, and she looks up at me.

"What does he say?" I know this is a slippery slope I'm going down but it's too late.

"He asked me if you had a boyfriend."

"When?"

"Last night. He read me my book and he kept asking about you." She picks her doll up and places it against the wall with the others before grabbing another one and bringing it over. She sits back down and begins to brush this one's hair now.

"Did he say anything else?" I feel like an asshole interrogating a five-year-old and now that I think about it, I'm not sure how accurate information is from a five-year-old, but I'm desperate to know more.

She shakes her head no. "He just asks if you, if you—" She loses her train of thought briefly. "If you talk about him."

I cover my mouth to hide my smile.

Holy shit... Mr. Graham Hayes totally has a crush on me and I know his secret.

1 6

GRAHAM

"I just don't trust her, sir."

I glance up from my iPad where I've been attempting to read the same article for the last fifteen minutes.

"Based on?" I take a sip of my espresso and double-check the time. It's almost seven forty-five a.m. I know Eleanor is most likely awake now, and she and Margot will be coming downstairs for breakfast soon. I'm not trying to ignore her; quite the opposite actually, but I don't trust that I'll be able to not grab her and kiss her, whoever is around be damned.

"She just seems deceptive, like she's up to something."

Her tone is that sickly-sweet one she uses with me when she wants something. She thinks I haven't caught on, like she actually has some sort of sway over me because of our *one night* of indiscretion years ago.

I don't know what's gotten into her lately now that I think of it. Every chance she gets she complains about Margot. She's either doing something wrong, letting Eleanor be too loud, too energetic, too... anything. It's annoying frankly and I'm about at my limit. I get it takes time adjusting to someone new underfoot in the workplace, but for fuck's sake, it's been months now.

"I can't go off a hunch here, Miss Perry. If you have a genuine concern, back it up with proof, then let me know, and I'll look into it. Otherwise, please try to get along with her. She's good for Eleanor."

Phil steps into the kitchen and points to his watch. "Be right there, Phil." I nod and stand up. I close my iPad and place my demitasse cup in the sink.

"I think she's trying to seduce you," she says finally and it stops me in my tracks.

I can't help it, I let out a loud laugh.

Oh, Miss Perry, if you only knew.

I turn and walk back over to her, thinking before I speak because what I want to tell her is to mind her goddamn business. I want to remind her about what she did.

I stupidly made the mistake of a lifetime about six months after Meredith passed. It was late. I had been drinking heavily and I was completely overcome with my emotions. Miss Perry came into my office and saw the state I was in and *she* seduced me. Yes, I could and should have said no, but she saw an opportunity. She saw a broken, grieving man and she took advantage.

"I'm only going to say this one time. Don't pretend to know what is going on in my personal life and don't try to gate-keep me or my emotions or my potential with someone else. I am your boss, Miss Perry." I wave my finger. "Nothing more."

She stiffens and offers a clipped nod before I turn and follow Phil out to my waiting car to head to work.

* * *

"We have a bet going."

What is with people today? It's not even nine thirty a.m. yet and already Garrett and Todd, his little minion that's always by his side like a damn remora always looking for leftovers, are bursting into my office unannounced.

"Which one of you will be fired first?" I lean back in my chair, crossing my arms over my chest.

143

"Who can get your nanny's number first?" Garrett laughs and elbows Todd.

Not this shit again.

"I didn't have the pleasure of meeting her when she came by the office or at the charity event, but I saw her. I was actually coming over to introduce myself when you whisked her away from Garrett."

"Yeah, what was that about anyway?" Garrett asks, taking a seat on my couch while Todd hovers.

"Don't you boys have some financials to be focused on?"

"We are actually heading out to go meet with the board in a few," Todd replies.

I'm so not in the mood today. I'm already having an impossible time focusing on work because all I can think about is tasting Margot again. The sounds she made when I made her come have been on repeat in my head since Saturday night. I purposely made sure I played a full eighteen rounds of golf on Sunday so I wouldn't end up with a chapped dick from jerking off so much.

"And you thought you'd come by and what? Ask me for her number or an introduction? Garrett, we've been through this. I'm sure Nadine, your *fiancée*"—I enunciate the word slowly—"wouldn't appreciate that."

"Hey." He crosses one leg over his knee as he makes himself more comfortable on my sofa. "I'm not acting on it. Just a friendly wager between men to see which of us she would choose."

They both laugh and I stand up, anger coursing through my veins.

"So you don't actually give a fuck that she's a human with feelings? You'll what? Get her number, then never call her? Lead her on? Make her think there's potential and then just ghost her?" My voice is getting louder and their laughs quickly turn into shock.

"We're just messing around, boss. No harm, no foul," Todd adds in his weaselly, ass-kissing voice.

"Yeah, Graham, she has a tight little body. We were ju—"

I slam both my fists down onto my desk. "Don't ever fucking talk about her like that again!" I shout and both men jump.

I'm not being too subtle right now, but I don't give a fuck. I might be emotionally damaged from losing my wife, but I'm not into playing games with people's hearts or emotions. That's childish, fucked-up shit, and I won't stand for it.

"I have told *you*"—I point toward Garrett's face—"more than once now to watch yourself, and you keep crossing the line. Learn some fucking respect and grow up. Respect Nadine and Todd, respect whatever fucking blow-up doll you sleep with every night, or at least attempt to respect yourselves. If I hear either of you say one more word about Margot, I'll not only fire you on the spot, but I'll destroy your personal and professional reputation. You understand me?"

The men are standing now, eyes wide as they listen. They both nod.

"I can't hear you!"

"Yes—absolutely, sir. Won't happen again," they both say.

"Good, now get the fuck out of my office."

I drop down in my seat after they leave. My heart feels like I just ran up ten flights of stairs. I loosen my tie and remove my suit coat.

"I'm losing it," I mutter, rubbing my hands over my face.

"Sir? Everything okay?" Olivia pokes her head into my office, a concerned look on her face. She clearly heard my outburst.

"Yeah, yeah," I mutter as she walks farther into the room.

"You have a pretty full day today. Your first meeting isn't until ten, though, so you have a few minutes yet. I moved your lunch meeting to a dinner meeting. I know you hate those, but it was the only time I could get Peter Vallow to reschedule while he's in Chicago."

I nod and tell her it's fine.

"You sure you're okay, sir? You need me to run out and get you anything?"

"I'm good, Olivia. Thank you."

I'm not good. I'm losing my grip. I haven't felt this out of control in… well, *ever*.

When I met Meredith, it was an instant attraction, sure, but it was more of a mutual respect we had for each other. She was gorgeous and driven. I was attracted to how she carried herself, her power, the way she commanded a room. But with Margot, it's different. She feeds a need in me. A desire to control her, to protect her, like she needs me.

I don't really want to open the can of worms that might be mentally. I'm sure a licensed professional would tell me there's some sort of repressed shit I need to deal with. That the desire to fully consume and own this woman is unhealthy... I don't doubt that at all. The amount of time I spend thinking about her is unhealthy, the way she occupies my entire brain and has me so wrapped around her without even knowing it or trying—seriously unhealthy.

Even the physical reaction I have to her is nothing like I've experienced with anyone. My relationship with Meredith was more emotional than physical. We had good sex—great sex even—but it wasn't pure carnal lust and desire.

With Margot, it's both and I haven't even fully had her.

I want to shield her from the Garretts and Todds of the world. I want to protect her like she's mine. I want to mark every single part of her body. I want to look at her and know there isn't one inch of her I haven't touched or kissed.

But guilt has kept me from fully taking her. I know she's young, has the world at her fingertips.

I glance at my watch. I have seven minutes until my first meeting. Just enough time to splash cold water on my face and get a second cup of coffee before falling headlong into another day.

By the time my day ends, including my dinner meeting, it's past eight p.m. I'm exhausted and just want to go home. More than anything, I want to see Margot. I haven't spoken to her or even seen her since Saturday night. I'm sure she thinks I'm avoiding her.

I close my eyes in the back of the car as Phil drives us home. I can feel the tinges of a headache brewing from the wine I had at dinner.

I climb the stairs to the second floor, pausing. I can hear Eleanor laughing in the tub over Margot's voice. They'll be done soon, then she'll put her to bed. I'm tempted to tell her I'll handle story time tonight but figure I don't want to interrupt her schedule.

Instead, I head to my bedroom, removing my suit coat and tie and kicking off my shoes. I walk to the large windows that overlook the backyard. I feel anxious, like I know there's something I'm trying to talk myself out of doing but I'm going to do it anyway.

I walk over to the wet bar in the corner and pour myself a couple fingers of bourbon. I sit on the edge of my bed but it's no use. I'm already making my way back downstairs toward Margot's bedroom before I can talk myself out of it.

The door is cracked; it's dark inside. She's in Eleanor's room now, putting her to bed. I step into the room, the moonlight casting a long tunnel of light across the floor. I walk over to the two chairs near the window and take a seat in the one that's still obscured by the shadows.

I've been sitting in there for a while when the door slowly opens and then closes as Margot enters. She lets out an exhale, circling her head around her neck as she stretches it.

"Good evening, Margot," I say, and as expected she jumps, clutching her chest as her eyes dart toward me.

"Oh my God!" she breathes out. "What are you doing?"

I raise the tumbler in my hand. "Enjoying a nightcap."

She walks toward me slowly. She's wearing a cute little sundress that hits just above her knee, a pale-pink cardigan over the top of it. She takes a seat in the chair opposite of me, perched on the very edge.

"I wasn't sure if you were avoiding me... after Saturday night." Her voice is soft and airy.

I shake my head. "No."

"You sure? You certainly seemed to be avoiding me before showing up to chase Hank off."

I don't say anything, just lean back in the chair.

"Are we good?" she asks.

"Good?" I'm confused.

"You seemed—I dunno. After that charity event I attended with you, you got cold, weird. It felt like you were avoiding me or mad at me. We left there in a rush, and then the whole thing on Saturday with you showing up and chasing off Hank."

"You're right; I was behaving poorly." I think through what I want to say, but then I stop myself. I don't want to give her a thought-out, curated answer. I want to just be honest with her. "I felt guilty after

147

what happened between us the night of the event. I was trying to avoid you, to put space between us. But I failed. I couldn't stop thinking about you with him, on your date."

"Well, that was my fault because it wasn't a date and it never was. I said that because…" Her words trail off.

"Because?"

"I dunno, to get a response from you."

I chuckle. "Well, it certainly worked."

"I'm actually glad you're here because I wanted to apologize for Saturday night. I was really unprofessional and I shouldn't have—"

"Don't," I say. I don't want her to apologize. I don't want her to feel anything but wanting to do it all again. She looks up at me, the corner of her cardigan between her fingers as she fidgets with it.

"I don't want you to be sorry."

"You don't?"

I shake my head and finish off the bourbon.

"No because I can't stop—thinking about you."

Her eyes widen in the moonlight, and she perks up even more. "What have you been thinking about?"

I run the tip of my finger over my lips, contemplating how detailed I should get.

"I want to do *things* to you, Margot." I see her throat constrict as she swallows. "I want to be rough with you."

"Rough?" The word sounds like it squeaks out of her throat.

"Mm-hmm, very." Her eyes never leave mine. I decide in this moment that I'm done holding back. If she wants to know all the filthy things I want to do to her, I'm not going to sugarcoat it.

"I want to tie you to the bed and handcuff your hands behind your back as I force my thick cock down your throat. I want to hear you beg and choke. I want to spank you while I bury myself so deep inside you you'll be screaming my name. But first, I want you to sit that pretty pussy on my face so I can devour you. I want you so spent, trembling, quaking from me stuffing every single part of you."

Her mouth falls open slightly as she grips the edge of the chair.

"Does that scare you, baby girl?"

She shakes her head and says, her voice trembling, "N—no."

"I think you're lying." I chuckle. "Lying should be punished."

"Punished? How?"

"Do you want to find out?"

I sink down into the chair a little more, my legs spread as I stretch them out in front of me.

She nods her head slowly.

I pat my lap. "Come here then, sweetheart."

She stands and starts to take a step, but I hold out my hand and she stops. "I want you on your hands and knees." She looks at me, then slowly drops down to the floor. "Crawl to me," I say.

Her eyes stay on mine as she slowly moves toward me, crawling on her hands and knees.

"That's right, baby. Come to daddy."

17

MARGOT

*T*hose three words...

Those three delicious, naughty words instantly set my body ablaze. I put one hand in front of the other as I crawl the few feet to where he's sitting. When I reach him I stop, sitting back on my feet and placing my hands in my lap.

He reaches down, his thumb coming to rest on the tip of my chin as the rest of his fingers hook beneath it. He tips my head up, dragging his thumb along my lip before sliding it into my mouth. Instinctively, I wrap my lips around the tip and suck.

"Naughty," he whispers, and then I softly bite it. He sucks in a sharp breath. "Do you understand what I'm going to do to you?"

I nod my head yes.

"I need you to tell me. I need you to tell me you understand that I'm going to take you upstairs to my bed and I'm going to spend the next several hours fucking you." He leans forward, slipping his thumb deeper in my mouth. "Over and over and over again."

He pulls his thumb out of my mouth. "I understand."

He reaches down and hooks his hands under my arms, standing up and bringing me with him. He spins me around to face the door and grabs my hand, walking forcefully out of the room. He's taking the stairs two at a time, pulling me with him as I struggle to keep up.

Halfway up the stairs, he turns and grabs me, tossing me over his shoulder and carrying me to his room. It's massive. I slide down the front of his body as I look around. It's dark, the only light the moon shining through the floor-length windows.

He grabs me and pulls me toward him, his lips smashing against mine in what I can only describe as a frenzied, passionate kiss. His hands are on either side of my head, his tongue demanding entrance. I open my mouth to deepen the kiss. His tongue dances with mine as his hands begin to wander my body. He pulls at my cardigan as he walks us deeper into the room.

He jerks it down my arms, tossing it to the floor as his lips trail from mine down my jaw, to my neck. I close my eyes, my head falling to the side as an unprompted moan falls from my lips. He feels incredible, the hardness of his body against mine.

Suddenly he stops and looks down at me, his fingers softly tracing the bite mark on my shoulder.

"Is that from?" I nod and his eyes look like they grow even darker.

He pulls my dress straps down my arms as I reach to the side and unzip it. He pushes it down my torso, then reaches around and unhooks my bra. It falls to the floor as he runs his fingertips softly over the bite mark on my breast.

"Do they hurt?" I shake my head no.

He must remember my hip because he pulls the dress the rest of the way off my body and stares at the spot where he bruised me. He presses it. "Does this?"

I whine a little because it does, and he drops to his knees and trails a row of kisses over the bruises.

"I like seeing my marks on you." He traces over it again with his fingertips as his eyes find mine. He stares at me as he hooks his thumbs into the waistband of my panties and drags them down my legs. I step out of them.

He reaches his hands around my ass, placing a palm on either cheek as he runs his nose right up my center. I gasp as his fingertips dig into my flesh.

"I've dreamed about this for weeks." He pushes me back a few steps till I feel the bed at my knees. "Sit," he commands, and I obey. He hooks his hands behind my knees and drags me to the edge of the bed. He grabs each foot, planting them feet apart. I feel so exposed, sitting on the edge of his bed, completely naked with my legs spread and him between them.

He runs his hand over his mouth as he stares directly at my mound. I grip the blanket in anticipation.

"Such a pretty little pussy," he groans as he reaches his hand out and runs one finger right up my slit. I close my eyes, my legs trying to close, but he stops them.

"You're already pulsing, baby," he says as he leans in, planting an open-mouthed kiss directly over me.

I let my head fall back as he begins his assault on me. It's heavenly, transcendent, the only way I can think to describe it. He's like a starving man. He growls deep in his chest as he grabs my inner thighs and spreads me even further, his tongue so deep inside me.

"I'm close." I can barely get the words out.

He's teasing me relentlessly. His tongue dances across my clit mercilessly as he pumps two fingers into me. I cry out, my legs shaking as I fall back on the bed, my orgasm coming in waves.

I'm panting, my body already feeling worked over, when he stands and looks down at me, his chin glistening with my arousal.

"I'm just getting started with you, sweetheart."

He reaches down and undoes his belt, the clanging sound sending another sharp pang of desire straight to my core. He wastes no time kicking off his socks and unbuttoning his shirt, slowly dragging it down his rippling biceps.

It hits me. This is the first time I've seen him naked. My eyes dart to his arm where a large sleeve tattoo covers his skin. I'm shocked. I didn't take him as the tattoo type. It's delicious and sexy and makes me wonder what other surprises lie in wait.

He slides his zipper down and I feel myself lick my lips in anticipation. He must notice because I hear him chuckle.

"Someone's excited to get fucked."

I bite my lip to keep myself from begging as he finishes sliding his pants down his legs. His massive cock bounces with the movement. It's thick and veiny. I can't help myself; I reach my hand out and grasp it.

"Mmm, fuck," he says, his hand flying to my hair as he grabs a fistful. His lips form an O as he slowly exhales, watching me as I wrap my hand around it. My fingers aren't even close to fitting. A glistening bead of pre-cum sits on the tip.

I look up at him, his eyes dark and heavy-lidded.

"You gonna suck me, baby?"

"Is that what you want?" I feel a surge of power as I grip him, like I'm in control even though I know that's not the case.

He grabs my hair tighter, tilting my head back with the force. "Put me in your mouth," he says. I do. I stretch my jaw wide open to accommodate his girth, wrapping my lips around the tip. He hisses.

"Now relax your jaw so I can fuck your mouth," he grits the words out as he begins to use my hair to move my head, back and forth down his shaft. I start to get the hang of it, and I use my tongue on the underside of him to stimulate as I suck.

He grunts and moans as he moves my head faster and faster, forcing himself deep into my throat. My eyes water as I take him. I worry I'll panic but I relax, breathing through my nose. I look up at him, his tan skin rippling across his defined chest that's peppered with black hair.

"Ohhh, baby." His voice sounds strangled. It's sexy and dark and I can feel my own wetness building. I reach a hand down and touch myself. He notices because he starts fucking my face harder.

"You're a greedy little thing, aren't you?"

His grunts come out with each thrust. He looks down his body at me, his abs flexing with each movement and I can tell he's close. He's frantic, his eyes rolling back in his head as his lips part.

"Swallow," he says as I feel his dick get even harder. His balls tighten as he comes, shooting hot streams to the back of my throat.

He gasps, stepping back so his dick falls from my lips. He pulls me up as I wipe the remnants of his release from my lips.

"You're such a good girl." He's breathing heavy but his cock is still just as hard as before his orgasm. He turns me so my back is to him. He kisses my neck again. "I love the thought of my cum in your belly, but now I want to fill your pussy. Are you on birth control, Margot?" I nod. "Good because I don't want anything between us. You don't have anything to worry about with me, baby."

He bends me over the bed, putting me on my hands and knees before gripping my hips tightly and pulling me back to the edge of the bed. I look back at him over my shoulder as he reaches between my lips and slides his finger inside me. He pulls it out, bringing it to his mouth to lick clean with an audible moan. He does it two more times before lightly spitting in his hand and bringing it back down to lubricate me.

Holy fuck, that was hot.

He doesn't wait; he lines himself at my entrance and steps forward.

"Ow," I gasp at the intrusion; it's painful.

"Does it hurt?" he asks.

"Yes," I say as I nod and take in a deep breath.

"I'm gonna need you to relax, baby. I can't hold back. I'm barely hanging on. I need to—" He pushes further inside me. "...to— Oh, yes. Oh, fuuuuuck." His voice echoes through the room as he slides back out of me and in again.

"Oh. Oh." My pants come out labored, the pain slowly starting to shift into pleasure.

There's no more talking, just the sounds of our skin slapping against each other and the moans that uncontrollably tumble from my mouth with every thrust.

He fucks me relentlessly before pulling out and flipping me to my back. He places his foot on the edge of the bed as he slams back into me. With one hand on my hip, the other massages my breast, his mouth quickly following. He sucks each nipple, worshiping them with his tongue before sucking and biting. It's painful but it mixes with the pleasure and feels like nothing I've ever experienced.

He reaches his hand around my throat, gripping it so tight.

"There won't be any part of you that I haven't tasted or fucked," he says in my ear as his body continues to piston back and forth. We're both so close; I can feel it about to explode. His movements grow erratic. I grip the comforter beneath me, grasping at anything to keep me tethered down.

My legs are over his shoulders, his hand still around my throat as he pumps into me. I close my eyes as my insides begin to spasm around him.

I cry out, my orgasm taking over just as he reaches his release.

He falls on top of me as we lie in a puddle of sweaty bliss, trying to catch our breath.

Our break is only momentary before he's hard again, pulling me to his lap to ride him with his back against the headboard.

"Again?" I say as his lips find mine.

"I told you, baby; you need to be punished." He reaches behind me and slaps my ass with one hand, the other grabbing my chin. "Make daddy happy and ride my cock."

The way he speaks to me is driving me crazy. I never thought I'd be the kind of girl that got off on calling a man daddy, but fuck me, this man could do anything he wants to me.

He leans back, slumped against the headboard as he holds my hips, helping lift me and bring me back down as I ride him.

"Your parents live around here?"

The question is unexpected. I lift my head from where it was resting on his chest and look up at him. Several hours and several orgasms later, we're both tapped.

"No. They did, but they're both gone now."

He lifts his head and looks down at me as he wraps his arms around me. "Shit, I'm sorry."

155

"It's okay. My dad died when I was seventeen, very unexpectedly in a car accident and my mom died about four years ago from cancer."

"Did your mom teach you music?"

I settle back against his chest and it feels so natural for us to just lie wrapped around each other like a real couple.

"They both did actually. My mom was a music teacher when I was growing up but before that she was a singer. She sang at some local jazz clubs and even did some small touring, had a really unknown album. That's how she and my dad met; he played the bass at the last jazz bar she performed at."

I lift my eyes to look up at him as he stares out the window on the other side of the room.

"What about your dad?"

"He died three years ago. Massive coronary event. Nobody was surprised. He lived on red meat and a pipe. He had a very unhealthy lifestyle, still ran himself ragged all through his sixties and early seventies."

"Were you two close?"

He shakes his head. "Not particularly. My dad wasn't so much of a dad to me as he was a boss. He started Hayes Communications when he was twenty-seven years old and never stopped working a day in his life. Of course, it was sad when he passed but we all carried on."

I wrap my arm around his stomach, pulling him closer to me. He leans his head down and kisses the top of my head.

"I was close to my dad; he was my best friend. I'm an only child so I was close to both parents, but we just had this bond." I smile, thinking about one of the last memories of him.

"What are you thinking about?"

"One of my favorite memories of him. We had this tradition. We'd go on what he called *dad dates*. I grew up in a small suburb, about forty minutes outside the city so there wasn't a ton to do but we always found adventures. We'd either go to the bowling alley or the arcade and Dad would always let me win whatever game we played. He'd let me eat nachos and drink my weight in soda because my mom never would. Then afterward we'd always go to Mike's Chill, this tiny little ice cream stand that had the best homemade ice cream."

"That sounds like a wonderful memory."

"Yeah, it was. That was the last thing we did before he died. We'd do that once a month and we had gone out that Sunday. The next day, he got hit by a truck driver who had fallen asleep at the wheel."

The room goes silent and I can tell he doesn't know what to say.

I sit up partially and crawl my way onto his body so I'm lying on top of him, our bodies touching from head to toe. I fold my arms over his chest and rest my chin on my hands.

"You're going to awaken something if you keep moving around on me like that." He smiles and snakes his fingers through my hair.

"How does it still have any... lift?" I say and he laughs.

"That's all you, baby. You drive me wild, like nobody has before."

I hate myself for it, but I immediately want to ask if that includes his wife. I don't, of course. I know that's a boundary I have no business crossing.

I reach up and trace the tattoo on his shoulder. "I didn't expect this."

He looks down to where my fingers touch his skin and pulls them to his lips, kissing them.

"That's a story for another time. It's late, baby. We need to sleep."

I pull myself from him and swing my legs over the edge of the bed, sitting up. He darts his hand out and grabs me. "Whoa, where are you going?"

"To bed," I say.

"You're in bed."

"Did you want me to sleep in here? With you?"

He doesn't answer; he just wraps his arm around my waist and pulls my body back against his, dropping his leg over mine and pulling the blankets around us.

I snuggle into him, my mind threatening to go down the road of *what will happen tomorrow*, but I tell myself not to ruin tonight. I close my eyes as my body relaxes against his.

"Good night, Mr. Hayes," I whisper.

"Mmmm," he groans against my neck as the hand on my waist squeezes me. "Don't tease me," he says sleepily. "Good night, temptress."

Within minutes, his nose is buried in my hair and we're both drifting off to sleep.

18

GRAHAM

I reach my hand out across the bed, opening my eyes when instead of Margot's warm body I feel the cold, empty sheets.

I sit up, looking around. I lean over and grab my phone. It's just after six fifteen a.m. Maybe Margot went downstairs to get coffee. Or maybe she works out in the morning. I realize I don't actually have a clue what time her day starts or what her routine is.

"Did I dream last night?" I say to myself as I look around once more.

I pull the sheets off my body and stand up to stretch. *Nope.* I definitely didn't dream that last night. I smile, my body already ready for a repeat.

"Down, boy," I say, walking to the bathroom to start the shower.

After I dry off, I get dressed, picking out a charcoal suit with a black tie. I make my way downstairs, stopping on the second floor briefly to see if she's with Eleanor. Both of their bedroom doors are closed. I lift my hand and knock softly on Margot's door, not wanting to wake Eleanor if she isn't up yet.

"Margot?" I say, but there's no answer. I contemplate opening the door but decide against it. As much as I've pushed her boundaries last night, I don't want her to feel like she doesn't have her own private space here.

I turn and make my way downstairs, in serious need of a double shot of espresso this morning.

"There you are." I find Margot standing in the kitchen, leaning against the counter with a cup of coffee in her hands.

"Thought I might have dreamed last night." I sidle up against her as I reach to grab a mug out of the cabinet to her right. I place my hand on her lower belly, planting a kiss on her temple. "You okay?"

She nods, taking a sip of her coffee.

"Margot?" I tip her chin upward.

"Yeah, I'm fine, just a little tired." Her smile seems halfhearted. "Needed this." She lifts her coffee.

I place my mug under the spout of the espresso machine and select the double option. The machine sputters and hisses to life, the scent of the coffee already making me a little more awake.

"Is that why you left without waking me?"

She stares at her pink fuzzy slipper as she draws little circles with her foot.

"Yeah, I know neither of us slept much so I just wanted to let you sleep in." I cross my arms over my chest, narrowing my eyes at her. She's lying. "Okay, fine. I was worried it would be weird this morning," she huffs before placing her mug on the counter next to her.

I reach for her hands. "Weird how?"

She sighs. "Look, last night was—well, I can't even put into words how good it was, but I also don't want to complicate things—for Eleanor. I don't know what this is and that's okay. I don't need an explanation or a label, but I also don't want to confuse her. You were pretty adamant about that a few weeks ago and I agree with you. She's too young."

I had a feeling that's what it was about and I don't blame her. I've had the same thoughts and concerns in the back of my head. It's part of why I tried to resist her.

"I get it and I agree. I'm not being irresponsible and not thinking about those things, about her feelings or yours. I want you to know

I'm considering all those things and I'm trying to make the right choices for my happiness, for—" I hesitate. "*Our* happiness. I am a father first and foremost; I don't want to confuse or hurt Eleanor either."

She listens quietly.

"Just promise me you'll let me worry about that—as her father. Trust me that I will make the right decisions for her?"

She nods, her smile a little less apprehensive this time, then she pulls her hands slowly from mine and goes to walk around me. I shoot my arm out, capturing her around the waist.

"You know I care about you, right?" She stares up at me and I pull her closer. "You mean something to me. I don't know what's going through that pretty head of yours but don't question that. Last night was"—I feel myself stir in my slacks with just the mention of last night —"special. I don't regret it this morning if you're worried about that."

"I know, I understand."

"Do you?"

I pull her back to stand in front of me, my hands resting on her waist as she places her palms on my chest.

"I know there's a lot of complications between us. I'm your boss and you are quite a bit younger than me. I know that things could always go south and you worry how that will be, living in my home, taking care of my daughter. And most likely, people will talk when it gets out I'm in a relationship with my nanny."

"A relationship?" Her eyes dart to mine, searching them. I can't tell if it's fear in her eyes or if she wants reassurance. I squeeze her waist a little tighter as I back her against the counter.

"I've tried to talk myself out of wanting you. All those reasons I just mentioned play on a loop in my head but no matter how hard I try"—I lean in and place a soft kiss on her neck—"I can't stop myself."

Her head lulls to one side, her fingers curling against my shirt.

"I don't want to stop myself anymore."

I run my tongue up the length of her neck, stopping only to kiss the same trail. I nip her earlobe. "I know you deserve better."

I suck her earlobe into my mouth, eliciting a small moan from her.

"But I can't stop and now that I've had you, Margot, now that I've tasted you, felt your body against mine, filled you so completely—there's nothing that will stop me. Nothing will stop me from making you mine."

I whisper the words against her ear as her hands dig into my chest. I don't give a fuck if she's wrinkled my shirt. I slide my hand up her neck, then the other hand, and I hold her head still as I tilt my own to lean in and kiss her. I'm a breath away when I hear Miss Perry's tell-tale heels clicking rapidly across the marble.

I step back, the moment dissipating as I reach for my coffee and put several feet between us just as Fiona enters the kitchen.

"Good morning," she says, eyeing us both suspiciously. "A little early for you, isn't it, Miss Silver?"

Gone is the heated gaze from Margot's eyes. Instead, she looks sad. I see her glance from me back to Miss Perry. "Time to get Eleanor up and ready for her ballet class." She exits the kitchen and I turn to face Fiona.

"Try playing nice, please," I remind her.

"I was perfectly pleasant."

* * *

I TRY to focus on work but the image of Margot's face after I jumped back from her this morning has me worried. I had just given her a speech about how much she meant to me, how I couldn't care less about all the reasons we shouldn't be together, and then I acted like a complete ass when Miss Perry walked in.

It's not that I don't want Miss Perry to know about us; I don't care. I try telling myself it's because I don't want to make any of the household staff feel uncomfortable with any private moments or physical touching between Margot and me. But that thought didn't seem to stop me one bit the other night coming home from the bar when I had Margot coming all over me and the back seat. Poor Phil.

The reality is, I know I need to tell Margot about the one night—

the mistake—I had with Fiona. Then again, why would I need to tell her that? She didn't know either of us back then and there's never been one ounce of feelings involved when it comes to Miss Perry.

I play this game in my head back and forth for hours, convincing myself that I'm making the right choice and then second-guessing it all an hour later.

I pull up Google and decide to plan our second date. I want to prove to Margot that she's more than just a hot fuck to me. I start researching bowling alleys and arcades, trying to find the perfect ice cream place to recreate the memory she shared with me last night.

* * *

"WHERE ARE WE GOING?"

"It's a surprise."

"Well, how should I dress?"

"Casual."

Margot hooks an eyebrow upward. "Do you even own casual clothes?"

"No, I was actually born in a suit; hell, I even sleep in one." She rolls her eyes and walks toward her bedroom. "Yes, I own casual clothes. I'm going to go change; you do the same. I'll be back down here in"—I look at my watch—"fifteen minutes."

I swat her ass and push her toward her door before bounding up the stairs to the third floor. My excitement is through the roof.

It's been two days since our first night together. I haven't pushed Margot to stay in my bed again. We also haven't slept together again. I figured some space might be good for her.

I sent Eleanor to her grandmother's house tonight. She's spending the night there so Margot and I can have a date night. When I told my mother that bit of information, she pointed her manicured finger in my face and threatened to *take me off the face of the earth* if I hurt Margot or break her heart.

Apparently the two of them have grown quite fond of each other, something I find both endearing and a little worrisome should they decide to gang up on me. Meredith and my mother got along very well, but I wouldn't say they were close. Meredith was very busy early on and she missed out on a lot of family stuff. After we were married, they both spent some time together, but they were too alike, both *very type A, had to be in control* women who didn't like to relinquish power. It never made for anything uncomfortable but there wasn't a kindred-ness between them like there is with her and Margot.

I think my mom wanted to mother Meredith, but Meredith was already grown and kicking ass by the time she was ten years old. Her own mother once said that she never felt like she raised so much as grew up alongside her.

Margot, on the other hand, doesn't have her parents and my mom never had a daughter.

I change out of my suit and pull on a pair of dark jeans, a plaid button-down, and matching brown boots and a belt. I splash on a little more cologne and give myself a once-over in the mirror.

I'm nervous. Actually nervous. I don't think I've felt this way since I had to perform a solo in the church choir when I was nine. I let out a deep breath and make my way back to Margot's room, seven minutes ahead of schedule.

"Oh my God." She smiles as I knock and enter her room. "I can't believe you're in jeans." She walks over to me, completely circling me like she's sizing me up.

"That a bad thing?"

"No, no. Trust me, this is a very good look." Her eyes rake down my body and back up, instantly putting ideas in my head.

"So is this." I reach out and grab the bottom of her ass cheek peeking out from the tiny shorts she's wearing. "I know I said casual, but goddamn, baby." I grab a handful this time, pulling her body against my firming erection.

"No, of course not." She swats my hand away, but I tug her harder against me. "You said fifteen minutes."

"I couldn't wait," I pant as I jerk her shorts and panties down her thighs. "I need a taste." I drop down to my knees, burying my nose in her mound.

"Ahh, we'll be late." Her plea doesn't sound very convincing.

"You want me to stop?" I ask as I look up at her, rubbing the pad of my thumb in little circles over her glistening clit.

She looks behind her, the bed only a few inches away. She falls back on it, kicking her shorts and panties to the side to give me better access.

"Good girl," I say before leaning forward and devouring her.

"OH MY GOD." Her hands cover her mouth as we pull up in front of the bowling alley, Lincoln Lanes.

I lace my fingers through hers as we exit the car and make our way across the parking lot.

"I thought for our second date, we could do something special." I drape my arm around her shoulders. "Also, I want to see how competitive you are."

"Care to make it interesting?" she asks. "Winner gets to choose the third date."

"A bet? I'll take those odds. Good to know there's already talk of a third date." I nuzzle her hair. "But I'll just go ahead and stick to the plans I already had for our third date, since I'll win hands down."

"Umm, I've been bowling since I was seven years old." She slips out from under my arm and points her fingers at me. "Prepare to lose."

I open the door and we step inside, the scent of stale popcorn and cheap beer filling the air.

We pick up our shoes and I pay for two games along with a pitcher of beer and their "deluxe platter" which includes a bevy of questionable fried foods.

"I'm a little uneasy about sticking my fingers in these used balls and then eating." I lace my shoes and watch as Margot grabs a chicken finger and takes a bite.

She shrugs. "It's part of the experience, Graham. Shitty food that probably has a ten-year shelf life, even shittier beer, and eighties music. It's what we used to call a Midwest night out in the sticks."

We both laugh as she grabs her ball, pulling it up to her chin and squinting her eyes to line up the shot. She takes two steps forward, pulling her arm back and letting it loose. It flies perfectly down the center of the lane, hitting the middle pin square on the nose and sending them all to the ground.

"A strike on the first bowl?"

"Told ya, old man." She winks as she saunters back to the booth and takes a swig of her beer.

I'm in trouble. She's in her element and she's about to wipe my ass with the floor.

* * *

"It wasn't even close, but it's okay. You didn't stand a chance." She sits on my lap, her arms wrapped around me as we look up at the screen and see our scores.

"Let's get you home. I think we both need a shower to get the grease off our fingers."

When we get home, we walk silently up the stairs, her hand in mine. We hit the second landing and she pauses briefly before glancing toward her room.

"You're mine tonight," I say, tugging her hand as I keep walking toward the third-floor stairs.

We ascend the stairs and walk to my room. As soon as I close the door my hands are on her. It's not rushed or frenzied. I just set about undressing her as we make our way to the bathroom.

I pull her shirt over her head, tossing it on the floor before reaching for her jeans. She stops in the doorway as I pull them over her hips and down her legs, pulling each leg free before tossing them to join the shirt.

I reach into the shower and turn on the water and the steam function before turning back to face her. She looks angelic, her pale frame leaning against the doorjamb as she watches me. Her full tits are on display in a white lace bra that matches her thong panties.

"I've wondered what was under that outfit all night," I murmur as I trail kisses over her shoulder.

"You're wearing too much." She reaches for the buttons of my shirt and I step back, allowing her to undo the buttons one at a time. It's agonizingly painful but she's enjoying undressing me and so am I. As much as I have to talk myself out of bending her over this counter right now and driving into her, I want to go slow, to savor every square inch of her body.

Soon, we're both fully naked. I put my hands under her arms and lift her to sit on the counter, settling between her thighs.

We kiss each other, our mouths hungry as her tongue finds its way inside my mouth. She pulls me closer, pressing her body against mine.

"You're so fucking beautiful."

I rest my forehead against hers, looking down her body as I cup her breasts, running my thumbs over her pert nipples.

"I've had so many fantasies about you. Imagined taking you in every way possible. But this"—I kiss her deeply, holding her head still so I can take it deeper—"has been my favorite fantasy. Savoring you, watching your body as I fill you."

I look down to where my cock is jutting out, the tip at her entrance begging to enter. I grip myself, stepping forward till I make entry.

"Ahh." She arches her back, holding on to my neck as I push in further. I watch as I pull back out, already slick with her arousal before pushing back inside.

We both let out an audible moan. I grab her behind her neck, kissing her harder.

It's slow and passionate, deep and intimate. It feels like we're both saying so many things with our bodies that we can't yet say verbally.

Our eyes are locked. I keep one hand on her neck, pulling her to me as I thrust inside her. Our lips can't get enough. With the other hand I hold hers, pinning it above her head against the mirror for leverage.

We make love like this for several minutes until we can't hang on any longer and we both fall over the edge together.

I help her off the counter, pulling her into the shower with me where I wash her, taking care of her body before bending her over the marble bench and fucking her so deep, so thoroughly we're both on the shower floor by the end, gasping and spent.

19

MARGOT

I wince as I stretch my arms overhead, letting out a yawn as I glance to my left.

The bed is empty. I listen for the shower, but I don't hear it. I bury my face in the pillow for a moment, a smile spreading lazily across my lips as images of last night flood my brain. The pillow smells like Graham.

I sit up and look around the room. "Graham?"

No answer.

I toss the blankets off my body and lean down to grab his shirt from the floor. Our clothes are still strewn about the room, the blankets never righted after our lovemaking.

Lovemaking?

I don't dwell on that thought too long. I'm not reading into things between us, and after the way he jumped back from me when Miss Perry came into the kitchen the other day, I'm not going to push things. Though I can't deny the lingering feelings I have about their relationship make me uneasy. I know it's none of my business, but he can't be that oblivious to the way she panders to him. The constant flattery and little touches, not to mention the way her voice morphs into a breathy version of what I assume she believes to be sexy or flirty is getting on my nerves.

I poke my head out of his bedroom and glance around, not that I expect anyone to be up on the third floor considering it's his bedroom. I walk down the hall toward the stairs when I pause, glancing around at the other two doors. I walk over to one and attempt to twist the handle, but it's locked. I check the other one— same thing. Suddenly I feel a little icky snooping; this isn't my home. I walk back over to the stairs and make my way to the kitchen.

It's only six forty-five a.m. and the house rule is Eleanor has to stay in her room until seven fifteen a.m., even if she's already awake. I tiptoe down the main stairs, looking for Graham. Maybe he's in his office.

I'm about to turn toward the hallway when I hear the clatter of something in the kitchen. I turn and walk in to find Graham in his pajama bottoms and a white t-shirt. His back is to me so I lean against the doorframe and observe him.

He picks up the spoon he dropped and tosses it in the sink before turning his attention back to the coffee he's making. He places two cups with saucers on a tray that already has orange juice and two fresh croissants with butter and berries.

"Thought you'd be in a three-piece halfway to the office by now." He turns around, a smirk on his face.

"Actually, I was about to bring you breakfast in bed." He reaches out and I walk toward him. He grabs my hand and pulls me into his chest, wrapping his arms around me and nuzzling my neck.

"I already set Eleanor up with her iPad. She's watching *Peppa Pig* so that we can have a nice, slow morning to ourselves."

He plants kisses up my neck between words as he speaks. A shiver runs up my spine.

"That sounds lovely."

"You look lovely." He drags his hand up my bare thigh and beneath the hem of his shirt. "Mmm, no panties." He softly runs a finger over me.

"Ohhh." A little moan escapes.

"You feeling okay this morning?"

I nod my head, closing my eyes and savoring the warmth of his large body pressed against me. It just feels so... right.

"How are your hips? I know that marble isn't very forgiving," he says, referring to when he bent me over the bench in the shower.

I reach my hands down instinctively as he pulls the shirt up to look.

"Fuck." He runs his fingertips over a slight bruise that has formed on my hip bone again. "I keep hurting you."

"It's a good hurt though," I say, trying to ease his conscience. I don't want him to stop or change; it's too exciting. "It was amazing if that matters." I reach onto my tiptoes as I turn his head so my lips find his.

He releases the shirt, letting it fall back down to my thighs, his hands going around my back to pull me back against him. He tilts his head, his tongue delving into my mouth as the kiss grows heated.

A cough interrupts us and we both break apart, startled by Miss Perry's intrusion.

"Good morning, sir," she says as her heels click swiftly across the floor.

I avert my gaze, not wanting to see the look of disgust or disappointment I know she's giving me.

"I should go upstairs," I say before excusing myself from the kitchen and running the three flights back to Graham's bedroom.

Once in the room I pull his shirt off, reaching for my clothes from last night. I find my panties and bra and put them on, then I step into my jeans.

"What are you doing?"

I turn around to see Graham in the doorway with the tray.

"Oh, I was just getting dressed to head down to my room."

"Like hell you are." He places the tray on the bedside table and walks over to me. "Take it off, put my shirt back on."

"Are you sure? I don't ha—"

"You want me to do it for you? It'll take twice as long because the moment I get your panties off, I'm going to have my fill of your pussy for breakfast."

My mouth goes dry. This man and the things he says. So brash, so vulgar... so hot.

"Maybe." I shrug and finish pulling my jeans back on.

Before I even realize he's moving, he has my jeans and panties off and he's tossed me onto my back on the bed with his shoulders between my thighs.

Ninety seconds later I'm clawing at his back as he draws another mind-blowing orgasm from my body.

"Now that's what you call breakfast in bed." I giggle as he wipes my wetness from his chin with a wink.

I pull his shirt back on as I climb into bed, then he settles the tray in front of us. We both sip our coffee and pick at the pastries.

"So, what's the deal with you and Miss Perry?" I finally ask.

"The deal?" He takes a bite of his croissant.

"Yeah. She clearly has a crush or something on you."

"A *crush?*" He arches an eyebrow at me.

"Oh, come on. You can't be that oblivious. All the little, *oh yes, sir; let me fix your tie, sir; let me make sure your pants are buttoned and zipped properly.*" I do my best impression of her voice and uptight attitude which causes Graham to burst into laughter.

"I gotta say the impression is uncanny. But seriously, she's just the house manager, Margot. She's never told me she has feelings for me, and I certainly don't have any like that toward her."

"I don't think she likes me very much." I watch his response, curious if she's ever said anything to him about me.

"I don't think that's true; she's just—cold. She was raised by British parents, stiff upper lip and all."

I nod. "You two ever have a relationship?"

He seems to think a little too long about this question but then smiles and says, "No, no relationship."

He moves the tray back to the table and slides his arm around me. "Enough about Miss Perry. Why don't we finish what we started in the kitchen earlier." He trails his lips up my neck.

"Do you not want her to know about us?" I cringe a little the moment I say *us.* "Not *us* like we're an *us,* but just that were—we've slept or been together." I'm getting flustered.

He sighs and sits back against the headboard, running his hand through his dark hair.

"I'm not hiding it, no. I just didn't think you'd want to openly be making out in front of her."

"It's just that, it was the second time."

He reaches out and brushes my hair away from my face. "What exactly are you asking, Margot?"

"I dunno—nothing really." I shrug and lean in and kiss him, hoping we can forget this entire conversation.

A few moments later he's inside me and we've both forgotten all about it.

* * *

"Did you sleep well?" I ask Eleanor as I pull her dress over her head.

"Uh-huh. I had a dream I was a unicorn." Her eyes are huge as she pretends her hand is a horn on top of her head. "And, and I had pony friends."

I laugh as she tells me about the magical land of ponies and unicorns from her dreams.

"That sounds wonderful."

I help her with her socks and shoes, and we pack her bag for her pre-K class. Once a week she attends an extremely fancy and exclusive pre-K class in the city. It's a drive but it's a full day from nine to four. I've never even heard of a pre-K program this exclusive. I'm pretty sure the tuition costs more per year than an average home in the suburbs.

But Eleanor loves it. They have equestrian days, which are her favorite, etiquette lessons, tea time every day because why not, and of course different language courses.

We finish getting ready and head downstairs to where Graham is waiting to tell her goodbye.

* * *

"Good morning, Miss Eleanor." Miss Grace Tillmore smiles as Grace runs into her classroom. "Hi, Margot, how are you?" She's a genuine and sweet woman and since learning about my music education background, she's been trying to get me in the door to teach at La Crème Academy.

"Hi, Grace. I'm good. How are you?"

"Oh, busy as usual. You have a minute?" she asks, ushering me out into the hall. "I spoke with Dean Woods and he is very interested in speaking with you about heading up the music program here." She's giddy with excitement.

"Oh, wow." I place my hand over my chest in genuine shock. "Heading up the department? I thought it was just about a teaching position?" Suddenly I'm worried about how I would be able to head up a department *and* be a nanny—the reality is I can't.

When she first propositioned me about teaching music, it was a part-time position that I could do on the days that Eleanor had class. It would have worked out perfectly. But this, this is a whole new job and I'm not sure I'm ready to walk away from being Eleanor's nanny quite yet... I don't know if I'll ever be ready for that.

"Just think about it. It wouldn't be until next school year anyway so you have time." She squeezes my hand before ducking back into the classroom to lead the class in their morning song.

I decide to walk over to the coffee shop Hank and I hung out at previously. It's only a few blocks away and I need to clear my head. Music has always been my passion, my life. I'm twenty-six and I only had less than five years actually teaching. I'm not ready to say goodbye to that career yet. But where does that leave me with Eleanor... and Graham? If I left, would that be the end?

I step inside the coffee shop, my head down as I walk to the counter.

"Margot?" I spin around to see Hank waving at me from a small table in the corner. I wave back, signaling I'll be over in a minute, then I place my order.

"Hey, what are the odds. You just live here now or...?" I joke, pulling out the chair and taking a seat across from him.

"Nah. I don't have to be at my first class until eleven a.m. so today is my easy-slash-lazy morning day. How are you? How are things since...?" He trails off and I know he means since the night we hung out. "Sorry I haven't really been in touch since then. I, uh, I didn't want to cause any issues."

"Issues? What do you mean?" I scrunch up my face as they call my name for my coffee. I go grab it and return to the table, taking a long, slow sip.

"Well, your—boss?" he says questioningly. "He kind of threatened me, chased me out. He clearly didn't want me around you."

"Wait. I was pretty tipsy, but I wasn't that drunk. I—" I stumble over my words. I'm confused and a little angry. "He threatened you?"

He shrugs. "Yeah, nothing crazy, just that I had no business letting you get that drunk. I think he thought I was trying to get with you."

"Oh my God." I reach across the table. "I'm so sorry. I had no idea what he said."

"So you two then?"

I nod slowly. "Yeah. Wasn't supposed to happen, certainly wasn't planning on it, but yeah, we, uh, slept together."

He laughs and shakes his head. "Hey, as long as it's consensual and he's not being a dick, I'm happy for you."

"Thanks." I blush. "I'm not reading into it. It's just some stupid if not irresponsible fun. Getting involved with your boss isn't exactly what I thought I'd be doing with my life." I take another sip of coffee. "How are things with you and Shelly?" I haven't spoken to him since the conversation I had with her at the house where she confessed her love for him. I knew I told him I'd keep him in the loop, but that's a confession that needs to come from her.

"Good." He nods, hiding a smile before he chuckles. "Great. Amazing. Can't get enough," he says with a full-blown smile. "We're official now, a couple."

"Oh my God!" I squeal. "I'm so happy for you guys; oh, this is amazing."

We laugh and joke about them getting married and where they'll live and how many kids they'll have.

"So what are you going to do next year? You thinking about applying at different schools again?"

I shrug. "Honestly, I don't know yet. I took the nanny job because I desperately needed a job, but I've fallen in love with Eleanor, the little girl. It would break my heart to abandon her. She's already been through that with the other nanny and her mother dying."

"You know it's not abandonment, right? It's a job, Margot. You're not her mom."

The words hurt but they're true.

"I know. Speaking of, she takes class over at La Crème and they were in talks to offer me a part-time music teaching position that I could do the days she's in class, but then this morning the teacher I've been talking about it with told me they want to offer me a position as head of the music department."

"Hot damn, Margot. That's fantastic! And at La Crème." He whistles. "That's a resume in and of itself. There's gotta be so many connections there. They say what the salary would be?"

"No, no specifics yet. It wouldn't start till next school year and they haven't even talked with me personally about it, more just to Grace, the pre-K teacher. Her husband is one of the administrators which is why she's involved. I sent her a copy of my resume."

He narrows his eyes at me. "But you'll take it if they offer, right?"

I sigh. "I don't know, Hank."

"Margot, come on. You're not thinking clearly. This thing with the boss is getting your wires crossed."

I swallow down the lump in my throat. Maybe he's right.

"I don't say this to be an asshole, but you're not their family. You're a hired member of the staff and they could fire you tomorrow without reason. You need to think about your future, long term. Don't sacrifice your future just because he wants you *right now*."

"I know. I think it's all just so fresh and new, ya know?"

"The offer or the dick?" He laughs and I reach over to playfully smack him.

"You're in the dick-sand stage; you're dickmatized." We both howl in laughter and it feels good.

I'm in a funk when I leave the coffee shop, my brain no clearer than this morning. I spend the rest of the afternoon running errands, getting in a workout, and reading in the park before picking up Eleanor and heading home.

"Snack tiiiiime," Eleanor sings as she marches through the front door toward the kitchen, dropping her backpack and shoes by the front door.

I pull open the fridge. "Grapes and cheese?" I ask, and Eleanor nods, sipping from her juice box.

Miss Perry walks into the kitchen. "Afternoon, Eleanor," she says, ignoring me as usual. Normally I can let it go, but her coldness toward me is growing increasingly arctic at this point and it rubs me the wrong way.

"Good afternoon to you too, Miss Perry."

I say it louder than necessary, making sure she hears me. She breezes past me, placing a plate and glass into the sink, most likely leftover from Graham's lunch since he worked from home today.

"Afternoon, Miss Silver," she quips before pausing, her shoulder brushing against mine. She lowers her voice, then says, "Nice to see you fully clothed." She looks down her nose at me and I curl my hands into fists at my sides.

I spin around to chew her out when Graham comes waltzing into the kitchen with a big smile.

"There's my girl," he says, planting a kiss on Eleanor's cheek. "How was school?" He looks up at me and winks, settling my nerves a bit. I give him an attempt at a smile, but I'm not in the mood.

"L'école était amusante," Eleanor responds in what sounds like perfect French, but I have no idea what she said.

"I'll be doing laundry," I say before exiting the kitchen and grabbing Eleanor's backpack and shoes and walking upstairs before Graham can stop me.

I know that Miss Perry's comment to me isn't what really has me upset. I'm upset at the mess I've gotten myself into because the reality is, I think it's way more than just an exciting sexual encounter or two with Graham. Feelings are very much involved, at least on my end.

I can either swallow them down and face the facts for what they are—I'm just a nanny and a current, exciting distraction for a broken-hearted billionaire who is used to getting what he wants and when this is all said and done, I'll walk away—or I risk it all and tell him how I feel.

20

GRAHAM

"**W**hen do I go more days to school, Daddy?" Eleanor swings her legs on the barstool as she finishes her snack.

"Not till this fall, sweetie. You'll be six and you'll be in class a few days a week instead of one. You like your class?" She nods her head, pushing her empty plate away from her.

I walk over and grab it, placing it in the dishwasher as Margot re-enters the kitchen. She looks positively delicious in her flirty little dress. I try not to stare but it's no use. The small dip in the neckline draws my eyes straight to her tits. It's not a sexy dress; it's cute and fun, leaving me wondering what she has on underneath.

"And how was your day, Margot?" I ask, giving her a flirty smile.

"Fine." She barely makes eye contact with me as she helps Eleanor down from the stool. "Come on, we need to go unpack your backpack and look over your assignments for the week."

I reach out and grab her hand as she walks by, but she pulls it away and continues out of the kitchen.

What the hell was that about?

I have about two hours before the chef has dinner ready so I throw on a pair of shorts and a t-shirt and head outside for a run. I crank my favorite metal playlist as I pound out a quick five miles.

I'm anxious. Lately I can feel it in my chest. It's like there's an impending storm brewing. Normally, I'm good with stress. I can sense when something is off, but I feel out of my element and I can't put my finger on it.

I think about Margot's comments this morning regarding Miss Perry. I didn't lie—*technically.* Yes, I fucked up royally a few years ago and slept with Fiona but it was purely physical, a release of emotions during a period of grief. Nothing more. We never had a relationship and that's what she asked.

I push the last half mile, running at a very clipped pace. My lungs feel like they're on fire as I double over, attempting to catch my breath.

I know what she meant. In so many words she was asking if we'd been intimate and I said no. I know it's a detail that I should tell her, but now it feels too late, like I'll risk losing her if I fess up now. Then again, why would it ever come up?

I wipe the sweat from my brow and turn to head back to the house to shower for dinner.

When I get inside I poke my head around the kitchen corner—no Margot, no Eleanor. I check the sitting room with the piano; nobody there either. I walk up the stairs and hear talking coming from Eleanor's room.

"Knock, knock," I say as I open the door.

Margot is sitting on the floor, her legs crossed, a tiara on her head and several fake rings and necklaces on.

"Daddy, nooo," Eleanor says, standing and waving a hand toward me. "We're playing princess and no boys can play."

I lean against the door and smile down at Margot. She offers up a smile back, but it feels weak, sad even.

You okay? I mouth at her. She nods her head once, still not convincing.

"Okay, okay," I say, backing out of the room. "I'll go take a shower. I'll see you royal ladies at dinner." I give Eleanor a wink before jogging up the stairs to my bedroom.

It's hard to believe that Margot only came into my life just a few months ago. She's changed it so dramatically in such a short time and I don't even think she realizes it.

I feel my walls coming down slowly. I crave time with Eleanor. I'm sad for all the dinners and bedtimes I missed in the last few years because I was scared of seeing her mother when I looked at her. It still stings but I can't hide from my future anymore because of my past.

I find myself imagining a life with Margot. Expanding our family together. Traveling the world with her and Eleanor. Growing old with her.

Fear grips my heart. Is this something I really want to go through again? Risking my heart all over again?

Right now, I'm not sure, but I know that the feelings... the cravings I have for Margot are only getting stronger each day.

All through dinner I can see her avoiding me. I try to send her subliminal messages across the dinner table, but it doesn't seem to be working. She either averts her gaze or is talking to Eleanor, her answers short and clipped when speaking to me.

"So what did you do today?" I ask her as Eleanor digs into a slice of cake for dessert. She's fully preoccupied so I take the chance to draw something out of Margot.

"I had a few errands to run in the city while Eleanor had class."

"Anything exciting?" I prod.

"Not particularly. Just stopped for coffee. Ran into Hank."

My eyes snap up when she says that and this time she's not averting her gaze. She's staring at me, arms crossed firmly over her chest.

Ah, so that's what this is about.

"And how is he?"

"Great. He's very happy with my friend Shelly whom he's dating." Yup, she's mad. "I set them up actually. They're happy and in love."

I chuckle and nod my head, her message received loud and clear.

"Come on, Eleanor. Let's go watch your show and then get ready for a bath." She grabs her hand as she hops down from the stool.

"Bye, Daddy. See you later," she chirps before running out of the kitchen.

* * *

"Miss Silver, a word in my office, please."

Margot looks up at me from where she's seated in the sitting room. Her tea mug is almost empty and she's nearly halfway through the book she's reading. I hate to interrupt her little moment of peace and serenity, but I think it's time we cleared the air about today.

I take a seat behind my desk and a moment later she enters.

"Close the door," I say, and she obliges.

She doesn't say anything, just stands in front of my desk, an amused look on her face.

"Please, have a seat." I gesture. "What's troubling you, darling?"

"You already know, so let's not play this game." When she has this expression on her face and her flat tone, she reminds me of a petulant teenager.

"Hank?"

"Yes, Hank. He told me what you said to him that night at the bar. Had I known then, you would have gotten an earful from me and I wouldn't have—" She trails off and I smile.

"Wouldn't have let me kiss you? Wouldn't have let me get you off in the back of my car?" She narrows her eyes, clearly attempting to prove that my words have no effect on her, but I call bullshit. I lean forward and lowering my voice, I say, "You seemed to rather enjoy what I did to you in the car, baby girl."

"Stop. I know what you're doing."

I lean back and shrug, feigning innocence.

"Look. Hank is a good friend and has been. He really is in love with my friend Shelly. We are like brother and sister; we've never had a moment or a kiss or anything. You can't go running him out of my life or anyone else for that matter."

"Anyone else?"

"I just mean in general. The way you wouldn't even let Garrett speak to me at the charity event, then Hank. You can't run around trying to shield me away from men."

"I'm not trying to shield you from *all* men... just the ones who want to sleep with you."

She huffs and stands up. "That's exactly what I mean!" she shouts. "Hank didn't want to sleep with me. I've made that clear, and the other guy, you think I would have, what? Run to the coat closet with some stranger and slept with him?"

I'm not expressing myself clearly. "Margot, no. I don't think that and I'm sorry. I didn't mean to upset you." I walk around my desk and grab her arms softly.

"You embarrassed me in front of Hank," she says softly, and I hate that I made her feel that way.

"Hey, I'm sorry. I didn't mean for that to happen. You're right. I need to respect your boundaries and next time I see Hank, I'll make sure I apologize to him."

She lets her forehead fall against my chest as I wrap my arms around her body.

"I don't want to be a secret," she murmurs against my shirt. I reach down and tip her chin upward.

"A secret?"

"From Miss Perry. I know things should be kept private between us. I respect that, especially with Eleanor. But I guess I just felt like a dirty little secret or something you were ashamed of."

"You're not a secret, sweetheart. Trust me, she's aware of what's happening between us, and I know Phil knows as well as Hank and Garrett after how possessive I was about you. I won't ever sit back and let a man hit on you in front of me, which is what Garrett would have done, trust me. I feel protective of you."

Her big eyes are trained on mine and I can't stand being this close to her without kissing her. I place a hand on either side of her face and pull her lips toward mine.

God, I'll never tire of kissing her full, pouty lips. I walk her backward around the desk, lifting her to sit on it in front of my chair.

"We still need to talk," she says as I trail kisses down her neck, pulling aside the strap of her dress to expose the skin of her shoulder.

"Mmm, we will, baby." I let my other hand wander down her body, gliding up her leg till I reach the hem of her dress. "After."

"After?" she whispers as her eyes close. I look at her, her head back, her hair falling down her back as she leans on her arms.

"Yes, after I have my dessert." I lick my lips as my eyes drop down to her legs where I'm pulling her dress up over her thighs. I reach beneath the dress, removing her panties.

I take a seat in my chair, placing her feet on the edge of it. "Spread your thighs."

She slowly lets her legs fall open wider, and my mouth pools with saliva at the sight.

"I'm going to defile you on this desk. I'm going to remind you who you belong to."

I don't wait for a response from her. I dive in.

I grip her waist, pushing my shoulders against her thighs as I savor the taste of her. I drag my tongue up her folds, her wetness growing quickly as she moans. I devour her, my tongue swirling around her bud before plunging inside her.

I can feel her thighs begin to quiver as she pants, but the moment is ruined when a sharp knock on my office door echoes through the room.

"Mr. Hayes?" It's Miss Perry's shrill voice.

"I'm busy. I'll find you later." Margot stiffens, staring at me. "I'm not finished with you yet," I tell her.

"Mr. Hayes, I really need to speak with yo—" She opens the door, barging into my office as my face is inches away from Margot's sopping wet pussy.

"Oh my goodness." She clutches at her nonexistent pearls, her eyes falling to the floor.

"I said I'll be with you later," I grit the words out as Margot struggles to pull her dress down, attempting to dismount from my desk.

"I said I'm not finished with you yet." I stare at her, speaking loudly enough Miss Perry hears what I said as I hold her in place.

Miss Perry scurries from the room, her face glowing red.

"Oh my God." Margot covers her face with her hands in embarrassment.

"You didn't want to be a secret," I say. "Now get on all fours."

"On here?" Surprised, she points to the desk.

"Now," I bark and she jumps before getting on all fours. She looks back over her shoulder at me and it's a fucking fantasy.

"Goddamn," I mutter as I drag my hands over her ass, gripping her cheeks to pull them apart. "Stay still," I command as I lean in, dragging my tongue up her slick pussy before swirling it around her asshole.

"Oh." She lurches forward at the foreign sensation, but I grip her hips back and pull her harder against my face.

I continue eating her out from behind as she grips the papers on my desk. Her moans fill the room and drive me absolutely fucking wild.

I'm not even close to getting my fill when she calls out my name, coming undone.

"You're not?" She looks at me in confusion as I pull her dress down and help her back off the desk.

"Trust me, baby." I kiss her lips softly as I help her situate herself. "Denying myself is the last thing I want right now." I reach down and grab my cock that's at full mast.

"But if I fuck you right now, it'll turn into a marathon session, and I won't get any work done tonight. I have a contract I need to look over for a very important meeting in a few days. Otherwise, I'd be buried in you right now, and honestly, after that view, it wouldn't be in your pussy."

I can see the shock settle on her face. "I told you I'll have all of you someday. There will be no part of you I haven't touched, tasted, or fucked." I plant a soft kiss on her lips.

"You did taste." A soft blush creeps up her neck. "It felt—good, really good."

"Was that your first time?" I'm praying she says yes. I want to be the only man who's had some part of her. She nods her head.

"Mmm." I inhale sharply. "That makes me want to do it again all the more."

"You can." She wraps her arms around my neck, pressing her breasts against me. My cock is now pressed so firmly against my zipper it's painful.

"Temptress," I whisper.

She juts her bottom lip out in a pout. "Fine, but you're missing out."

She's teasing me, and it's adorable.

I reach out and poke her lip. "I'll be up in a few hours. Make sure you're in my bed. I promise that I'll give you another orgasm between now and the morning."

I spin her around toward the door and slap her ass. "Now, obey me before I lose my mind."

21

MARGOT

"Mmm." I push my naked body back against Graham's hardened cock. "Looks like someone is happy to see me."

"Very."

I look over my shoulder and realize he's several inches away from me.

What the?

"Is that your—?" I roll over. Yup, it is. "How are you poking me from that far away?" I laugh.

"Nine inches away to be precise," he says, gripping the base as we both look at his impressive size.

Damn, how have I not realized just HOW huge he is?

"You're telling me you're just now realizing?" He laughs as he pulls me against his chest, burying his nose in my hair.

"Sorry, I'm always a little—preoccupied when your trouser snake is loose."

That gets me a hearty laugh.

"I'll run down and get us some coffee. You stay right here." He reaches down and pinches my ass. "Or there will be consequences."

A tingle settles in my belly at the way he says the word *consequences.*

He slides out of bed, my body immediately missing his warmth as he pulls on his pajama bottoms and a t-shirt and heads toward the kitchen.

I roll over, staring up at the ceiling. I feel a sudden warmth settle over my body as I remember last night—Miss Perry walking in on Graham going down on me on his desk.

I groan, dragging my hands over my face.

"She's never going to let me forget that."

I quickly scamper to the bathroom, realizing my morning breath is a bit too ripe. I use my finger and some toothpaste to freshen up before walking into Graham's closet.

As I suspected, it's immaculate. Suits hang in color-coordinated rows followed by a row of perfectly pressed, crisp shirts—also color-coordinated. Everything is a beautiful light wood, maybe maple or oak. I reach over and flick the switch, and the lights set to an ambient, soft glow.

There are a few shelves of shoes, mostly dress, some casual. There are also several drawers but I feel a little too nosy opening any of them. If I had to guess, I'd say they're full of watches and ties, probably those fancy cuff links he's always fidgeting with as well.

I glance to the other corner where casual clothes are sorted. I grab one of the black t-shirts and pull it on, bringing it to my nose. It smells like him, a soft soapy scent with hints of teakwood. The only reason I can pick up on that scent is the candles I'm forever buying at Bath & Body Works.

"Margot?"

I turn the lights off and walk back through the closet and bathroom. "Hey, I was just grabbing a shirt. Coffee smells amazing."

I walk across the room and go to reach for a mug just as he steps toward me, wrapping an arm around my waist.

"Thought I said don't move. Now you have to be punished."

He tosses me on the bed, pinning my arms overhead with one hand as he tickles me with the other.

"Stop! Stop!" I laugh hysterically. "Oh my God, I'm gonna pee!" This doesn't deter him.

He leans over me, pretending to bite my neck just as Eleanor's sleepy voice interrupts us.

"Daddy, you're loud."

"Oh God." I pull my hands free from his grip as I scramble to get off the bed. Not that it would make a difference; Eleanor has clearly already seen us.

"Good morning, sweetie. What's wrong?" Graham stands and walks over to Eleanor. She holds her arms out to him, her favorite bunny in her hand. Graham scoops her up and walks her back toward the bed.

I grab the sheet and pull it tightly around me. "Good morning, Eleanor," I say, attempting to sound normal.

"You're out of your room before seven fifteen a.m., sweetie." Graham settles against the headboard as she curls into his chest, bringing her thumb to her mouth and cuddling her bunny.

"I can't find Muffin," she pouts.

"I'm sure she's exploring somewhere. When did you see her last?" he asks.

"Last night."

I look over at Graham and nod. "I'll go check on her," I say as I try to extract myself from the sheets. My stomach is in knots. Graham doesn't seem bothered at all that Eleanor just walked in on me in his bed.

I'm about four steps down the hall when I hear Muffin's bell jingling as she trots up the stairs. I crouch down. "Muffin, psst, psst."

She runs over to me meowing and I scoop her up, carrying her back toward the room.

"Muffin!" Eleanor squeals, her arms outstretched. I place the kitten in her arms and stand awkwardly by the bed.

Graham eyes me and I avert my gaze, instead grabbing a cup of coffee and sitting on the very edge of the mattress.

"Did you have any dreams? More unicorns?" Graham smooths Eleanor's hair down as she sits in his lap, completely distracted with Muffin.

"No. But, but Muffin was biting my toes last night." Eleanor laughs.

"She bit your toes? Was she being mean?"

"No, she was playing, Daddy!"

As nervous as I am for the conversation after this, watching Graham hold Eleanor as they both play with Muffin has my ovaries and my heart about to explode.

"I need to get ready for work, sweetie."

"Whyyyy?" Eleanor pushes her lip out.

"How about we have a family movie night tonight when I get home?"

"Yay! Movie night!" Eleanor scrambles to her feet and jumps on the bed.

Family movie night?

Graham swings his legs over the edge of the bed and stands in front of me. "That includes you."

I look up at him, my coffee still in my hands. He smiles at me softly as Eleanor goes back to playing with Muffin.

I watch as his eyes drop to my lips. He leans in, but I turn my head to avoid his kiss. The smile instantly falls from his face. I glance back at Eleanor, hoping he understands, but he doesn't seem to feel the same.

"Eleanor, sweetheart, take Muffin downstairs and go pick out something to wear. Miss Margot will be down to help you in a bit."

After she leaves the room, he turns his attention back to me. "Am I allowed to kiss you now?"

Here it comes.

"I wasn't trying to deny you. I just was taken off guard when Eleanor came into the room."

"Weren't you the one who said you didn't want to be a secret?" He takes a sip of his coffee.

"It's not that." I sigh. "I don't want to confuse her. It's one thing if Phil or Miss Perry knows; it's another for a child, *your* child."

He doesn't respond, just looks at me.

"Graham, if this is just a fling, that's okay. But I don't want to make Eleanor think it's something it's not. You said yourself that you didn't want her confused on who I am, who her mother is… I'm trying to respect that and I care about her and you—deeply."

I can't tell if he's even hearing me and I'm not in the mood to argue.

I stand and put my empty mug back on the tray. "I'm going down to get Eleanor ready for the day. Maybe we should talk later?"

He reaches out and grabs my hand. "I have a work event coming up in a few days. I'd like you to attend with me."

"Okay, I can do that." I offer a smile but I'm frustrated. This is the second time I've attempted to get him to talk about things with us—or maybe it's the third, I can't remember—but he clearly isn't interested in having the conversation. At least not now.

I know I should just ask him outright, *what the hell are we doing*, but I'm terrified. I'm scared that the reason he's avoiding the conversation is because to him, this is all just a fling and if I put him on the spot and demand a straightforward answer, I'll risk it all falling apart.

He pulls me toward him and kisses me deeply. His tongue snakes into my mouth immediately but just as quickly he ends it and walks toward his bathroom.

I leave his room and head downstairs to get my day started, the lingering question of *would I rather lose him and have my answer or would I be okay living in denial* floating in my head.

The rest of the morning goes smoothly. All through breakfast, morning music lessons, and the drive to ballet class, Eleanor never once mentions what she saw this morning.

Relief washes over me. Although, I still have to navigate our *family* movie night. My stomach tightens again at that word.

Instead of heading back to the house during Eleanor's class, I pull into a Starbucks. I scroll through social media, check a few news articles, and then flip over to my email. One at the top catches my eye. It's from Grace Tillmore.

Margot,

I hope you're doing well. I wanted to reach out and follow up with you regarding our conversation about the upcoming position at La Crème Academy. I've spoken with my husband Jeff about your background—he was super impressed with your resume!—and your education. He feels like you would be a fantastic fit! You are already familiar with our standards and culture here at La Crème so I know you'd fit right in.

They do plan on posting the job position but not for another month so you have time to think about it. Although, I really, really hope you'll take it!

As always, if you have any questions feel free to send them over. Jeff will be reaching out to you in a few days to set up a phone call.

All the best!

Grace Tillmore.

My heart sinks. This is the kind of opportunity I've dreamed of and to be considered for it at such a young age means so much to me.

I think about my mom and dad, how proud of me they'd be. They'd also encourage me to take it. But then again, they both always preached to me to follow my heart.

"Mom, why'd you give up your dreams of being a singer?"

It was a warm summer night and she and I were sitting on our front porch watching fireflies as we snacked on some popcorn. It was only a few months after Dad passed.

"Well, doll, dreams change. I loved being a singer so much; it was my dream, you're right, but then you came along and my dreams changed. I realized I wanted to not only share music with the world but teach youngsters like you. It wasn't just about sharing my gift with the world anymore. It was about teaching them how they could have it too."

I think about that conversation often. I know dreams can change. I just don't know if mine actually have or if I'm trying to justify not following them.

I stare at the email again, my eyes glazing over as nothing feels clearer. I'd give anything to have my mom here right now to talk through it.

My phone buzzes and I see 'Maybe Warren Dorsey' across the top. I always hit ignore. I don't know why I haven't blocked him. But something in me hits the answer button this time.

"Hello?"

"Margot, is that you?" His scratchy voice instantly sends a chill down my spine, the kind you get when you can smell the scuzziness coming off someone.

"What do you want?"

"Now is that any way to speak to your father? I just want to get to know my little girl. Don't you think it's time we put things behind us?"

I can feel bile rising in my throat.

"Fuck you!" I shout, not caring that I'm in public. "You had your chance, you piece of shit, and you were never my father. You will never be my father!"

Tears sting my eyes as I end the call and walk out of Starbucks, a few people staring after me.

* * *

I FASTEN the delicate necklace around my neck. It's a simple gold music note that once belonged to my mother. She gave it to me on my eighteenth birthday.

The royal-blue dress I picked out for Graham's work event hugs my slight curves intimately. The neckline swoops across my chest, dipping just low enough to expose my cleavage. The real showstopper is the back. It swoops all the way down to my waist, just above the two dimples at the base of my spine.

I let out a shaky breath as I stare at my reflection. I angle my front away so I can check the back again.

"You look breathtaking."

I turn my attention to the doorway where Graham is standing.

"You look pretty mouthwatering yourself." I drag my eyes casually up his finely clad body. "New tux?"

He pulls himself away from the doorway. "It is."

He comes to stand behind me, placing his hands on my upper arms.

"Don't worry about the dress. Trust me, every neck will break when you walk through that door."

I can feel his warmth against my exposed back and it's comforting. We haven't spoken about things since Eleanor found us in bed together earlier this week. I didn't want to ruin the family movie night which ended up being so much fun.

We watched a *Barbie* movie and a *My Little Pony* movie while eating 'unicorn popcorn' that was just regular popcorn coated in chemically sweet neon colors. Eleanor had the time of her life with us and Muffin and ended up passing out between us halfway through the second movie.

"That's what I'm afraid of. I don't really like being the center of attention."

He pulls a small box from his pocket and opens it, pulling out a small gold bracelet.

"Give me your wrist." I lift it toward him, and he wraps the bracelet around me, clasping it.

"I thought of you when I saw this. This one isn't borrowed; it's yours to keep."

"Graham," I gasp. "You shouldn't have."

I look down at the small plate in the center of the chain. "What is this?" I ask, referring to the black etching on it.

"Let me see your phone." I reach over and grab it, handing it to him.

He opens the Spotify app and points the camera at the bracelet, scanning it. Instantly, "In Your Eyes" by Peter Gabriel plays through the speakers.

My heart catches in my throat and I wonder if he chose the song or if he just picked a random one.

"That's amazing." I smile as I look down at it again. "You're amazing," I say, sliding my hands up his chest and around his neck.

"Promise me something?"

"Of course."

"Never doubt how much you mean to me."

I pull his mouth down to mine, not wanting to ruin the moment by trying to figure out if there's a hidden meaning or an ominous warning lurking behind those words.

Tonight, I'm going to just let it all go and pretend that maybe Graham Hayes is falling in love with me too.

22

GRAHAM

"So what is tonight's event for?"
I settle in the back seat next to Margot as we make our way into the city.

"It's for my company. We do two of these a year. This one is held at the end of June as a thank you to our clients and the second one, held in December, is a thank you to our employees."

My eyes drop to where her hand has settled on my upper thigh.

"That's very nice of you. Is it similar to the last event?"

"Yeah, somewhat. Open bar, dancing, mingling. This one has raffles, casino games, and I think there's some famous singer who is the close-out entertainment."

"You think?" She giggles, nudging my shoulder.

"I didn't plan the thing. I just have to show up since my name's on the building." I wink at her and she leans in.

"Mmm." That's a lovely way to start the evening. I pull her in for a second kiss.

"So what kind of stuff is raffled off?"

"Well, it's a free raffle; they don't pay for the tickets. Same with the casino chips. It's free for them to participate and they can win anything from gift cards to a month-long vacation to a location of their choosing or a car or money."

"Damn." She whistles. "I'm in the wrong business."

"Last year the big prize was $100k."

"A hundred thousand dollars?" Her eyes bug out. "Holy shit!"

I chuckle. "Yeah, in this world, a lot of my top employees get more for their Christmas bonus so it's not a big deal to them. It's like an average salaried person winning five or ten thousand. It's a nice surprise, free money and all, but it's not like they're winning the lottery."

"So do I get to play? Since I'm... one of your employees."

I look over at her, not sure if she's making a joke. She has a coy smile on her face so I play along.

"I guess that depends. Who are you going to take with you when you win the month-long trip?"

I place my arm over her shoulder as she leans in closer to me, that hand on my thigh trailing dangerously close to my hardening cock.

"Hank, probably." She laughs and I flex my arm around her. She falls forward a little into my lap, her hand now resting fully on my crotch.

"You're just begging to get punished, aren't you?"

"Maybe." She drags her teeth across her bottom lip. She has the kind of lips that beg to be kissed—to have my cum dribbling off them.

I look down her dress, my mouth watering. I slip my hand right inside, pinching her nipple, her look growing from flirty to needy in a matter of seconds.

"How should I punish you?" I continue to roll the tight bud between my fingers as I reach over and slide up the divider. Phil does not need to be witness to what's about to happen.

"Do I get to choose?" I nod my head yes as she slowly slides off the seat, settling between my thighs.

Her eyes stay trained on mine as she reaches forward and undoes my pants, her hand reaching inside my underwear and fishing out my cock.

I reach out and slide one strap off her shoulder. "Don't want you getting messy." I do the same with the other, the dress falling off her naked breasts and pooling around her waist.

"God, you're fucking beautiful." I cup her cheek, letting my hand linger for a moment before she leans forward and takes me in her mouth.

I let my head fall back against the seat, my eyes fluttering closed as she slowly takes me all the way into her mouth till I hit the back of her throat. She repeats the process slowly a few more times, drawing a guttural moan from the back of my own throat.

She picks up the pace a little, sliding her hand up my shaft as her mouth comes down.

"Oh, baby," I groan, reaching down to put my hand behind her neck.

I guide her, my hips begging to thrust forward, but I don't want to be rough with her. I'm too afraid to screw up her makeup.

"Goddamn, your mouth was made to be fucked." I grit my teeth, pleasure building rapidly.

"That's right, baby girl. Take all of me," I pant, my breaths coming out in quick, shallow puffs.

I can't hold back. I tighten my hold on her neck as I empty myself down her throat.

"That's a good girl. Swallow down every fucking drop."

I glance out the window. We have less than ten minutes before we're at the venue.

I reach down, pulling her mouth from my cock with a pop sound. I lift her dress up and pull her panties to the side, turning her so her back is to me before sliding her down on my cock.

"Ahh!" She reaches down, her hands gripping my knees at the intrusion.

"Sorry, baby. I don't have time to get you ready. You're gonna have to take me." My words are strained as her tight little pussy milks my throbbing cock.

She moans as she finds a rhythm. I grab her hips, helping her raise and lower herself down on me.

I continue my verbal assault, not holding back on every filthy thought that I have in this moment.

"I want your belly and pussy full of my cum tonight."

I move one of my hands to her shoulder, forcing her down onto me even harder. Her yelps and moans only spur me on.

"Everyone will know you're mine. This pussy. Those tits. Your lips."

I bring my thumb to my lips and get it wet before pressing it firmly against her back entrance. "This ass."

She sucks in a sharp breath as I press harder, sliding an inch of it inside her. I feel her cunt tighten around me. "You like that, don't you, filthy little girl. Fuck, I knew you would. Just wait till my cock fills you like this."

We're both teetering on the edge, hanging on by a thread when it finally snaps. I explode inside her, my vision blurring as my head falls back against the seat. My chest feels like it's on fire.

Her legs tremble as I help her up. I reach into my pocket and pull out a handkerchief, sliding it between her thighs.

"I didn't plan that, honestly," I pant as I help her clean herself up before we both adjust our clothes and right ourselves.

"Your dress okay?"

"I don't really care." She smiles, her eyes sparkling.

"We've got a few moments to catch our breath. Here." I hand her a bottle of water and open one for myself.

The event space looks fantastic. I throw two of these a year and each time I'm more impressed. I make a mental note to thank the team who handles it.

"I need a drink," Margot whispers in my ear as she clings to my arm.

I don't blame her for being nervous. This is an entirely new world to her and these people are sharks, wolves—predators. They can sniff out new blood from a mile away. Most of them are fine; I trust them with business, but when it comes to humanity, not as far as I can throw them.

I tighten my grip around her waist and steer her toward the bar. "That sounds like an excellent idea."

"Old-fashioned and—"

"Prosecco, please."

I chuckle.

"What?" She gives me that smile again. It's flirty and cute. Inviting and dangerous.

"It's just that"—I lean in close to her ear so no one can hear—"you order this sweet drink with such a sweet demeanor, and nobody would know that not fifteen minutes ago you had my cock stuffed down your throat."

She bites her bottom lip, a pink glow spreading across her cheeks.

"Nothing to be embarrassed about, baby. I love that only I get to see that side of you."

We stare at one another and it's almost like there's something being exchanged between us, something we haven't expressed to each other before. But the moment quickly dissipates when the bartender places our drinks down in front of us.

"So, you already lost to me in bowling. What game can I kick your ass in here?"

"Damn, one glass of Prosecco and she's already cocky."

We do a quick round of obligatory meet and greets.

"Grayson, good to see you." I shake his hand as his father approaches from the left.

"Graham, you son of a bitch, you did it again with this year's party." He claps my shoulder.

"Ted, I couldn't do it without you and Grayson and your continued business. Just a small token to say thank you."

I see Grayson's eyes travel to my right where Margot is standing. I put my arm around her and pull her a little closer.

"This is Margot Silver, my girlfriend."

It's only a second but I see a small flash of something flutter across Margot's face before she smiles widely. "Pleasure to meet you both."

No, we haven't discussed titles but it's something I know we need to discuss and she's made it clear it's on her mind.

The conversation carries on for a few moments, quickly taking a deeper dive into some business discussions. I feel bad; this isn't something Margot has any interest in and I see her gaze slowly drift from the group.

"I'm going to go get a refill," she whispers in my ear as she lifts her glass.

"Sorry, it'll just be a moment," I say, giving her an apologetic look. She offers me back a sympathetic look of understanding and walks over to the bar.

I'm trying to stay engaged in the conversation as I watch Margot across the room. She smiles at the bartender, clearly making a joke because they both laugh. A flash of jealousy rears its ugly head, but then I feel at peace. Seeing her happy, laughing and enjoying herself, is all I want for her.

I turn back to Ted. "Well, listen, Ted. I'm never going to turn away more of your money. I'm happy to double down in the second half of this year. What do you think, Grayson?"

"I'm all for it, Mr. Hayes."

"I'll let you men get back to your evening, and Ted, I'll have Olivia reach out and get something on the books."

I step around them to head toward Margot when Steve Buckner steps in front of me.

"Graham!" His rosy cheeks tell me he's already about three sheets to the wind.

"Steve," I say, giving him a handshake as I attempt to keep moving.

"Listen, I need to chew your ear for a minute. Won't be long." He laughs heartily.

I sigh. This is an appreciation event and I need to keep that in mind.

"Of course," I say as he launches into it.

I stay focused even though his speech is a bit slurred, but then my eyes drift back to Margot and I can see she's visibly agitated. I can't see who she's speaking to; they're obscured by a group of people.

One by one they dissipate and I see who it is—Warren fucking Dorsey.

He reaches out, touching her arm that she quickly jerks away.

Is she crying?

She shakes her head, pointing her finger at him as she says something. I'm too far away to hear and I can't read her lips. Suddenly she pushes past him and storms off.

"Steve, I'm sorry to cut you off but I need to step away. I'm sorry. I'll find you a bit later, okay?"

I push through the crowd and follow Margot down a long, dark hall.

"Margot?" I hear her sniffles as she stops and turns around to face me. "What happened? What did he say to you?"

"Are you in business with Warren Dorsey?"

I shake my head, confused. "I mean, technically. He proposed a deal that hasn't gone through but we're in talks. Why? What happened?"

I'm growing frantic. I grab her arms but she pulls them away.

"That's not what he said." She wipes a tear away. "He said you guys are in bed together, that it was your idea."

I'm growing more frustrated.

"No, it was his proposition. He came to me but that's neither here nor there. No contracts have been signed yet. I was considering it, yes, but I'm so confused. Did he say something to you? What's going on?"

"I didn't think you were the kind of man to do business with someone like him." Her words are sharp, like daggers.

"Margot, yeah, he's sleazy. We all know it but it's nothing personal. This is money; it's business, that's it. I don't like the guy if that's what you're worried about."

"Not personal? What does that even mean? To *you* it might not be personal, but it is to others. What about people he's hurt or people he's wronged?"

"It's a good business opportunity." I raise my voice a little. Frankly, I don't like being lectured. "It's called diversifying your portfolio, Margot, and it's very important in this world."

"Fuck this world!" she spits. "Don't talk down to me like I don't know what diversifying means."

"I'm sorry." I reach for her but she smacks my hand away.

"No. I want to go home." She crosses her arms tightly over her chest like she's trying to protect herself and it breaks my heart.

"I—I don't know what happened or what's going on right now, but I can't leave, sweetheart. I can tell Phil to bring the car around and he'll take you home."

She nods.

I pull my phone out and send Phil a text.

"He'll have the car out front in two minutes. Will you please be in my bed when I get home? I'd like to talk through this."

She doesn't say anything, just stares at the floor.

I walk to her, placing my hand softly at the small of her back, and guide her to the back exit where I told Phil she'd meet him. She doesn't say anything as she gets in the car and Phil drives away.

I try to put on a happy face for the rest of the event. I check my phone every few minutes to see if there's anything from Margot.

I went in search of Dorsey, but he'd already disappeared. Probably for the best because most likely I'd be in a jail cell right now, staring down the barrel of an assault and battery charge.

It's after midnight by the time I return home. The party was still in full swing with about half of the crowd still there, but I gave my speech, made my toast, and rubbed enough elbows I felt fine leaving.

I walk through my bedroom door and immediately I can see the bed is still made. I turn around and walk downstairs to Margot's room.

I knock softly but there's no answer. I open the door and slip quietly inside.

She's on her side, facing away from me toward the window. I take a seat on the edge of the bed, but she doesn't turn toward me.

"Margot?" I reach my hand out and rest it softly on her hip.

"We need to talk."

She sniffles. "I don't want to."

"Just tell me what's wrong, please."

"I already told you. I know what kind of man Warren Dorsey is, more than most, and I thought you were the kind of man who would never do business with a snake like that."

I hang my head because she's right. There's no point in groveling, telling her how much I didn't want to do business with him and that I tried to get out of it. Because the reality is, he didn't put a gun to my head; he didn't threaten me. He gave me the dollar amount I asked for and I was willing to throw away my principles for it.

"Have a good night, Margot."

I stand and leave her room, my heart feeling things I haven't felt since I lost my wife.

I hate that I hurt Margot. It's a terrible feeling. But even more, I hate that I've disappointed her because she's right; I am a better man than that… or at least I've convinced myself I am.

23

MARGOT

I toss and turn for most of the night, guilt pulling at me for the way I reacted last night.

I feel like I was hit by a bus and dragged for a mile. The sun has just started to peek over the horizon. I grab my phone and check the time. It's 5:04 a.m. Way too early to get up.

I roll over and stare at the ceiling, attempting to assess my feelings. There really isn't much assessing that has to be done. I'm falling in love with Graham Hayes and it's right in front of my face.

There's still so much we don't know about each other, but I know in time we'll share and learn.

Graham doesn't know my past. He doesn't know who Warren Dorsey is to me and honestly, the thought that I'd have to even explain it to him never crossed my mind. It *should* have. They're both billionaire businessmen in Chicago who run in the same circles, but I just didn't put two and two together.

I know I owe him an explanation and I'll give it to him fully. I'll be honest and tell him about how Warren is technically my biological father, but he's played zero role in my life.

I can't shake the nagging feeling that Graham chose to do business with him, knowing all the other unethical and gross rumors that circulate about him. I thought Graham was different than the others, truly. The bottom line is, maybe I built him up in my head based on what I wanted him to be.

He has a good heart, I know, but maybe the reality is once you reach a certain level of wealth, even principles become too expensive and you toss them out for a healthier margin and bottom line.

"Ugh." I sit up and decide that it's useless to try and go back to sleep. I reach for the journal I keep in my bedside table and walk to the window in the adjoining sitting room to watch the sun rise. I curl my legs against my chest, wrapping my arms around my knees.

If Graham doesn't see an issue with continuing business with Warren, then I think I'll have my answer—about everything.

Lately, I've been writing in my journal as if I'm talking to my mom. I miss her wisdom. She wasn't judgmental. I just remember her telling me consistently that she wanted me to be happy in life and content with who I was.

"There's no point in pretending, Margot. The only person you're fooling is yourself. If you can't be happy with who you are as a person at night when your head hits the pillow, only you can change that."

She had been holding my chubby little sixth-grade cheeks in her hands when she said that to me. I'd been crying to her about how all my friends wanted to join the Pompettes, our middle school dance team, but I wanted to join band. I ended up doing what my friends wanted and was disappointed. I hated that I was pretending to not be a "band geek" when all I thought about was music.

"But I want my friends to like me," I had cried to her.

"Sweetheart, there's no point in others liking you if you don't like yourself."

She poked my nose and then kissed it softly, reminding me that no matter what I chose to do in life, she'd still love and support me. She also reminded me it wasn't a failure to join the dance team and hate it; we have to try different things in life to find out what we love and sometimes, it's an uncomfortable choice that lends the best reward.

I glance down at my wrist. I'm still wearing the gold bracelet

Graham gave me last night. I run my finger over the delicate gold chain and the etching on the small plate.

I think about the offer from La Crème and my chest tightens. I close my eyes and clutch my journal to my chest, inhaling deeply and slowly letting it go. I try to clear my head, praying that an answer will just pop in and reveal to me what the best decision is, like my brain is a magic eight ball.

In truth, I'm going to have to put my big girl panties on and figure it out myself. Even if my mom were still here, she'd never tell me what to do—what the best decision is. She'd tell me to search my heart.

It's just after seven a.m., and I've been sitting in this chair for two hours now, attempting to figure out my life and very much avoiding running into Graham. I'm sure he's gone to the office by now, so I stand, stretching a few times before heading into the hall to wake up Eleanor.

As much as I want to avoid Graham, I will do the right thing and speak to him tonight, explaining my reaction last night and praying that he'll see the light and walk away from Warren Dorsey.

"Chocolate chip or blueberry?"

"Blueberry!" Eleanor shouts, her arms over her head like it's the most exciting decision of her life.

I place two blueberry pancakes on her plate along with some strawberries.

"What's your favorite color?" she asks between bites of pancake.

"Hmmm, probably orange. It reminds me of a pumpkin and I love fall and Halloween."

"Halloween is scary, but candy!" She goes back to chewing and then perks up again. "Do you like butterflies?"

I giggle and nod. "I do, very much."

"What about snails?" She crinkles her nose up when she says it.

"I don't think so; they're pretty slimy."

"Uh-huh." She nods her head in agreement.

I make myself a cup of coffee and look through today's schedule. Eleanor doesn't have any classes today. We'll have a music lesson after breakfast and work on our flash cards later for colors, animals, and the alphabet. She has a late birthday so she won't be attending kindergarten until this fall.

"How about some pool time today?" I ask, looking up from the iPad, and she cheers. That always tires her out pretty successfully after a few hours and she tends to need a nap after. Which is perfect for me so I can get the laundry done and clean up her playroom.

"Do you love Daddy?"

The question takes me by surprise.

"What, sweetie?"

"You and Daddy are in love."

I can't tell if she's teasing, but I knew that her seeing us in his bed would lead to this. I close the iPad and place it on the counter as I lean forward on the island.

"Your daddy and I are good friends. I care about you and him so much."

"But you had a sleepover?"

I drop my head forward between my shoulders. Part of me feels like this is something her father should discuss with her, especially since he didn't seem to mind her seeing us. But then again, I'm the other part of this equation.

"How about your daddy talks to you tonight and you can ask him all the questions you want about it?"

She cocks her head to the side, and I'm fully prepared to bribe her, but she shrugs and says, "Okay."

If only if it were that easy to convince Graham...

* * *

ELEANOR CAN BARELY KEEP her eyes open after our late lunch. The two hours we spent in the pool completely wore her out.

She's snoring softly before I even finish one book. She looks like a little angel. I tuck her in and plant a soft kiss on her head as I tiptoe out of her room just as my phone buzzes.

I pull it out and slide the screen open to see a text from Shelly. I smile as I click the image attached to the message. It takes up my entire screen.

Shelly: *Greetings from Mexico, bitches!*

It's her and Hank, their sunburned faces smooshed together as they hold up brightly colored cocktails that are overflowing with fruit.

I don't know the details about this getaway, but they look incredibly happy. Honestly, with how in love they are, I wouldn't be shocked if she came back with a ring on her finger.

I send back a kissy emoji and wish them all the fun. A slight tinge of jealousy shoots through my chest but I ignore it.

I head downstairs to clean up Eleanor's lunch mess and make myself a cup of tea. A few cozy episodes of *Schitt's Creek* are in order to help cheer me up.

I'm reaching for a tea bag when I see something drop onto the counter out of the corner of my eye. I glance to my right and see Miss Perry casually strolling past me.

"I believe those are yours." She spins around to face me, her eyebrow arched almost comically high.

I look at the measly scrap of material on the counter.

"No, afraid not."

"You sure? I found them while tidying up Mr. Hayes' office this morning."

"I'm positive. There's a little more material to my underwear and I don't own any in a bright red like that."

My stomach tightens. I don't know what kind of game she's trying to play, but I'm not in the mood for it. I turn my attention back to the box of tea, pulling out a bag and placing the box back in the cabinet.

"Oh, silly me, they must be—" Her words trail off. I turn back around to see what she's up to. She grabs them, a smile on her lips as she stuffs them in her pocket.

"Dear me, I guess you're right. I should have looked closer." She shakes her head with a skin-crawling laugh before muttering under her breath… "I would have recognized them as my own."

"Excuse me?"

"Yes?"

"What did you just say?"

She waves a hand at me like I'm an insignificant nuisance and I snap. I slam my hands down on the counter and shout, "What? If you have something to say to me, Fiona, then say it!" I make sure to use her name just to turn the knife a little.

She scowls at me before her stoic mask slips back into place. "Why, whatever do you mean?"

I laugh out of frustration. "Seriously? Don't you ever get tired of playing this twisted game? It's exhausting, honestly. You have had animosity toward me since the moment I met you and I did nothing wrong. I've been polite and respectful."

"Respectful?" She spits the word out in mockery.

"Yes, I've been respectful."

"You call parading around here, throwing yourself at Mr. Hayes respectful? Lying across his desk spread-eagle?"

I laugh. "That is none of your business and when did I ever throw myself at him? That's your thing. And last time I checked, he was a pretty willing participant in me being 'spread-eagle' on his desk."

Her face grows red and her hands curl into tight balls. "I tried to warn you, you will never be the woman he needs. You're just a silly little girl."

"Oh, and let me guess. *You* are the woman he needs? Well, isn't that convenient." I shake my head and turn to leave. "Forget the tea, I'm done with this."

"I *was* the woman he needed. I was there for him when his wife died." She points her finger at her chest dramatically every time she says the word *I.* "I was the woman that held him when he was grieving, when he was at his lowest. And I was the woman who he came to for physical release and intimacy."

I shake my head. No, this can't be happening. He said—

"Oh yes, little Margot." She steps closer, her menacing eyes boring into mine and I know she's eating this up. "He's been in my bed too."

My stomach lurches and I feel like I'm about to lose my lunch on the kitchen floor. I'm in total shock.

"I—I don't understand."

Our interaction is interrupted when a clueless Graham comes waltzing through the kitchen door.

"Afternoon, ladies. Thought I'd come home for lunch and finish the workday here."

He gives Miss Perry a curt nod and turns to me with a quick smile before grabbing the refrigerator handle.

My face must look like I feel because he spins back around to me. "What's wrong, Margot?"

"You slept with her?" My voice is shaky with emotion as I point my finger toward Miss Perry.

His eyes dart from me to her, then back to me, his skin going pale. I don't need him to confirm it; it's written all over his face.

"How could you? When? You said—" The words catch in my throat and I feel like I'm about to hyperventilate.

"It was years ago; it meant nothing, Margot. A mistake." I see him flash an angry look toward Miss Perry.

"It certainly didn't seem like it," she snips and he shouts at her.

"Leave the fucking room!"

He doesn't have to tell her twice; she stiffens before quickly exiting.

"Margot, please—" He reaches out for me, but I step back, recoiling.

"I asked you point blank and you lied to me. I gave you an opportunity to be honest with me."

He opens his mouth and then closes it again. "Technically I didn't lie because you asked if there was ever a relationship between her and me. There wasn't. It was one time and I wanted to forget it happened."

I shake my head. "You fucking asshole." Tears start to fall.

"Margot, baby, please. I was wrong and I'm sorry I kept it from you. I fucked up."

"You knew that's why she hates me. When I brought it up the other day you acted like I was making it up. I heard you guys talking a while back and she was telling you to fire me, that she didn't trust me. You know that's why she didn't call me back after my first interview. You knew all that!"

"Now, Margot, please. You're making accusations. Let's focus on the issue at hand. Don't blow this out of proportion."

I can feel the anger radiating off my body. I can't look at him right now.

"I can't do this," I say and walk out of the kitchen.

He follows after me, grabbing my hand and spinning me around. "We are going to talk about this like adults. I'm sick of you being irrational and running away when we have problems."

"How am I supposed to talk to you when you're gaslighting me? I just told you how I feel, how *your* actions made me feel, and you just invalidated all of them. Telling me I'm irrational and blowing things out of proportion?"

He stares at me, eyes wide.

"How would you feel, Graham?" I take a step toward him.

"How would you feel if I'd slept with a man that I worked with. That I saw every single day. That lived in my home and I didn't tell you about it."

I can see he's getting uncomfortable. He drags his hand nervously through his hair.

"Even worse, what if I lied to you about it? A lie of omission is still a damn lie. How would you feel? You certainly acted irrational when you thought there was something between me and Hank. You certainly were blowing things out of proportion when Garrett said two words to me."

He shakes his head. "That's different."

"Ha! How? Enlighten me."

"I was trying to protect you from guys who just wanted to sleep with you, use you—"

"First of all, Hank wasn't trying to sleep with me!" I shout the words and I don't care if I'm being childish. "I'm sick of explaining that to you. And Garrett? If you trusted me, even if he was trying to sleep with me, then you'd be fine letting me talk to him because you'd know I wouldn't do that to you. But clearly, you don't trust me, and you know why? Because you're shady. You can't be trusted so you think I can't."

I jab my finger in his chest and he reaches out and grabs it, pulling me forward. I stumble into him, and he grabs the back of my head, his lips crashing down on mine.

He kisses me hard, painfully. I pull away and cock my hand back, landing a slap square across his jaw. The sound of skin-to-skin contact echoes through the atrium.

"You're not going to use sex to avoid this. I don't even know who you are anymore. You used me."

He reaches out to me again, but I jerk my hand away.

"Margot, please, I—I love you."

I stare at him, his eyes pleading with me but instead of elation, I feel nothing.

"I'm in love with you," he says again, this time just a whisper.

"I need to be alone."

I turn and walk toward the stairs, getting halfway up.

"One other question." He looks up at me.

"Why did the other nanny leave?"

He looks confused. I don't elaborate on why I'm asking. On Miss Perry's ominous warning about her time here. No, I want to see how he answers.

"She, uh…" He rakes his hands through his hair again. "She had a family emergency, and she had to move back to Vermont. Why?"

I don't answer him; I just turn back to the stairs and make my way to my room.

I close the door and lean against it. All the pain and emotions I was keeping a lid on boil over and I slowly sink to the ground in a puddle of tears.

The rest of the day is a blur.

Graham must have gone back to the office because I don't see or hear him, and Miss Perry stays out of my line of sight.

I do my best to put on a happy face for Eleanor but it's a struggle. Every time I look at her, I want to break down and sob. I don't know if I'm losing her too in all this.

When I finally put her to bed, I drag myself back to my room. I don't have any tears left. I feel numb. I lie on my bed and contemplate how I got myself here. I blame myself for falling for Graham, but I also blame him for lying to me.

None of this would be happening if he would have just been honest. It's not just about the lie—it rarely ever is—it's about the reasoning.

Am I not important enough for the truth?

Or is he hiding something else? If you truly never felt feelings for this person, why lie and hide it?

I torture myself like this for hours, rhetorical questions going round and round in my head and getting me nowhere.

I decide that my mom is right. At the end of the day, I have to be happy with myself or I'll never truly find happiness.

I walk over to the table by the window and pull open my journal to a blank page. I let out a sigh as I begin a letter to Graham.

When I finish, I tiptoe downstairs and place the letter on his desk.

24

GRAHAM

I stare at the letter that Margot left on my desk two days ago.

I haven't seen her since our fight. I've been too afraid and this letter confirms my worst fears.

I read it over again.

Dear Mr. Hayes,

I have appreciated the opportunity you gave me to look after Eleanor. I have enjoyed and loved every second I spent with her. I have also appreciated your generosity with the salary and accommodations.

However, I have to put my well-being and mental health first and I do not feel I am the best fit for this position.

Please consider this my official notice of resignation. My last day will be two weeks from tomorrow.

-Margot Silver

"Mr. Hayes, Mr. Dorsey to see you, sir."

Olivia's voice breaks through the intercom.

"Send him in," I say as I fold the letter and place it back in my drawer.

"Graham, you ready to make millions?" He laughs as he steps into my office and gives me a stern handshake.

"Warren," I say as I unbutton my suit coat and sit back in my chair.

"I called you in for a reason. I won't take up much of your time as I know we are both busy men. I'm not going to sign your contract."

He smiles, that gross smile that could make a snake recoil.

"What's it gonna cost me? Forty percent? I won't go over forty, son, so don't get greedy." He points his fat sausage finger at me.

I lean back in my chair. "You could offer me ninety-nine percent, Warren, and I'd still say no."

His smirk falls from his face, instantly replaced with disgust.

Ah, I've hit a nerve. Nobody says no to Warren Dorsey.

"What changed?"

"Nothing changed. I just thought long and hard about who I'll be *in bed with*." I make sure to use the same phrase he said to Margot. "And I don't want to be in bed with a man like you."

He laughs and leans forward, resting his elbows on his knees as he levels his eyes at me. "I thought my daughter might cause an issue for us."

"Your daughter?"

"Margot, your nanny."

I stare at him blankly. *What the fuck?*

He laughs harder. "You didn't know?"

I shake my head no.

"Margot Silver." He leans back in his chair, his belly spilling over his belt. "She's got a different name, but she still came from my sack."

My stomach curdles at his putrid response. I don't want him to know he's getting to me; he gets off on shit like that.

"Well, it doesn't matter anyway; she's put in her resignation. As of two weeks from now, she'll no longer be my nanny."

I point my finger at his purplish face, his collar cutting off the circulation as it digs into his fat rolls.

"So if you thought you were going to use that relationship as some sort of leverage or blackmail into getting me to sign the contract, you can fuck right off because I'm not the kind of man that will kowtow to that behavior."

"You think I need to do that to get someone to sign a contract to work with me?" He stands and straightens out his jacket. "Boy, you've still got a lot to learn in this city. I run it. You might have a bigger dick, but I've got a bigger bankroll."

And with that ominous threat, he turns and walks out of my office, slamming the door behind him on his way out.

Seconds later Olivia pokes her head into my office. "What was that?" she asks, her eyes round with concern.

"Nothing to worry about, Olivia. The trash just took itself out."

She smiles. "Good. I never liked that guy anyway. Gives me the creeps."

* * *

I PUT off going home for as long as possible but I can't keep ignoring Margot. I owe her an apology and a conversation to clear the air and let her know that I will respect her wishes to resign.

But first, I need to have a conversation with Miss Perry.

I call her into my office. She hurries over to where I'm sitting behind my desk and places her hand on my shoulder.

"How are you doing, sir?" She tilts her head to the side in a sympathetic gesture.

"Fine. Please have a seat."

She hoists her leg a little and slides onto the edge of my desk.

"In the chair, Fiona," I say a little more exasperated than I intended.

She reluctantly moves to the chair across from my desk.

"We need to have a talk about what happened the other day."

She smiles sweetly at me, like I'm confessing my love to her instead of reprimanding her. She's perched on the edge of the chair, her hands folded neatly in her lap as she leans toward me.

"What are you doing?"

"I—I don't understand, sir. I just—" She stands again and takes a step toward my desk, her hand outstretched as she reaches for mine. "I just want you to know that I'm here for you. That I'll always be here for you. Just like I was when Meredith passed."

I snap, standing up. "Stop! Just stop it," I say firmly and she jumps back, sitting back in the chair.

"We both agreed years ago that it was a mistake. I'm not trying to be cruel, but it didn't mean anything. I was lost and grieving. I know you're a human with feelings and I hate that I used you back then, but we both said it meant nothing."

Her expression goes from hurt to smiling again like she's a robot... or a sociopath.

"You can't still be upset about Margot's unprofessional outburst from the other day. She's just a silly young girl."

"You were unprofessional. You provoked her. You've been obviously cold toward her."

She waves a hand dismissively. "She's just being sensitive, Graha—"

"Enough!" I shout again. "It's Mr. Hayes to you."

She straightens and folds her hands back in her lap, her stoic expression back in place.

I reach into my desk drawer and pull out Margot's resume. I place it on my desk.

"Why didn't you call Margot back after the first time you interviewed her?"

She stares at me, not saying anything, her eyes blinking rapidly.

"Shall I read over her qualifications?" I pick up the resume and start to read off the bullet points.

"She has several years' experience working with children, dedicated her life to them really. She volunteers at the library. Is CPR and lifeguard certified. Has a double degree in early childhood and music education." I glance over the paper at her. "Shall I go on?"

"I was going to call her back. I just got distracted with my upcoming vacation, sir. I apologize, sincerely. You know me. In all my years working for you, I have delivered exceptional service. Just this one little thing slipped through my fingers."

I don't say anything. I just stare at her, a tactic I've used in negotiations over the years. A tactic that never fails. If you stare at someone long enough, especially someone who's trying to bullshit you, they'll eventually break.

It takes less than a minute for her.

"Sir." She begins to cry. "I just did it because—" She gulps in air and I'm pretty sure she's faking it. "Because I'm in love with you. Can't you see that?"

She lunges forward and grabs for my hand, but I pull it away.

"I've dedicated my life to serving you. I've loved you through so much. I've been there for you, picking up the pieces of your heart and putting them back together."

I'm unmoved by her outburst. Frankly, I have no idea if any of it's true. If it is, it's far too late for me to care. Had she told me in the past, I'd have been sympathetic, but for her to torture Margot and try to trick me into turning against her, it's unforgivable.

"Why did Margot ask me why the last nanny left?"

She sniffs and wipes at the nonexistent tears.

"What?"

"You heard me."

"I—I don't know why."

"Don't lie to me."

She lets out an exasperated exhale. "I may have insinuated that you were involved with the last nanny and that's why she left."

I can feel my blood pressure rising and it takes everything I have not to flip this desk.

"Here's what's going happen. You're going to go upstairs and pack your things. Then you're going to leave and never show your face around this house, my daughter, my company, or Margot ever again."

"Mr. Hayes, ple—" she interrupts, but I hold up a finger to silence her.

"I will give you three months' pay, but if you fight this or try to cause a problem"—I lean forward on my desk, wanting to make sure she doesn't miss what I'm about to say—"I will fucking destroy you."

Her mouth snaps shut.

"Do you understand me?"

She stands. "Yes." Then she turns and exits my office.

While it's only one small part of the bridge I need to fix with Margot, it's a start. I'm just praying the rest hasn't been completely burned to ash.

I give Fiona a few moments to exit before I take Margot's resignation letter and walk up to her quarters. The door is ajar and I knock softly.

"Come in," I hear her say softly. I step inside. She's sitting on her bed, her eyes red from crying.

"Got your letter," I say, holding it up as I sit on the edge of the bed. I place it on the comforter and slide it slightly toward her.

"Is there room for negotiation in these terms?"

She rolls her eyes. "It's not a business deal; there are no terms or negotiation. I'm quitting, plain and simple. I was offered my dream job and I accepted it. If you can't—"

I reach forward and press my hand to her lips softly, and she stops speaking.

"I'm not here to fight with you or upset you. It was merely a question."

I'm curious about this dream job she got offered. Not because I want to talk her out of it, but because I truly want to know what kind of job is Margot's dream.

"I also came up here to apologize." I slowly remove my hand from her lips. "First for the way I acted the other day. I shouldn't have invalidated your feelings. There were other things at play that I truly wasn't aware of."

She looks at me as if I'm crazy.

"I know. I think I turned a willful blind eye to those things. That wasn't anyone's fault but my own. For what it's worth, you were right about Miss Perry. About her trying to sleep with me, I mean. But for the record, I have and had zero interest in her like that."

I glance up at her, our eyes connecting briefly before she looks away.

"I fired her. She won't ever be an issue for you again, not that it matters at this point. I also wanted to clear the air about the last nanny. There was nothing ever between me and her, not even remotely. I barely spoke to her. Miss Perry told me about the lie she told you regarding my relationship with her. It wasn't true."

Her eyes dart back to mine.

"Margot, I can't express to you how sorry I am that I hurt you. I never wanted that to happen and I know it's too late but I have to tell you that now."

I stand, waiting for her to say anything. Hoping she begs me to stay or runs into my arms but she doesn't.

"And I also wanted to tell you that I will respect your wishes and boundaries while you finish out your time here. I will give you the space you need to do your job and care for Eleanor, and I'll have the conversation with her about you and me and you moving on."

I see her shoulders fall. I debate bringing up the whole Warren Dorsey thing, not because I'm hoping to get brownie points for doing the right thing and cutting the shitbag loose, but because I want to hold her and apologize on his behalf for being her father—even if it is only biologically.

In the end, I decide against it. It's her business and if she wanted to share that part of her life with me, she would have.

"Are those terms you can agree to?"

She nods her head yes and I smile at her, hoping she can't see my heart breaking into a million little pieces right now.

"Good night, Margot," I say as I leave the room and shut the door softly behind me.

25

MARGOT

Ten days… I can make it.

I can resist his tempting looks.

I can resist the way his body calls to me.

I can resist the way his fingers move across the toast he's buttering as he grips the knife. I will not think about all the delicious toe-curling things he's done to me with those fingers…

I choke on my coffee, shooting up from the chair I'm sitting in. It skitters across the hardwood floor, clattering to the ground.

"You okay?" Graham looks up at me.

I don't respond; I just run out of the kitchen as my cheeks burn from embarrassment. I take the stairs two at a time, launching myself into my bedroom and slamming the door.

"You're fine. You got this."

I pace back and forth in my room. I grab my iPad and settle into the chair.

"Just look at apartments. Keep focused."

After my conversation with Hank and my outburst at Graham's office event, I replied to Grace's email and told her I'm fully onboard. Jeff called me a day later and we discussed the position at La Crème, the salary, job expectations, and start date.

During the summer, La Crème offers limited programs but this position won't be starting officially until the second week of August. Since I'm giving Graham two weeks here, that will take me into the middle of July. With the amount of money I've saved working here, I'll be fine without a paycheck for a month, but still, trying to find an affordable apartment in Chicago near the academy won't be easy.

I scroll through the listings, flagging a few to check on their availability. I sigh. The reality that I'll be leaving Eleanor soon is hitting me hard.

I still feel so torn. I love her so much and I know I'll see her at La Crème, but it's not the same. She cried when I told her I'd be leaving but cheered up a little when I told her about my new job. I don't think she fully understands though.

My phone rings, interrupting my thoughts. I see it's Shelly.

"Hey, girl, how was Mexico?" I haven't spoken to her since her whirlwind vacation with Hank.

"*Oh. My. Gaaaawd.* It was fantastic. We lay on the most beautiful beaches. We swam in the Cenotes; we drank margaritas—it was beyond anything I've ever experienced."

"Awww, yay! I'm so happy for you guys. Did you come back with a ring?"

"What?" She laughs. "No, I'm not *that* impulsive. We have talked about it a little though."

"See, I knew it was brewing."

She fills me in on some of the funny things that happened on her trip, and it makes my heart feel full to know that she's so happy.

"So what about you? What's going on?"

I let out a long, labored sigh.

"Uh-oh," she says, picking up on it.

"Yeah. So, I put in my two weeks' notice."

She gasps. "Wait, hold up. Let me grab my water. Okay, I'm ready."

I explain everything to her. The Warren Dorsey drama. The Fiona Perry drama. How I'm conflicted on my feelings for him and if I should forgive him and give him a second chance or just move on.

"Wow." She puffs out a breath of air. "That's a lot. That's a whole lot."

"Yeah," I echo her sentiments.

"Are you in love with him?"

I roll my head around, hesitating.

"That sounds like a yes to me."

"I am. I think that I feel guilty for wanting this other job when I took this nanny job and committed to it. I feel like I'm flaking on both of them. It's just all screwing with my head right now."

"I can see that dilemma. I think you need to first, be honest with yourself about your feelings in all of this; they're valid. Second, you need to ask yourself what you really want. You can take this teaching job that is one hell of an opportunity that you've worked hard for and earned and feel guilty about it and let it ruin your ability to lead and nurture these kids or you can realize that life changes. Graham clearly isn't angry at you for taking this job, right?"

"I don't know for sure. I do want to talk to him about it and clear the air. He apologized to me but I never apologized for how I reacted to things and I never explained to him that this is my dream job."

I flop back on my bed after wearing a path in the area rug around it. I let out a frustrated huff.

"All that to say, I do need a place to live in less than ten days and I don't know how I'm going to make that happen. I've found a few places I can afford, but you know how availability can be in the city. They'll waitlist you or you never even hear back after your application."

"Why don't you move in with me?"

I laugh. "Babe, your studio is barely enough room for you."

"No, seriously, I'm never there. I stay at Hank's almost every single night now. Trust me, you won't be in the way, and it doesn't have to be long term. Just until you find the right place."

"It is super generous of you." I rub my temple. "And I really don't want to be stuck taking the first place I can find. I'll pay your rent while I'm staying there; I'm not freeloading."

"I don't require that, but I appreciate it, Margot. And I mean it.

Take the time to think about things. Just because things with Graham are rough and he screwed up doesn't mean that what you have isn't real and worth fighting for."

"Look at you." I laugh. "Miss true love expert now. Never thought I'd see the day."

"It's your fault, you know, for introducing me to this perfect guy."

We both giggle and I hang up.

I feel better about knowing I have a place to live, but I still need to find my own place long term. Part of me is holding back because I want things with Graham to work out so badly. I want to stay here and live with him and Eleanor.

Not as the nanny, but as his partner. His lover. His everything.

* * *

Eight days... *You've got this.*

I feel like I'm constantly on the verge of losing it.

The passionate looks he flashes at me. The way his eyes linger a little too long when I walk away. The small, intimate touches when he's reaching for something near me.

Why the hell is he always around now? Doesn't he need to go to his office or something?

"Easy. The toaster didn't do anything to you." He smirks as I smash the handle down.

I glance at him before turning to the fridge to hunt for the butter and jelly.

"You okay, Margot?"

Ugh, my belly clenches at the deep timbre of his voice. Flashbacks of him whispering my name in my ear as he did unspeakable things to my body flood my brain.

"Great," I say—a little too loudly. "Sorry, yeah, I'm great. How are you? You've been home a lot."

He leans against the counter, crossing one leg over the other as his fingers grip the edge.

"Well, this is my home."

I sloppily butter Eleanor's toast and apply a thick layer of jam. Normally the chef makes breakfast for the household but he's off today. I put the butter and jelly back in the fridge, then I quickly leave the kitchen and head upstairs to fetch Eleanor, praying Graham has retreated to his office before I return.

Eleanor has her daylong class today so I drive her to the city and we chat about how excited she is to finally be in what she calls "big girl school" this coming fall. I try to remain positive with her about my leaving, telling her how she won't need a full-time nanny anymore anyway since she'll be in school. I tell her that she'll make lots of fun new friends and have the time of her life.

I grab a coffee and head to my first apartment showing I lined up this week. I'm about five minutes' walk away from the leasing office when my phone rings and I see his name on my screen.

"Hello?"

I don't know why I haven't blocked dear old dad yet. Maybe I'm waiting on the courage to finally sit down and talk to him, attempt to get some answers.

"I hope you're happy." He doesn't even bother with pleasantries.

"About anything in particular?"

"Oh, don't play coy with me, Margot; it doesn't suit you. The fucking business deal."

I stop on the sidewalk. "What about it?" I say, growing impatient.

"Your boyfriend pulled it. Refused to sign the contract and more or less told me to go fuck myself with it."

I hang up the phone. I'm not interested in hearing anything else from Warren.

"Move, lady." Someone bumps into my shoulder and I realize I'm just standing in the middle of the sidewalk still, clutching my coffee and wondering if Shelly is right.

Am I making a big mistake now letting Graham fix the issues I had with him? I told him how he hurt me and he's done everything within his power to fix it and make it right, and here I am, stubbornly refusing to allow my heart to give him a second chance.

I slide the phone in my pocket and head to my appointment. I try to focus on the apartment and amenities, but I'm completely lost trying to figure out what exactly my heart wants.

* * *

Six days... six more days and then I'll be gone from him, possibly forever.

My heart feels like it's slowly dying.

I pause outside Graham's office.

The door is ajar. I look inside and see him sitting in a chair, facing the window with a drink in hand. I knock softly and enter, walking up behind him. He doesn't look at me right away, keeping his gaze trained forward as I approach.

"I know what you're doing," I say softly.

He continues staring ahead for a few seconds before slowly turning his head to look at me.

"And what am I doing?"

I exhale and take a seat in the chair next to him.

"The way you look at me. The little touches and glances and comments."

He chuckles as he looks into his tumbler before taking a sip.

"Margot, just because I've fucked up royally and possibly lost you forever..." He pauses, his eyes looking at me questioningly before he continues. "Doesn't mean that I don't still find you attractive... or want you. I'm sorry if I've made you feel uncomfortable."

I shake my head. "No, you haven't." I stand up and walk to the window, looking out over the expansive backyard. Lightning bugs dance in the moonlight.

"You know, when I met Meredith, my wife, she was hell-bent on not dating. She was focused on her career and so was I. I admired that in her. I saw myself in her."

I listen as I continue to watch out the window, unsure where he's going with this.

"I was like her. I was rigid in my commitment to my preconceived notions I had about myself in life and business. I had set these rules for myself and I wouldn't change any of them because if I did, I felt like I was compromising, and compromise was failure in my eyes."

He grows silent for a moment, clinking the ice around in his tumbler before continuing.

"When Meredith got sick, it was like a light switch came on and I realized that I was boxing myself in. Life is short and unpredictable and there's no point in having these stringent rules for yourself if your heart's not in it. I'm not even sure what I'm saying here. It's just that with you, I didn't have any of those ideas or rules in place. I just followed my heart and my feelings, and they led me to you."

It feels like there's a vise around my heart, squeezing it so tight.

"Do you miss her?"

He nods. "I do. I miss seeing her with Eleanor. It kills me that she won't get to see her little girl grow up. I've processed my grief though. I did have some unhealthy reactions to it, I won't lie. You know that already. I avoided Eleanor for some time because every time I looked at her, I was reminded of Meredith, of her not getting to raise her. I felt guilt that I still got to do that."

He stands, placing his glass on the small table next to the chair, and walks up next to me, his chest partially against my back.

"I can't express to you how sorry I am, Margot. I hate that I've hurt you and made you doubt your faith in me not only as a partner but as a friend and a person. I—I hoped things would work out so differently with us. I had hoped you were my future, that you were Eleanor's future."

I lean my head forward, pressing it against the cool glass. I feel him step closer, his hand reaching out to brush my hair away from my neck. He leans down, his warm breath coming out in puffs against my skin.

"Do you ever think about that night on my desk?"

I nod my head.

"Me too. I think about it too, probably too much. All those little looks you mentioned I give you? I'm remembering that moment,

Margot. I'm remembering the way your body trembled beneath my tongue. The way your taste filled my mouth."

My entire body is burning with desire. My heart is telling me to just tell him how I feel. To fix it and make it work.

I spin around to face him, placing my hands on his chest.

"What did you do with my panties?"

He gets a devilish grin and walks over to his desk, leaning down to open a drawer. He reaches inside and produces the panties, holding them up so I can see them.

I watch as he brings them to his nose, closing his eyes and inhaling.

Holy shit. I clench my thighs tighter.

"Do they still smell like me?"

"A little."

I feel a sudden surge of confidence soar through me and I capitalize on it, maintaining eye contact with him as I slowly walk toward his desk. I lift myself, sliding my backside onto his desk. His lips part in anticipation as I slowly spread my thighs open and lift my skirt.

I watch as he grips the panties in his hands, slowly sliding down into his seat. He reaches his other hand forward, but I smack it away, shaking my head.

I pull my skirt all the way up to my waist as I lean back on one hand, the other dragging down my body and into my panties. I close my eyes and allow myself to get lost in the moment as I begin to explore my womanhood.

I tease myself. Running my fingers through my wet folds and around my sensitive nub. I don't hold back. I moan and bite my bottom lip, letting myself enjoy every second of this, not questioning what will happen after or tomorrow or next week.

I can feel my wetness soaking my panties as I slide my fingers inside. I thrust over and over again, bringing them out to play with my clit before delving them back inside. My release builds. My thighs tremble and shake as I fall over the edge, my orgasm shooting through my body to my toes as I come undone.

Graham is gripping the armrest of his chair so hard his knuckles are white. His jaw is clenched and tight and the tenting in his pants tells me he's just as excited as I am.

I remove myself from the desk, reaching beneath my skirt to wipe myself with my panties before sliding them down my legs and bending to pick them up.

Without a word, I drop them in his lap and exit the office.

26

GRAHAM

Four days...

I stare at the ceiling in my bedroom as rain taps against the glass of the window. It's soothing but it's no use, I can't sleep.

I sit up and lean forward, scrubbing my hands over my face, debating if I should take another shower to help me relax. I glance over at the clock on the nightstand: 1:23 a.m.

I pull on my pajama pants and trudge downstairs, opting to bury my feelings in Oreos. I think I saw a pack in the pantry yesterday.

I flick on the light above the stove and open the pantry door.

"Can't sleep either?"

I spin around to see Margot sitting at the kitchen island, a mug of tea in her hands.

"Thought I might drown my sorrows in Oreos. Want some?"

She nods and pats the stool next to her. I reach inside and grab the package, bringing it over to where she's seated.

We both take a cookie. I watch as she splits it in two, eating the plain cookie first before scraping the cream off the other with her teeth. She then proceeds to eat that cookie as well.

"That's an interesting method."

"What's yours?"

I too split the cookie in half. "I eat the naked one first and then"—I pause as I pop it into my mouth and chew—"I eat the other one, with the cream still on it."

"Isn't that what I did?" she asks.

"Close but you ate the cream alone."

She shrugs. "Guess I don't even pay attention to how I eat Oreos."

Silence settles between us as we each eat another cookie.

"I want to tell you something." She turns in her stool, angling her body to face me. "You opened up to me about you and your wife the other day and I appreciated that."

She reaches for another Oreo but doesn't eat it, just fiddles with it between her fingers.

"Warren Dorsey met my mom at the jazz club that she used to sing at—The Bluebird. She was young, really young actually. He was close to twenty years older than her at the time. She was only nineteen.

"She was naive and she thought that his infatuation was love. He showered her with gifts and even paid her rent. He'd show up to the jazz club and woo her basically. All the time she had no idea that he was already married with a family. She didn't know who he was; he wasn't as well known back then as he is now. He was certainly rich—richer than anyone else she'd ever met—but he was just making a name for himself."

She places the cookie on the counter and wipes the crumbs off her fingers, taking a sip of tea.

"Anyway, she fell head over heels for him and she thought he loved her too because he told her he did. He made her all these crazy promises about running off and getting married. Traveling the world. None of it actually happened and none of it was genuine. It was a whirlwind romance. They met and fell in 'love' all within like three months. By month five she was pregnant and he was gone."

"What a fucking prick," I mutter.

"He literally just ghosted her. Poof. Everything seemed perfect between them, she told me. She said that she was excited about being pregnant and he seemed genuinely excited and happy too. He told her he was going to move her into his high-rise apartment in Manhattan.

He left one night, telling her he had a business trip so he'd be out of town for a few days and that was it. She never saw or heard from him again."

"Not even when you were born?"

She shakes her head no.

"Nope. He never paid a single cent of child support. Never sent a birthday card or asked how she was or I was. She had no idea what happened to him until one day when I was around seven, she saw a new headline about this up-and-coming billionaire, Warren Dorsey."

"Wait. Did he lie about his name to her?"

"Not completely. He did say his name was Warren, but he gave her a fake last name. She recognized him in the photo and she realized as she read on that it mentioned his wife Cheryl and three kids, two of which were older than me."

I shake my head. I didn't think it was possible, but I hate that fucker even more now and I feel especially horrible for the fact that I almost did business with him. Now I understand her reaction toward him.

"Glen Silver, my adoptive father, is my real dad to me. He raised me. He met my mom when I was nine months old and stood by her side till he passed." I laugh, recalling a memory. "Mom told me that Dad called her his desert rose for two reasons. Because he felt like his potential to find true love at that point in his life was dry and barren and because my mom was a redhead."

"Did Warren ever reach out when your mom died?"

"No. He randomly did though for the first time about a year ago. He started calling my cell phone. No idea how he got the number. I never picked up."

"Did he say why?"

"He left me a few voicemails saying he wanted to get to know me. I have no idea what prompted it. After those two voicemails, he stopped reaching out. It wasn't until I started working for you that it started again. I think he knew I was your nanny and he wanted to try and manipulate me to get you to do business with him. I don't know for sure; I'm just speculating."

"I don't think it's just speculation. That man would sell his own mother if it meant he'd make a dollar. "You were right about him and me for that matter... I am better than that, Margot. I knew better."

I turn to face her, our knees brushing against each other.

"I terminated my business with him. I'd like to say I would have anyway but I can't say for sure. I actually had told him to go fuck himself before but I got greedy when he threw a big number at me."

"I know. He called me."

My head snaps up. "Did he threaten you or anything?"

"No, just thanked me for ruining his business deal. I hung up before he could say anything else. I'm not interested in his life in the slightest."

"So," I say, changing the subject. "What's this new dream job you accepted?"

A genuine smile spreads across her face as her eyes light up.

"It's actually at La Crème, Eleanor's school."

My eyebrows raise. "That is a dream job. Congrats." I bump her shoulder.

"I didn't go looking for it, just to clarify. Grace Tillmore, Eleanor's teacher, and I would make small talk when I would drop her off. I told her about my background in teaching and she said if a position in the music department ever opened up, she'd keep me in mind. Her husband Jeff is one of the head administrators that overseas hiring new staff and he told her about an opening to be the head of the music department."

"Holy shit! That's fantastic, swee—" I catch myself before I finish the sentiment. I don't really know if I'm allowed to call her that... I'm not sure what we even are.

"Yeah, I'm—happy, excited about it." She stares down at the mug in her hand.

"You sure about that?"

She sighs. "Yes and no. I'm struggling... a lot."

I don't push for more. I just wait till she feels comfortable enough to elaborate.

"I don't want to lose Eleanor. I feel like I'm abandoning her." Her lip quivers and it breaks my heart that she's been struggling with this alone.

"Oh, Margot," I say, standing and pulling her in for an embrace. "You're not losing her. You'll see her every day at school."

"It's not the same. I'll miss spending one-on-one time with her, teaching her piano and singing with her." Her lips turn down into a frown as tears pool in her eyes. "I'll miss watching her line up her My Little Ponies every night before bed."

She brings her hands to her face as sobs rack her body. I pull her against me, wrapping my arms around her tightly as I rub her back.

"You can come over anytime and see her, Margot. I promise."

I release her and place my hands on either side of her face, looking in her eyes. "I'll never keep her from you."

She nods her head and I wipe away a few stray tears that have tumbled down her cheeks.

"It's just not going to be the same though. I'll miss it all."

"Margot, it doesn't have to change, you know."

She looks at me, blinking several times. "What do you mean?"

I reach down and grab her hands, bringing them to my lips. I place a kiss on each one.

"You're following your heart, taking this job that will allow you to fulfill your dreams and goals. I would never want you to change that because you took this job and felt like you were abandoning Eleanor. I want you to be happy. I want you to be fulfilled and love life."

"What do you want?" she asks softly.

"Total transparency?" She nods.

Fuck it.

"I want to marry you. I want you to be my wife. I don't want you to move out, unless it's moving out of your room and into mine. I want us to both build a life together and memories with Eleanor."

She stares at me, her eyes unblinking this time.

"You're good for me. You remind me of the value in life and love. You make me a better man. I don't say all this to pressure you or scare you. I'm not asking and I don't need an answer. I'm just being honest. I love you, Margot Silver, with every fiber of my being."

A small smile spreads across her lips and it feels like the elephant on my chest gets up, the tension slowly releasing that I didn't even know was building as I expressed my feelings.

"Do you love me?"

I've wanted to ask her that so many times, but I've been too scared.

"Yes," she says, nodding her head.

"Tell me again."

She smiles wider this time. "I love you, Graham Hayes."

She launches into my arms, and I bury my nose in her hair as I hold her tight. Finally, we break our embrace and step back. I grab her hands and look into her eyes.

"So," I say nervously. "What happens now?"

27

MARGOT

ONE MONTH LATER...

"Are they happy tears?"

I nod my head, cupping my hands around my mouth as we step out of the bar.

I turn and throw my arms around Graham.

"I can't believe you remembered it was The Bluebird."

He grabs my hand and ushers me inside.

"I came here once about five years ago. Mom was still alive, but the cancer had already taken so much of her. I barely stayed through two songs because I couldn't keep my composure." My breath is a little shaken, but I squeeze Graham's hand to calm my nerves.

We approach the hostess. "Hello again, Mr. Hayes. Your table is right this way," she says, smiling with an outstretched arm.

"Hello again?"

"I stopped in after work to make the reservation."

I look around the dimly lit space as we snake our way through some tables and up onto a platform that has a red velvet booth.

"Here you are. A waiter will be with you momentarily. Enjoy your evening."

We thank the hostess and I slide into the booth when a photo on the wall behind it catches my eye. I freeze, my eyes taking a second to register the image. It's an 11x15 photo of my mother.

She looks radiant—in her element. Her red hair is pinned back at the sides, her bangs curled off her forehead. Her hair contrasts against her forest-green dress that cinches at her waist, creating an hourglass shape, her delicate shoulders highlighted with capped sleeves. She looks like a young Susan Hayward.

"How?"

"When I stopped by, I asked the manager if they happen to have any old photos. He put me in touch with the owner's son Bobby who still runs the place and he let me go through all these old boxes in the back."

I can't stop staring at the photo. I've never seen it before. I turn my head to Graham. "Are there others?" I ask hopefully.

"Yes, only a handful but there are. I'm having them restored and framed at a photo shop."

My lips tremble and I fan myself so I don't completely fall apart and ruin my makeup. I look below the photo and see a gold plate with an engraving that reads: *In loving memory of Lydia Silver, our desert rose.*

I can't hold back the tears any longer. I sink into the booth as Graham's arms engulf me. Our waiter approaches, confused, but Graham asks him to give us a moment.

Finally, I compose myself after excusing myself to the ladies' room to freshen my makeup. I look at myself in the mirror over the sink and I see so much of my mom in me. I smooth down my dress, a similar style to the one my mom is wearing in the photo, and I smile.

I lean my back against Graham's chest in the booth. The music fills the room. I feel like I've been transported back in time. Men and woman sip fancy cocktails. A few take spins around the dance floor—it's simply magical.

"Shall we?" He stands, extending his hand out to me with a flirty smile, and I join him. We walk to the dance floor, his arm snaking around my waist as the other holds my hand.

"Are you happy?" he asks as I let out a content sigh.

"Very." He holds me close, our bodies swaying to the music through several songs.

"Thank you," I say against his chest.

He looks down at me. "How are you feeling about things? About us? How our relationship is going?"

I can't help but smile because it feels amazing. After we both confessed our feelings for each other, I realized that he was worth a second chance. He didn't just tell me he was sorry; he showed me.

"Great. I'm happy, very happy actually."

"And are you excited about starting your new job next week?"

I nod. "A little nervous too. I'm still worried they'll realize they hired *me* and rescind the offer."

"Not possible. You're perfect for it and you're going to do amazing things at that school."

We go back to dancing for a few moments.

I never ended up actually quitting the nanny job. I realized that I acted on emotion and I also realized I didn't want to quit the job. Eleanor will be going to school full-time in two weeks. While I start the new job in one week, her grandmother will help out with the childcare aspect for the interim week, and Graham has decided to take the week off to spend more time with Eleanor.

He's been spending more time with her recently anyway and it's been beautiful to witness. We've even gone on a few outings all together. We went to the Brookfield Zoo, the Shedd Aquarium, and Legoland.

I was nervous about the conversation we agreed to have with Eleanor about our relationship. I don't know why I doubted how she'd react. She was elated that me and Daddy were now officially "kissing friends" as she likes to put it.

"Speaking of jobs, I think a promotion is in order."

I furrow my brow and look up at him.

"Well, since you've officially moved into my—our—bedroom and we are officially a couple, I think it's only right."

I'm still confused.

"And don't worry, I ran it by the boss Eleanor first. She actually made you something for the occasion."

He reaches into his suit pocket and pulls out a folded piece of paper and a black velvet box. My heart catches in my throat.

"Oh my God—"

He slowly drops down to one knee in the middle of the dance floor.

"Margot Roxanne Silver, I could spend a lifetime expressing to you how much you mean to me. How you made me believe in love again. How you helped to heal my heart. I would love more than anything for you to allow me to do just that, spend my life showing you how important you are to me and how much I love you. Will you marry me?"

Tears fall down my cheeks as I nod my head excitedly.

"Yes. Yes!" I say as he removes the ring from the box and slowly slides it on my finger. It's an exquisite marquise solitaire with a gold band. Simple and elegant.

The crowd claps around us, bringing me back to the moment as I stare at the ring.

"Wait, what abou—"

Without a word he stands and hands me the folded piece of paper. I look from his eyes to the paper, taking it from his hand and slowly unfolding it.

It's a picture by Eleanor. It's three stick figures of me, Graham, and her in the middle with big sloppy letters that reads, *Will you marry my daddy?*

"This next song is dedicated to the future Mr. and Mrs. Graham and Margot Hayes." The singer's smooth, melodic voice fills the room as Graham takes me in his arms once again and leads me around the dance floor.

28

GRAHAM

SIX MONTHS LATER...

I stare down at my wife's naked body tied to our bed and bite my fist.

"Goddamn, baby girl, you were made to be fucked."

She tugs on the restraints, her back arching.

"You ready to be fucked by your husband?" I reach my hand down between her thighs. "Oh, you're soaked, sweetheart; you're definitely ready."

I bring the wet fingers to my lips and savor her taste as she whimpers.

I grab my belt and slowly undo it, followed by my zipper.

"Please," she begs, and it's like music to my ears.

"Please what?" I ask, pausing my movements.

She squirms again and I crawl up her body, the cold of my belt buckle making her jump as it makes contact with her skin. I lean down and circle her hardened nipple with my tongue, swirling it around before taking it in my mouth and biting.

"Ah." Her eyes close and she arches into the pain.

I turn to her other full breast and repeat the process.

"Please, daddy." She finally says the words; they're filled with need and it drives me wild.

I remove myself from her quickly, kicking my pants and underwear off. I place a knee on the bed as I push her thighs further apart. I grip the underside of her thighs, pressing them upward so she's fully exposed to me and there's nothing she can do about it.

I lean down, dragging my tongue up her in one long, slow lick from her asshole to her clit. Her body shudders.

"You're so close already, aren't you?"

"Ohhh," she moans as I flick my tongue repeatedly over her swollen clit. "Please," she begs again.

I've been teasing her for close to an hour. It's been torture for me to watch her come over and over from my tongue and hands while remaining in my tuxedo pants.

I grip my cock, positioning it at her entrance before pushing my way inside her sweet, wet pussy. She grips me tightly, and I lean my head forward, trying to stop myself from coming on the spot.

"Oh, fuck, Margot; you're so tight. So—" I pull out and thrust back in further this time. "Fucking—" I repeat it again until I'm all the way inside, buried. "Good."

I try to go slow. I try to be gentle, but she begs me not to.

"Harder," she begs as her tits bounce with every thrust. Her head falls back on the pillow as her hands grip the restraints at her wrists.

We're both panting. The sound of our bodies slapping against one other fill the room as the headboard slams against the wall.

"Fucking take my cock, baby!" I'm delirious. I feel her tighten around me as she shouts something inaudible. I can't hold back any longer; I explode inside her, my body shaking as I hold myself up over her swollen belly.

I catch my breath and lean over her, releasing her restraints from her wrists and ankles before kissing and rubbing each one.

"Are you okay?" I ask as I lie back down beside her.

She nods her head. "Can't talk." A lazy grin spreads across her face as she turns her head toward me and kisses me, her tongue dancing with mine.

"Mmm, careful. That's how you started this whole thing."

She giggles as I drag my hand up her thigh and place it on her lower stomach.

"How's my son doing?"

Her belly is just now starting to really show, a round bump protruding over her waistband.

"He's doing okay," she says, nuzzling into me.

We started trying about three days after I put the ring on her finger, and she was pregnant two weeks after that.

"What time is our flight tomorrow?"

I push her hair back from her face, a few strands clinging to her sweaty temple.

"We leave at eleven a.m. so you can sleep in. Everything is already packed and ready to go. We just have to get in the car and Phil will drive us to the private airfield."

"I can't wait to feel the sun again. These Chicago winters are the worst."

"I can't wait to see you in a string bikini." I plant another kiss on each of her nipples and I see her toes curl.

"You are so responsive to me while pregnant." I continue teasing her for a few moments before she's begging me to get her off again. It only takes about thirty seconds of my fingers inside her before she's coming. "It does wonders for my ego."

"It's always been that way. From the moment I met you my body was on high alert."

"Same. Pretty sure my blood pressure was dangerously high the first two months you were here."

We lie in bed and reminisce about how nervous we made each other. All the secret thoughts we had, the stolen glances.

After our engagement, we both agreed we didn't want a big wedding. I think since Margot doesn't have any family it made sense and I certainly don't have a large social circle. Instead, we opted for a small, private ceremony today in the atrium of our home. It was elegantly decorated with ivory roses and pale-pink details.

My mother, Eleanor, Phil, Hank, and Shelly were the only guests in attendance. We enjoyed a small dinner afterward, and then I basically kicked everyone out so I could have my wife all to myself.

"Eleanor asked that we bring her back a sand castle from St. Lucia."

I laugh. "I'm shocked she didn't ask us to bring her back a damn pony."

I rub Margot's belly. "Hank said that Shelly insisted on picking a wedding date after Glen is born."

She rolls onto her side and props herself up on her elbow to look at me. "Yeah, that's what she told me too. I told her she didn't have to but she said they want to do a destination wedding in Mexico. It will be nice not to be pregnant at their wedding, then I can enjoy some margaritas and dancing the night away."

"My mother said she has a surprise for you when we get back from our honeymoon."

She arches a brow at me. "Oh boy, a surprise?"

I kiss her forehead. "Don't worry. She's just having the nursery finished. She wanted to contribute her design eye and I told her that you would appreciate not having to tackle that beast. I sent her your Pinterest boards."

She sighs. "You are so wonderful, you know that? So is your mother. I still can't believe that I get to have all of you in my life. That you all love me and accept me. I never thought I'd get to have a family again." She sniffs and a tear is close to falling over the rim of her eye. She's been extra emotional lately with the pregnancy hormones.

"You think people are meant to be?" I ask.

She nods. "Sometimes I do, yeah."

"Me too. I think about how we both lost a lot in life, and then it was like we were these two perfect puzzle pieces that came together and filled those empty spots for each other."

I reach down and pull the comforter over our bodies as Margot wraps herself around me.

"I have a question," she says, breaking the silence.

"Hmm?"

"When did you know it was hopeless for you with me? That you weren't going to be able to resist any longer?"

I think about her question. "I was instantly attracted to you, I knew that. That's why I didn't help you up when you tripped that first night. Just shaking your hand had my body buzzing and I didn't trust myself. But probably that night I walked in on you talking orgies."

She laughs.

"I'm sorry it's not a more romantic moment," I confess. "But dammit, woman, you had me so wound up. What about you?"

She bites her lip, dragging her teeth slowly across it. "Well, I'm afraid my moment isn't much more romantic either."

"Do tell." I bite her earlobe softly.

"Those three words…" she says as her eyes flutter close. "*Come to daddy.*"

The words sound way more erotic when she says them. I drag my tongue down her neck as my hand comes up to plump her breast.

"Oh, you're a naughty girl," I say as she melts against me.

"Only for you, sir."

Did you love *Those Three Words*? Be sure to check out my other stand-alone billionaire boss romance books in this series.

(ALL books in this series are complete stand-alone books and can be read in any order).

Dirty Little Secret

I'm the type of man that gets what I want.
Hell, I didn't become a billionaire before forty-five by playing by the rules.
But then she waltzed into my life…

Keep reading for a preview!

JUST THIS ONCE SNEAK PEEK

I swore to myself that I'd never cross that line with her.
But when Savannah Monroe, my chief operations officer, shows up
on my doorstep with a proposition that starts with her in my lap and
a promise of *just this once...* The line disappears.

At fifteen years my junior and the smartest woman I've ever met, she's
by far the greatest asset at Baxley Tech.
From the moment I hired her, we had a connection.
As friends, as a mentor, but always with an unspoken attraction that
lingers just beneath the surface.

So when she reveals a painful secret she's been hiding from me that
involves my CFO, I don't hesitate...I take care of it immediately.
Or so I thought.
But the lies and corruption go much deeper than I ever realized and
now we're in a tangled web of passion and secrecy.

After our one night together, everything changes.
The thought of her in the arms of another man turns me into
someone I don't recognize—insatiable, hungry.

Indulging in every filthy thought I've had about her for three years is one thing, but losing my heart in the process wasn't part of the deal.

But here's the thing about forbidden fantasies…they usually come at a price.
And this one, just might be deadly.

When a blackmailer threatens to destroy her life and everything she's worked for, I take matters into my own hands.
Because when it comes to Savannah Monroe, there is no negotiation.
No backing down.
No Limits.
No Rules.
No losing her.

We promised each other it would only be *just this once*.
But now that I've had a taste…I want my fill.

PROLOGUE

SAVANNAH-THREE YEARS EARLIER...

"I got an interview!" I thrust my hands in the air in celebration as I stand up, my desk chair shooting out behind me.

I glance around nervously, trying to judge if anyone heard me. Probably not the best idea to be shouting about a new interview at my current job.

I sit back down and read the email again for a third time.

"Oh my God, I got an interview," I repeat in disbelief.

When I applied for the open Chief Operations Officer position at Baxley Technologies, I truly didn't expect a call back. Not to say I'm not qualified for the job; I feel I am, but most companies want to see at least fifteen years on your resume before they even consider you for the COO role.

I close my office door and grab my cell to call my best friend Callie.

"Hey, this is a lov—"

"I got an interview," I blurt out, cutting her off.

"An interview for—oh, for Baxley?"

"Yes!" I'm attempting to whisper but with my excitement it's coming out more in a whispered shout. "I'm in complete disbelief, like me? Seriously?"

"Of course you, why not *you*? First of all, you're very qualified. Your insane work experience in just six years speaks for itself, not to mention the MBA and undergrad from an Ivy League school, both of which you got into on merit and not because your family had money."

"I know. It's just that I don't want to get my hopes up if they're not serious about me."

"These are billionaires, sweetie. They wouldn't waste their precious time if they weren't serious about you. Now stop doubting yourself and get ready to go out and celebrate tonight. Think about where you wanna meet for drinks."

I smile into the receiver. If there's one person who will always have my back and gas me up, it's Callie. She's been my ride or die since the day we met freshman year at Northwestern. I didn't think she'd associate with me at all. She comes from a very wealthy family, old money, from the North Shore and I... well, I'm an only child, that I know of, raised by my grandma after my mom went to prison and my dad abandoned me.

I put my phone on my desk and turn back to my computer to finish up my workday. I feel too giddy to focus, but if this interview does actually turn into a new career opportunity, I don't want to leave this startup I've been at for the last three years high and dry. I need to finish up a few projects before I officially leave this place.

I knew from a young age I wanted a career, a big one. I busted my ass in high school, opting for any and every extracurricular and after-school program, even summer school. I graduated early with honors and was accepted into Northwestern University with a focus on business and finance.

Even through high school and college I worked any and every odd job I could find that would pay my bills and give me experience. I started in fast food, working my way up to a management position and then the corporate office that happened to be located in Chicago where I lived. Even through getting my MBA, I continued to move up the ladder until I was brought on as a project manager and financial advisor here at this software startup. In only three years we've grown from nothing to a multimillion-dollar company that's in the final stages of IPO.

I was determined to break the cycle of failure in my family if it was the last thing I did. Sometimes I still struggle with imposter syndrome when I look in the mirror. Like who is this girl who came from nothing and why does she deserve this opportunity?

I shake the thoughts from my head and power through the rest of my day before sending a text to Callie.

Me: *Leaving here in the next twenty. Mitzy's for martinis?*

Thirty minutes later I take the first celebratory sip of my dirty martini.

"Will Todd be surprised when you put in your notice?"

"*If* I ge—"

"When," Callie says emphatically with an arched brow.

"When," I start over, "I get the job, I think Todd will be sad to see me go for sure, but I think he knew from the get-go that I didn't plan to stay long term. I think when you jump in at the ground floor of a startup, it's a much quicker burnout period than other jobs, you know?"

She nods and takes a sip of her French martini, her eyes rolling back in her head for a brief second. "Yeah, for sure. You have literally put blood, sweat, and tears into that place. I hope he knows what he has with you."

"He does. He's always been extremely generous with pay, but as we all know, there's zero work-life balance when it comes to a startup. I'm only twenty-seven and I already feel like between school and all my jobs over the years, I've never had a chance to just breathe, enjoy life, and take some downtime."

I do feel a little guilty wanting to move on from Code Red Software, but I'm beyond excited that I even get the chance to interview at a tech giant like Baxley Technologies.

I SWALLOW down the fear in my throat as I stare up at the massive mirrored building on Franklin St.

I close my eyes for a brief second and take in a deep breath. "You've got this. You deserve this. You're going to nail it."

I square my shoulders back, lift my chin up, and march up to the massive revolving door emblazoned with the world-famous gold BT symbol.

"Please have a seat, Miss Monroe."

I take a seat in front of a large table where six other people are sitting across from me. "I'm Pierce Denton, Executive Vice President here at Baxley." The rest of the individuals follow suit with their name and title.

Round table style interviews are nothing new to me. I had to do them for my MBA program and when I came onboard with Code Red, but this one is intimidating. Not only is it filled with department heads, but the collective net worth in this room alone is more than I'll see in ten lifetimes.

"Mr. Baxley won't be here today for this interview. If we decide to move forward with second rounds, he'll be present for that one," Mr. Denton says.

I nod and try to consciously make eye contact with each person while not looking crazy at the same time.

"You have an impressive background, Miss Monroe. I'm sure it's not the first time someone has told you that."

I smile. "Thank you. Yes, I have heard that from previous employers."

We go through some general questions about my background, education, and then come the fun ones… the ones about how I'd be an asset to the company, why I should be considered, what value I'd bring to the company… a fight for my life or basically a modern-day version of a mock execution.

But this is where I come alive because I'm not just trying to blow smoke up these people's asses; I'm serious about my career and where I see myself, and I see myself at Baxley Tech.

I feel confident as I stand and shake each of their hands.

"Great job today, kid." Eric, the CFO who introduced himself earlier during the round table, gives me a wink and touches my elbow.

An instant *ick* feeling settles in my stomach but I don't let him see.

"Thank you. I feel very confident about the next steps." I maintain solid eye contact with him, refusing to let him make me feel out of place with his subtle comment about my age.

I'm more than aware that I'd be the youngest person in an executive position at this company, but that doesn't scare me one bit. It just stokes the fire of determination inside me.

"I have no doubt we'll be in touch shortly," Mr. Denton says after walking me to the elevator.

"Thank you and I look forward to it, sir." I step into the empty elevator and press the button for the ground floor. The moment the doors close, I toss my hands in the air again and do a happy dance.

* * *

IT'S BEEN four agonizing days since my interview and I am a nervous wreck. Every time I turn around, I'm either knocking something over or tripping over my own feet. My nerves feel like they've been juiced up with adrenaline and caffeine and all my breath work is for nothing.

I glance at the clock; it's 4:48 p.m. on a Friday. For most people, the workday is done already but for me, I'll probably be here till at least seven p.m. or later. I'm used to it at this point—that's not why I'm looking at the clock. I refresh my email for the fiftieth time, but there's nothing from Baxley.

"Hey, Savannah, doing anything fun this weekend?" Lynn, my coworker, pokes her head in my office.

I shrug. "Nothing on the books. Probably be here pretty late tonight. What about you?"

"Pete's uncle is taking his boat out on the lake so we'll probably join him. It's not exactly my cup of tea, fishing and drinking beer, but it'll be nice to get out in the sun."

"That does sound fun. And hey, maybe you can convince him to take you to that cute French bistro you saw the other week that you mentioned."

Her eyes light up, "You are so smart. I completely forgot about that."

I'm about to respond when my phone buzzes and I look at the screen.

Incoming call from Pierce Denton.

"Oh, I have to," I say, pointing to the phone, and she nods and waves, shutting my door behind her.

"Hello?"

"Hello, Miss Monroe. Apologies for the late callback. I know how annoying that is, but business gets in the way sometimes." He chuckles and I hold my breath. "Anyway, we would love to have you back for another round of interviews next week. That work for you?"

"Yes!" I attempt to readjust my volume as my excitement gets the better of me, "Yes, sorry."

"Great. I'll have Dorene from HR set it up with you. She'll send over an email with some proposed times."

"Will Mr. Baxley be there?"

"Yes, he will be—should be. You'll be interviewing with him and Eric Oliver, the CFO you met at the last interview."

"Oh, okay. Yes, I remember him." I try to sound positive, but I don't love the idea of having to speak to that man for several hours as these interviews can run long. At least Mr. Baxley will be there to hopefully correct him if he calls me *kid* again.

Per usual, I stay late tonight but with a little extra pep in my step. I double down and make sure I finish up as much as I can, knowing that there's a good chance I'll be gone from here in a few short weeks.

Normally, my Friday nights are a stressful battle between me trying to work late to finish things up so I'm not so stressed the next week and trying to appease my boyfriend via text with promises to spend every minute with him this weekend.

However, after several painful and teary conversations into the wee hours of the morning, Nick and I recently decided that after four years together, neither of us could offer what the other needed.

It wasn't easy but it was right, and we both agreed. The breakup was mutual and amicable, and I'm sure we'll stay friendly over the years. I promise myself that this time, I'll give myself at least a year off from relationships.

I grab my purse and head down to my car, already yawning. I received an email about an hour ago from Dorene with three times next week for my interview. I confirmed one for Monday morning so now I can actually relax over the weekend... at least until Saturday afternoon when I start panicking all over again.

* * *

I HOLD MY PURSE, plant, box of knickknacks for my office, and a bagel all in my hands as I walk through the revolving door of Baxley Tech, my new job where I, Savanna Grace Monroe, am COO. It still feels unreal.

Unfortunately and strangely, I have yet to meet Warren Baxley himself. He was called away on business before our interview so he was only able to attend via audio, sitting quietly on the call. I wouldn't have even known he was there if Mr. Oliver hadn't told me.

I purposely made eye contact with Mr. Oliver the entire interview because less than thirty seconds into it, his eyes dropped down to my breasts when I dared to look away for even a brief second.

"Hold it, please!" I say as my heels furiously click across the marble floor of the lobby. I dart through the closing doors of the elevator just as someone rushes up behind me to do the same.

I stumble as I feel two warm hands grab at my waist. I try to turn and see who it is when I hear his voice. "Whoa, kid. I'm sorry. Almost took a tumble on your first day." Eric Oliver flashes me a smarmy smile, acting like he isn't the one who caused me to stumble in the first place when his chest ran into my back.

I give him a slight smile and try to push my way to the back of the elevator.

"You need me to show you around? I can—"

"No, thank you. I know where I'm going. Much appreciated

though." I shut it down before he can offer anything else. "This is me," I say, exiting the elevator the second the doors open.

But it isn't me. I glance down to my right, then my left. I spot a bench and place my stuff down to pull up my email again to check the floor and suite number of my office.

"Shit, two floors up." I walk back over to the elevator and press the button. This time when the doors open, it's empty. I let out a sigh and step inside, but it stops after one floor and wouldn't you know it, he gets back on the elevator with me.

"You sure you don't need some help there, little lady?" He chuckles and pokes at my orchid that bobs over the top of my box.

"I'm sure."

"Well, listen, I mean it. If you ever want to get lunch and get a feel for the company or need a mentor, I'm here for you." It's like he has zero control of his eyes that once again look down at my breasts at least four times in that one sentence.

I spin around and exit on my correct floor this time, finally finding my office and placing my things down. I straighten out my button-down blouse and pencil skirt, second-guessing my very professional clothing choice... Maybe I should have opted for a damn potato sack.

I don't have many personal items to display in my office, not because I'm particularly private but because I have no family to have framed photos of or gifts or sentimental knickknacks. Besides my orchid, which I place on the corner of my desk, the only thing I have is a small five-inch-tall Eiffel Tower.

I click the button on the back of my iMac to turn it on, but nothing happens.

"The hell?" I mutter as I do it again and still nothing. I look under my desk and see that it's not plugged in. I reach under my desk and plug it in. I grab my chair to help pull myself back up, but it swivels, so I launch myself forward and land right on my belly on the floor.

"Glad to see you found your office. Everything okay?"

I hear a voice behind me as I right myself. I'm on my knees, read-justing my ponytail I just knocked askew. I am really not in the mood for this man's continued attempts at flirting or whatever the hell he's thinking. Time to let him know this won't fly with me.

"Sir, let me be very clear," I say with my back still toward the door. "I'm not your midlife crises, okay?" I stand up and brush down my skirt. "This is a professional setting."

"No, you're not, but I'm pretty sure I'm your new boss."

My spine stiffens and I feel my eyes bug out as I slowly turn around to face the man standing casually in my doorway.

Warren Freaking Baxley, in the flesh.

Shit.

CHAPTER 1

WARREN

"He broke up with me."

Savannah flings her arms in the air before flopping down in the chair across from my desk, her silky chocolate hair pooling around her shoulders as she slumps down.

"Are you more upset that *he* broke up with you or that the relationship is over?"

I don't look up from the document in my hand. This isn't the first time Savannah has vented to me about her relationship woes and I'm sure it won't be the last.

We're an... unlikely friendship. She's outgoing and friendly, young and not afraid to voice her opinion. Whereas I'm fifteen years her senior and do everything I can to avoid human interaction outside of my business.

Yes, I'm her boss, but I'd say we're also good friends. Completely professional, of course, which is why I leave all the filthy thoughts that wander into my head about her, in my head.

"What do you mean?" The V between her brow deepens.

I put the paper down and remove my glasses, folding them in my hands.

"I mean, is it an insult that he's the one who dumped *you* or did you really think he was the one?" She chews her bottom lip as she considers my question.

"I'm not upset that he was the one who ended things because I can't handle being dumped. I'm hurt. We've been together almost a year and a half and this just came out of nowhere. I thought he was asking me to move in with him or maybe proposing at the—"

"Proposing?" That gets my attention. Sure, they've been dating that long, but I've never heard her speak about him like she's ready to marry the guy. I swallow down the panic that forms in my throat.

"Yeah, or moving in together. It's just—frustrating. Another failed relationship at thirty."

"Savannah, you have plenty of time to find *the one*. Stop putting that pressure on yourself and live your life. I'm sure Nick will regret his decision soon enough." I offer her a tight-lipped smile, but she just glares at me.

"Nick? Nick was my ex from three years ago. His name is Easton and you've met him twice."

"I have?"

I shrug nonchalantly, knowing full well that I met the smug prick twice. The first time he tried to offer me advice on my company's latest software launch by telling me that someone *my* age should be taking tech advice from someone in their twenties. And the second time, he was sloppy drunk at our office Christmas party and knocked over an entire table of champagne flutes.

"Maybe I'm not the best person for these kinds of talks."

She lets out a dramatic sigh. "No, you're probably right. I'll save it for overpriced martinis with the girls." She stands up and stretches her arms overhead, the bottom of her blouse lifting just enough to expose a sliver of her flat stomach. She pulls her long hair into a high ponytail, wrapping the tie from her wrist around it a few times.

"You doing anything this weekend?" she asks, coming around my desk to look at the paper I've been studying.

"The usual—work, maybe a round of golf or tennis at the club, and more work."

She leans in closer. The familiar scent of her floral perfume still lingers at the end of a ten-hour day. Her long, delicate fingers rest on her hip as she eyes the paper.

"This the Code Red proposal?"

"It is."

She picks it up and hikes one hip up to rest it on my desk. My eyes fall to where her hips flare out from her waist. It's a spot that I often fixate on with her. She has that classic hourglass figure that leaves me constantly desiring to run my hand over that dip in her body.

Sometimes I wonder if there's overt flirty undertones with her body language and actions, but I always settle on no because she knows how important discretion is to me. But also because I don't think for one second she sees me as anything more than a boss or mentor—fuck, maybe even a father figure in her life. It hasn't gone totally unnoticed by some of my male colleagues that not only is Savannah young and beautiful, but that I'm also rather protective of her.

"Good thing I didn't sell my stocks after they went public and I left the company. If this acquisition goes through, I'm poised to become a very wealthy woman. Might even knock you off the richest man in Chicago pedestal."

She winks at me and tosses it back on my desk. I lean back in my chair, attempting to put some distance between us.

"What about your weekend plans?"

I'm trying my hardest not to look down at her smooth, tan legs left exposed by her skirt riding up a little. Sometimes—okay, often—I wonder what her reaction would be if I simply reached my hand out and ran my fingertips up her silky skin.

In my fantasy, she parts her legs a little further for me, allowing me a peek at what she's wearing beneath her proper pencil skirts. In this particular fantasy, her on my desk at the end of a long day, she'd simply slip her panties off and hike her skirt up, offering me her sweet, wet pussy to devour.

"Oh, general wallowing I suppose now that I'm a single woman." Her response snaps me back to reality and I realize I've let my gaze settle on her thighs, but she doesn't seem to notice.

"I'm sure I'll let it all out with Callie and then rapidly go through the phases of grief, convincing myself I'm better off while I get it all out over a grueling spin class."

"That sounds miserable but I'll wish you all the best."

"You're welcome to join us for martinis at Mitzy's if you're bored." She smiles and while I know she knows I'll never take her up on the offer, I do appreciate that every weekend she offers to let me tag along on whatever crazy adventure she's up to.

"I'm afraid I'd be a bore. You don't want an old man, let alone your boss, to tag along with your friends." I wink at her and I swear I see a slight pink hue spread across her cheeks. For as much as we have kept things professional between us, once in a while it feels like these little tender moments are laced with flirty innuendo.

"Maybe I'll become a sugar mama. Find some twenty-one-year-old smoke show that needs beer money." She scoots back a little further on my desk so that she's now fully sitting on it and reaches down to pull off her heels. "You ever done that?"

"Been a sugar mama? Can't say that I have."

She slaps my arm playfully. "No, have you ever entertained someone considerably younger than you that you knew wouldn't be anything serious, just a fling?"

I debate on saying something to the effect of *no, but I'd be happy to if you're offering.* Instead, I answer truthfully. "No. I'm not really the kind of man who wants to be used for my money, but there's no shame in those who desire that kind of arrangement. It's just not for me."

"And what kind of arrangement does work for you? What is Warren Baxley looking for?" She crosses one leg over the other, briefly drawing my attention to her exposed flesh. I look up at her and she's leaning on one arm, palm flat on my desk as she waits for my answer.

"Who says I'm looking for anything?" She rolls her eyes. "I don't think I'm looking for an arrangement of anything. Just open, I suppose."

It's a vague answer, but the truth is I'm not sure what I actually want. I'm not exactly wanting to die alone, but what I want feels wrong. It feels selfish to want Savannah. She's young, has her entire life ahead of her, and I'm already in the second phase of my life. Besides, I've convinced myself that the things I'd want to do to her would scare her away.

"Look at us, both single with an amazing career, but no prospects." Suddenly her face drops and she lets out a groan. "Dammit! I completely forgot that Easton and I have our annual benefit dinner next month for the Northwestern University Alumni Association."

"I'm sure he'll behave accordingly if that's what you're worried about."

She shakes her head. "That's not what I'm worried about. I just hate having to make a public appearance at a place where everyone knows he and I were previously dating. It's like a public statement letting everyone know we failed. Like back when your friend would change their Facebook relationship status to it's complicated."

"I think you're being a touch dramatic, Savannah. And if it's really that uncomfortable, just don't go. Make him be the one who has to tell everyone there that he made the biggest mistake of his life and dumped the smartest, most accomplished, and beautiful woman he'll ever meet. He'll look fucking stupid."

Her frown morphs into a huge, genuine smile that reaches her eyes.

"Look at you, Mr. Sentimental." She pokes me with her bare foot, and I bat it away, but she does it again, this time trying to poke me in the ribs, but I reach my hand out and catch her foot. The warmth of her skin tingles against my palm. The moment we make contact, it's like something shifts between us. The air grows thick with unsaid desires and tension.

Her smile fades and I swear I see a sharp intake of breath between her open lips. I don't let go of her foot right away. Instead, I do something so stupid—I run my thumb up her insole and her eyelids flutter. Something is definitely happening between us, and it feels magnetic, like I couldn't stop it if I wanted to. But then it's gone when a soft knock brings us both back to reality.

"Hey, boss, got a min—oh, sorry, didn't mean to interrupt." Eric shoves his hands in his pockets as he looks between us.

"Not interrupting. Come on in."

Savannah jumps down from my desk and scoops up her heels.

"I'm heading home," she says to me as she slips on her heels. "Have a good weekend, gentlemen."

"What was that about?" Eric asks the moment she's gone. He walks over to the bar cart in the corner of my office and pours himself a generous amount of my liquor.

I shake my head like I have no idea what he's talking about. "Nothing. We were just talking about our weekend plans and Code Red."

"Last time I checked, my secretary doesn't sit on my desk when she's making small talk with me."

That irks me. I narrow my gaze at him and sharpen my voice.

"She's not my secretary, Eric. Those digs won't fly with me so cut that shit out."

I've always known Eric was a little more than jealous when I brought Savannah on as COO. He thought as the current CFO, he was a shoo-in for the position. He could have managed it—I have no doubt—but he's better with finances. He's not as good with the big-picture decision-making that Savannah does.

He raises his hand in a silent apology. "Speaking of Code Red, are things still moving forward?"

"As expected, yes. We'll make the announcement sometime in the next two weeks. How's Kane doing? Still no interest in coming aboard Baxley?"

I stand and walk over to the bar cart to pour myself a tumbler of whiskey. I'm not a big drinker, maybe a drink a week, typically on Friday night. It's a ritual; usually after everyone has left the building, I pour myself a glass and slowly sip it as I put on a record, kick back, and watch the city below.

"I'm working on it. Kid still thinks he wants to focus on building his own app. I told him I'm all for it, but it could really help him to get a few years under his belt working here. Really help him land some connections, and then he could develop the app with us or sell it to Baxley."

"Well, he's still young. I'm sure he'll come around eventually. It's good that he's so ambitious though. Just like you."

Eric and I have known each other for the better part of two decades. He was my mentor out of grad school at my first major job. He was a director, and I was just starting out. He saw something in me, took me under his wing, and helped me become the man I am today. So when I started Baxley Technologies fifteen years ago, he was the first employee I hired.

"More like you. I still remember you telling me six months after you started at DataTech, you said *Eric, I give myself five years before I start my own company and ten to make it a billion-dollar enterprise.* I thought you were crazy but here we are." He raises his glass to me and we both drink.

"Shit," he says, looking at his watch, "the Mrs. will be calling me any second if I don't get home. Maybe if I'm lucky I can sweet-talk her into giving me some of that action you and Savannah almost had." He winks at me and I just ignore the comment. "Have a good weekend, boss. See you Sunday at the club. Nine a.m. tee off; don't be late." He points to me as he walks out of my office.

Eric is on his fourth, possibly fifth marriage at this point. I can't keep track. His penchant for chasing after his next wife while still married to his current usually lands him in divorce court every few years.

His comment about Savannah and me lingers as I dim the lights and walk over to my records. I leaf through them briefly, finally deciding on "Something Else" by Cannonball Adderley. The smooth sound of jazz fills the office as I take a seat in my chair. I lean back and close my eyes, allowing the melody to carry me away.

Pre-order Just This Once for a special price!

DIRTY LITTLE SECRET
SNEAK PEAK

I'm the type of man that gets what I want.
Hell, I didn't become a billionaire before forty-five by playing by the rules.
But then she waltzed into my life...

Wren Adler, my head of PR and the star of every one of my dirty fantasies.
She's driven, fiery and more than ten years younger than me.
In other words, she's off f-ing limits.
But when a psycho stalker starts to terrorize her and her narcissistic ex keeps making mysterious appearances in her life, the only way I could make sure she stays safe—was to have her move in with me.
So now I'm not just tortured at work, but every night as she permeates every inch of my life.
I've been a saint for three years.

I've kept my hands off her curvaceous body and my filthy thoughts to myself.

Until last night when she asked if I had any dirty little secrets and my
resolve finally snapped.
I should have walked away.
I shouldn't have tasted her.
I shouldn't have let my hands roam.
And I sure as hell shouldn't have told her to grab the headboard.
Instead, I finally let myself indulge in the ultimate fantasy of
pretending she's mine.

**Now, she thinks that she's my dirty little secret but the truth is, I'm
not only lying to her, I'm lying to myself.
I have to decide to take a chance on finally getting what I want, or
walking away forever.**

CHAPTER 1

THEO

"You know I don't speak just to hear myself talk, right?"

"Hmm?" Wren Adler, my head of PR, makes a questioning response but doesn't turn her focus to what I'm actually saying. She's clearly lost in thought, staring out the window of my downtown Chicago high-rise office.

I take the opportunity to drag my gaze up her curvy body. Before you judge me too harshly, I know... I'm her boss and it's unprofessional as shit to lust over your employee. I don't make a show of it; I'm discreet, but a man can only handle so much voluptuous temptation. For three long years I've had to talk myself out of bending her over my desk every damn day. I'd like to think it's because I'm a noble gentleman but I'm not sure that's the case. Apart from my very strict no fraternizing policy at my company, she's also still twenty-nine years old and I'm weeks away from forty-two. Whatever the reasons, I just know she's absolutely off-limits.

"Wren, I'd like to get this press release out today so if we could focus?" I say a little more sternly.

She shifts her weight from one leg to the other, drawing attention to the seductive seam that runs up the back of her pantyhose. Or maybe they're thigh-highs? I imagine the top of her sheer black stockings encased in lace, gripping her thick thighs.

Fuck. Rein it in, I tell myself.

"Oh, sorry," she mumbles, turning and walking back toward my desk. "What—which part did you want to go back over?" She fumbles with the iPad a little as she tries to refocus her attention to the task at hand.

I roll my eyes and let out an exaggerated sigh. I'm moody and demanding; I know it and she knows and so does everyone else. I didn't become a billionaire by wasting my time and catering to people's feelings.

"Or you can be childish about it and throw a tantrum?" She cocks her eyebrow and juts her hip out. She may be daydreaming, but she's quick to snap back to reality and give me a touch of attitude. She's the only one that can call me on my bullshit.

"You know I don't like wasting time, Wren," I say in my calmest voice, plastering on the cheesiest grin I can muster.

"Oh, calm down, Theo. It was two minutes and I'm pretty sure you're wasting time right now with this petty lecture. *Anyway,*" she says dramatically as she places the iPad on the desk in front of me.

I grip the end of the armrest tightly, my knuckles turning white. *Petty lecture?* I want to tell her that I'll bend her over and teach her a real lesson while turning her plump cheeks a bright shade of pink.

"As you can see here, I've made notes where I want you to double-check and let me know if you want anything added or deleted. The facts and figures have been triple-checked and it's ready to go to publication."

I lean forward, looking over the notes and trying my damndest not to inhale her scent. What is that? Gardenia? It smells florally with a hint of spice. She bends down a little farther to drag her finger across the screen.

"This part right here is the only section I assume you'll actually care about so just look it over and let me know if I can submit it."

I glance to my right briefly; it's the perfect view right down her blouse to her glorious tits, but I pull my eyes away just as quickly. I know it doesn't make sense that I feel guilty sometimes and sometimes I don't. It's lunacy what this woman does to me, but it feels like no matter how hard I try to fight my attraction to her, the more she infiltrates my every thought.

"Looks excellent as always. I don't require any changes." I look back up at her and she's staring off into space again, nibbling on the edge of her thumb.

"Wren?"

"Perfect! I'll get this published right now." She scoops up the iPad and starts for my office door.

"What's going on, Wren?" She likes to think she knows me more than I know her, but it's not the case. I can read her like a book and I know when something is off.

I see her shoulders fall a little as she stops, spinning around to face me with a big smile on her face.

"Nothing. Just didn't sleep well is all. Plus, ya know... Penn."

I see her face drop at the mention of her ex's name, and I feel my own hands ball into fists. The guy is a piece of fucking work. Grade A douchebag and frankly I never understood what she saw in him. I know, cliché to say when I'm lusting after her but I'm not a dick. I want Wren to be truly happy.

"Didn't you break up with him months ago?" I know exactly how long it's been—seven months—but I don't lead on that I do. "He still causing problems?"

She bites her bottom lip, something she does when she's full of shit.

"Not problems, no. He's just having a hard time letting go of things." I want to roll my eyes again but I refrain.

"Seriously? Tell the baby to move the fuck on already."

"We're not all robots without feelings, Theo. Some people take time to heal, especially after four years of dating."

Ouch. That stings a little but she's not wrong. Somewhere in my forty-plus years of life, my feelings and heart went out the window.

"Want me to... help him get over it?" I'm not sure what I'm insinuating with my offer, maybe just have a talk with him and tell him to grow the fuck up and move on with his pathetic excuse of a life. My blood pressure is rising; it's time to calm down.

"*No!* Trust me, you getting involved would only make it ten times worse. I got it; don't worry about it."

I'm about to ask her what that's supposed to mean when my assistant, Cheryl, walks into the office with a stack of folders.

"Sorry to interrupt, sir, but you need to look over these contracts before your lawyer gets here for your meeting in"—she looks at her watch—"seventeen minutes."

Cheryl is a helluva guard dog when it comes to my schedule, something I'm extremely grateful for. She peers over her half-moon glasses that are permanently perched on the end of her nose as if to tell me to get a move on.

"Thank you, Cheryl. I'll get right on it." I turn to Wren who is already moving back toward the exit. "We'll finish this conversation later," I tell her. She just shakes her head and waves a hand in the air as she makes her way toward the elevators. I'm tempted to linger a little on her round hips as they swish back and forth, but I'm well aware of Cheryl's presence.

I grab the stack of contracts and open the first one to look it over, but Cheryl is still standing in my office, a knowing look on her face.

"Just say whatever it is you're thinking, Cheryl; I know that face."

"When are you going to wake up and smell the fact that she likes you?"

I take it back. Cheryl and Wren are the only two people who regularly give me their very unsolicited input. I toss the file back down onto my desk and run my hand gruffly over my face.

"And when are you going to understand that she's too young for me, she's my employee, oh, and most importantly, it's none of your business. Contrary to popular belief, Cheryl, I'm not just another entitled billionaire asshole that feels he can take whatever he wants."

She crosses her thin arms over her chest, her move of defiance that she always does when she's about to speak her mind.

"We both know that isn't the only way to go about this. I see the chemistry between you too and it would be a damn shame for you to just throw away something like that because of principle."

I do not have the time or energy to deal with her high-horse rants today. I look at my watch and then point to it. "I now only have fifteen minutes to look over these contracts before Will gets here to discuss them. So if you could kindly take your delusional ideas elsewhere, I would greatly appreciate it so that I can get back to work and make sure that we keep business running. Okay?" I know my tone is cutting and borderline rude at best, but I'm tired of Cheryl reminding me of the fact that I can't have Wren. It's a conversation that needs to die.

She gives me one last harsh look before turning and briskly walking out of my office, slamming the door a little harder than necessary behind her.

After four meetings in a row, a missed lunch, and God knows how many cups of coffee later, I hit the button on the intercom on my phone.

"Cheryl, will you bring me everything we have on the Newcombs, please?"

"Absolutely, sir. Be there shortly." Moments later my office door opens and Cheryl walks in, her pin-straight dark hair flowing behind her with her quick pace. She puts a thick file on my desk. "This is everything I could find."

"Thank you."

"Is there anything specific you're looking for? I may be able to help," she offers.

"No, nothing specific. Just trying to get myself familiar with the client."

"Okay, well, if there isn't anything else, I'm going to take off for the day."

"What time is it?" I ask, looking at my watch to see that it's already pushing five thirty.

"It's almost five thirty, sir," she answers with a smirk.

I shake my head at myself. "I'm sorry. Time has completely gotten away from me today. Yes, please feel free to get your evening started."

She nods. "You got any big plans this evening?"

I want to roll my eyes. Didn't we just broach this subject a few hours earlier? It might sound like a genuinely innocent question, but Cheryl's questions are never innocent; there's always an ulterior motive. I manage to hold back; she already knows my plans.

"I'll probably grab some dinner, read over more of these notes and files. No big party for me," I say as I keep my eyes focused on the paper in my hand.

She shakes her head. "When are you going to slow down and finally take a break? You're over forty. It's time to settle down. Get back out there."

I scoff. "Cheryl," I say a little long-sufferingly, "I thought we discussed this earlier? Leave my personal life out of work stuff."

She laughs and puts her hands on her hips. "Well, I'm pretty sure it's well past five so, this is my personal time and not company time."

"Good night, Cheryl."

She takes the hint. "Good night, sir." She steps out and closes the door behind her quietly so I can get back to work.

I lean back in my chair and let out a long breath as I bring my hand to the bridge of my nose and pinch it. My eyes have gone blurry from reading too much today and I already feel the headache setting in. There's no way I can call it quits just yet though. I still have mountains of work to get through before our meeting with Mr. Newcomb tomorrow. I'll work for another hour or so, and then I'm getting out of here.

I open my eyes and sit up straight, forcing my gaze back to the stack of papers on my desk. I start reading where I left off.

The next hour passes in a blur and before I know it, I'm driving home, playing the same sick, twisted game I play with myself about once or twice a week. I let my brain run wild with thoughts of Wren. And before you assume they're just sex-crazed fantasies, they're not… at least not all of them.

Wren is like no other person I've ever met. Apart from being knock-you-on-your-ass beautiful with brains and wit that would give anyone a run for their money, she's kind and warm. She's genuine. She hasn't let the assholes and shitty hand that life sometimes deals wear her down or leave her jaded. She's always the first one to offer a helping hand or give someone encouragement. She goes out of her way to listen to others. She's a ray of positivity in the sometimes soul-sucking darkness of corporate America.

She deserves a meaningful and fulfilling life and I know she'll have it; it just won't be with me. It's not that I don't know how to love or that I was fucked over royally by some woman in the past; it's just that I'm a grumpy asshole that's married to his job and I have no business corrupting a bright young mind. That's the last thing I want, her ending up like me. I already see it happening at times, her staying at work long after the sun has set or getting in before it's risen. She skips lunch far too often and I'm pretty positive that in three years, she's never taken a vacation. I make a mental note to fix that.

I step on the accelerator as I take a left onto my street out of the city. The orange glow of the setting sun blinds me momentarily as I hit the button to drop the top on my Aston Martin. This is my favorite part of the drive home. It's serene and calm; you wouldn't know that Chicago is a short twenty-minute drive away. I know a lot of people who work downtown prefer to stay downtown, but not me. The last thing I want at the end of a long day is to stay downtown in the constant buzz of people, cars, and hot garbage. I bought a penthouse not too far from the office a few years back, thinking I'd use it —can't remember the last time I set foot in it. Another thing I make a mental note to address.

Don't get me wrong, oftentimes my thoughts drift to much less noble places. Sometimes involving Wren screaming my name as she's bent over my desk and other times I just want to get lost in touching, kissing, licking every square inch of her body while I'm buried deep inside her heat. I subconsciously run my tongue along my bottom lip like I'm licking the sweet, forbidden nectar of the peach off my chin.

I told you it was a sick game. It's like allowing myself to smell and touch the ripest, juiciest peach, knowing full well I'm fucking allergic to peaches.

CHAPTER 2

WREN

"That's right, baby, take me deep just the way you like it." Theo's deep voice whispers naughty fantasies in my ear as his hot breath puffs against my neck. I groan and grasp at the hard desk beneath me but there's nothing for me to grip.

A pile of papers falls to the floor as I let out an animalistic groan I've never heard myself make before. I feel like I'm about to explode; my body is tight and on the edge; my tits bounce wildly with every hard thrust of his cock. I look up into his dark eyes; a thick lock of his black hair has fallen over one golden eye, and a thin sheen of sweat glistens on his brow.

I reach up and grab his tie that's dangling loosely around his neck. I fist it, pulling his lips toward mine just as I hear a loud beeping sound invade my thoughts.

"Wha—what is that?" I say between thrusts. He doesn't seem to notice it. I glance around, confused as the sounds grows louder and more persistent.

The annoying sound of my alarm pulls me from the deepest sleep I've had in a long time.

"God, not again," I groan as I roll over and feel for my clock to turn off the alarm. I was so close to finishing this time. This is the third sex dream about my boss in as many weeks. At first I thought it was just a stupid brain dump after spending a few late nights in his office, being surrounded by his scent and close proximity, but now... I think it's something more. Something I can't help but blush about when I remember the way he had me convulsing in pleasure on his desk.

I've always had an attraction to Theo; it's almost like biology didn't give me a choice. He's pushing six four and built like Chris Evans. Yeah, it's disgustingly unfair. His eyes are a shade of gold I've never seen before and sometimes, I feel like they linger on me a second longer than needed but maybe that's all in my head. His thick black hair still doesn't have a single gray and his Disney prince-like jaw could probably cut glass. I've pretty much only ever seen him fully clothed but I would bet money he's got the most mouthwatering six-pack beneath his bespoke suits with the way he wears them. And judging by the small patch of black hair at the base of his neck, I'd guess he has a perfect little happy trail that leads alllll the way down to his huge... I roll to my side and look at the clock on my bedside table to check and see if I have time to finish what I started in my dream.

"Shit." It's going on six a.m. already and I like to be at the office by eight. I need to get my ass in gear if I don't want to sprint for my train.

I roll to my back and stare up at the bright-white ceiling, trying to work up the energy to get out of bed. With a little mental pep talk, I manage to sit up and get my feet on the floor. First stop, coffee. The scent wafting from my kitchen already has me in a better mood. I have my coffee pot set on a timer so by the time I reach the kitchen, it's already done brewing. I'm not one of those *just a splash* of cream type girls. I like it rich, sweet, and creamy. My recent obsession is a Madagascar vanilla creamer with a dash of cinnamon on top. I reach into the fridge, deciding that today calls for a healthy dollop of whipped cream on top, and then I squirt a generous amount directly into my mouth before placing it back in the fridge.

I place my cup of coffee on the highest shelf in the shower and climb in. My little routine makes getting up at the ass crack of dawn bearable. I bring my coffee into the shower with me so that I can savor little sips while I wash and shave. It's like a little spa experience in my head—only there's no plinky music and fresh cucumbers. By the time I'm showered, slathered in lotions, creams, and serums, I've finished my first cup and am heading to the kitchen for the second.

I take my second cup of coffee to my room and sip on it as I open my iPad and hit the Spotify app and select a *Women of Pop* playlist. The first song that comes up is "Work from Home" by Fifth Harmony and I grab my hairbrush to sing along as I dance around the room.

I love all things girly—the makeup, cute clothes, and bright colors. To me, fashion is a way to express myself. I love my job, but it's not very creative so being able to doll myself up and add a punch of color with bright-red lips or a bold smoky eye is a form of self-expression. Also, I'm not one of those *dab on some lip gloss and mascara* kind of girls and run out the door. I like to take my time, choose the perfect lip color with the perfect outfit, and make sure I feel and look my best before I head out the door.

I place a few drops of Argon oil in my palms, running it through my bouncy barrel curls before walking over to pick out an outfit from my closet. I've never been one of those stick-thin girls and I never will be. For years I struggled with the fact that I matured before anyone else in my class. I went to great lengths to try and hide my body, but it was no use. They didn't exactly make clothes for girls in sixth grade that already had D's. It wasn't until I was forced to defend myself that I realized how grateful I am for the body I have. It's healthy, gets me places I need to go, and looks fucking phenomenal in a pencil skirt.

I'll never forget the second day of my sophomore year in high school. Kyle Westmore, the class jerk-off, told me that if I wasn't careful, the friction between my thighs was going to start a fire. I just ignored the comment, but my friend Whitney told him to fuck off and that he wished he was the reason for the friction between my thighs. I tried hiding my giggle, but Kyle saw it and replied with, *"No, thanks, I don't date fat chicks."*

And that was the day, the exact moment actually, that I gave up trying to hide or care about what others thought of me. I'll never forget the surge of courage I got in that moment. I froze, turned around, and marched right back up to Kyle and told him that maybe if he had half as much dick in his pants as he did in his personality, a girl like me might consider him. The crowd that had gathered around us laughed and jeered as Kyle slammed his locker and shouted some unmemorable comment back to me.

I giggle to myself, grabbing my favorite red heels, or as my best friend likes to call them, *fuck me* pumps, and slip them on with my high-waisted pencil skirt and polka-dot blouse. Looking myself over in the mirror, I smile with excitement. I look like I just stepped out of the fifties and I love it.

I gather my things for work, pour my unfinished cup of coffee in a to-go cup, and leave my tiny apartment to make my train on time. I'm a few minutes early so I take a seat on my usual bench and pull out the newest book I picked up from a local bookstore. It's about an ordinary girl who meets and falls for a guy who just so happens to be a prince. I know it's unrealistic but hey, that's why we read romance, right? To get lost in the fantastical stories about average people falling in love with a secret prince and dirty scenes so hot you have to fan yourself so your cheeks don't catch on fire.

My phone beeps from my bag and I suddenly remember that I forgot to take it out yesterday and charge it. There's no telling how many calls and messages I've missed in the last twelve hours. I just hope none of them were about work. I pull the phone out of my bag and notice the battery bar on the top of the screen is red. It's on its last bit of life and I remind myself to plug it in the moment I get to my desk. What captures my attention next is the fourteen missed calls and the nine unread messages—all from the same person. My ex, Penn.

My stomach tightens when I see his name. It's not the fact that he's reaching out to me that's bothering me; it's the feeling that his behavior is becoming unhinged and erratic. It's not normal in the slightest to call someone fourteen times outside of an emergency, especially someone you broke up with seven months ago.

Penn and I had what I thought was a good relationship—until it wasn't. We met four years ago and started dating pretty much immediately. I felt like we had an instant chemistry and connection that I'd never experienced before, but really, I only felt that way because he constantly told me that's how he felt. I've since learned it's what my therapist calls "love bombing." It's a trick narcissists use to make you feel like what you have with them is so special and can never be recreated and it slowly turns into guilt and manipulation to keep you with them.

He really is a nice guy—or was a nice guy. I have to remind myself constantly that being controlling, projecting his insecurities, and making ridiculous accusations isn't being nice. It felt like he changed somewhere along the way and I completely missed it, but my therapist also told me that this is what narcissists do. He hid who he was from me until he'd gained my trust.

"They are parasites, Wren. They will latch on to you and use you and use you until they suck you completely dry. They will not change because they do not believe they need to. They believe that you are the problem. That if only you loved them more, just did what they said, didn't upset them... then everything would be perfect."

I let her words bounce around in my head for the hundredth time. It's something I do when I start to feel the guilt creep in that I "abandoned" him and start thinking that maybe I could fix him.

According to him, everything was perfect and me asking for space came out of nowhere. But that wasn't the case. He had a lot of problems with my relationship with Theo and how much time I spent away from home traveling with him. He would often comment about how I got a raise, convinced that I didn't earn the money but was given it for pleasing my boss in one way or another. I finally had all I could take and I called off the relationship. However, I still haven't managed to get him to release me completely.

I glance up and see my train approaching. I shake the thoughts of Penn from my head as I put my book back into my bag and pull it higher up on my shoulder to board the train. The usual hustle and bustle of everyone boarding pulls me in and I find that my usual seat is still open so I grab it and settle in by the window to resume reading my book. I've ridden this train to and from work every day for three years so I know by counting stops when I need to get off without ever really leaving the world of the book I'm lost in.

I start reading before the train is even done boarding and don't take notice of the other passengers around me. I'm too lost in the story of poor girl Ann Cummings and her prince William Shotright. As I make my way through the story, I can't figure out why I'm so distracted. Maybe I'm just still feeling uneasy about the amount of missed calls and texts from Penn. I look away from my book to inspect the faces of everyone around me. I scoot to the edge of the seat, glancing at the people on the train. That's when my eyes land on the man I've been seeing a lot lately.

I grip the book a little tighter as I peer around the page at him. He has dark stubble growing across his chin and jaw. His hat is pulled down low over his brow so I can't see his eyes. I'm not a paranoid person but something is off about this guy. He appeared basically out of thin air a few weeks ago and has been riding my train every day since. I know he very well could be new to the area or got a new job around here, but he doesn't get off at the same stop every day and that little voice inside my head is sounding off alarms. This might sound silly but when you ride the same damn train every weekday for three years, you get to know your train mates.

The whole time I'm looking at him, his gaze is focused on the window, seemingly unfazed by my gawking. When I turn away, it feels like he's looking at me again but I tell myself to stop. I open my book and do my best to focus all my attention on the story. When the train begins to approach my stop, I put my book away and get ready to get off. I turn my attention back to the guy and it's like the moment I look at him, he looks away. I even see his hair move from the quick action.

The train stops and I'm more than happy to get off. I hike my bag up on my shoulder and make my way toward the exit with a dozen other people. I start making my way away from the train station and in the direction of the office. It's only three blocks and I walk it every morning and evening. I usually enjoy the walk, but today, my paranoia is on overdrive and I feel like I'm being followed. This is a new development. I've seen the guy quite a few times lately and he's always given me an uneasy feeling, but I've never felt that he'd follow me.

I try to think back over the past few weeks to remember how many days I've seen that man so close to me. He always gets on at my stop, but I've never noticed him get off when I do. I try to figure out if he's on the train when I get on in the evening, but I don't remember if he's already on or if he gets on with or after me. I pick up the pace and walk a little quicker. Rounding a corner, I decide to look back. When I do, I see the man, walking in the same direction I was headed before I turned the corner. This is the first time he's ever gotten off at my stop. This makes my heart race and I push myself to go faster.

I don't look back again until I'm walking up the sidewalk to the office. When I do, I see a whole sea of people but don't zero in on his face even though I can't shake the feeling that he's still there. I walk up the steps to the building and before I walk through, I turn back one last time. I scan the crowd in front of me. I catch a glimpse of something out the corner of my eye and I turn my head in that direction. In a café across the street, there is a man with the same colored hat pulled down low. It's too far away for me to see the man clearly, but it feels like he's watching me. A chill races up my spine as I turn and rush into the building.

I feel out of body as I make my way to the elevator.

"Morning, beautiful." Bob gives me his usual greeting with a head nod, but I'm too lost in thought to return the greeting which isn't like me at all. I avoid unwanted conversations on my way to my office, and when I reach my office my assistant, Julie, is there waiting with my cup of coffee. I take it even though I have one in my hand.

"Thank you," I tell her, practically flying by her.

She follows me into my office. "Either you've already had way too much coffee today or something is wrong." She puts her hand on her jutted-out hip.

I fake a smile and a nervous laugh slips out. "I'm fine. Just excited to start the day. And maybe I've had a little too much coffee," I say, holding up my hand and showing her a *little bit* with my thumb and forefinger while I wrinkle my nose.

She laughs and shakes her head, causing her shoulder-length red hair to bounce with the action. "I left your messages and appointments on your desk. Let me know if you need anything."

"Thank you. I'll be just fine," I say, urging her out the door. She walks out and I close it behind her, leaning my back against it. I feel like I can finally breathe, like nobody is watching me or following me. I take a deep breath and let it out slowly while closing my eyes and resting my head back against the wood.

Taking my seat behind my desk, I turn on my phone and remember to charge it. I start up my computer and start sorting through emails and replying as needed. I have a few questions to answer in response to the recent rumor that Mr. Carmichael is thinking of selling the company which isn't true at all. How these rumors get started is beyond me. I give a typical response stating that the rumor isn't true and the company is doing better than ever and that people can start watching for the amazing things to come, and I send the email back to the reporter at *The Business Blog* website.

After I send the email, I gather my things and head out to my first meeting of the day. I have to prep the new interns on how to respond to questions that may be coming their way on future press releases. It's all typical and boring and something I have to do every six months when we bring on another round of new interns.

The meeting lasts an hour and when I get back to my office, Julie greets me with a smile. "You have a message from Mr. Carmichael's assistant."

I breeze by her desk and into my office as she follows me.

"He's asking for you to come up to his office."

I let out a long sigh. "Does it say why?"

"It does not." She holds out the paper and I take it, looking over the message. "Okay, thank you."

My nerves are shot today and dealing with Theo won't exactly help matters. The last thing I need with my already fried nerves is staring at him while I remember every filthy thing he said to me in my dreams while trying to dodge whatever mood he's in. Every moment I'm around him, I have to remind myself not to stare, not to flirt, not to say something inappropriate. It's tiring to say the least.

I take a deep breath and push myself up, heading for the top floor. The elevator ride seems quicker than normal and when I step off, his assistant greets me.

"Theo wanted to see me?"

She nods. "I'll let him know you're here." She picks up her phone and whispers into the receiver. She hangs it up moments later and looks back at me with a smile. "He'll be just a moment, dear."

I nod. "How's the new kitten?"

She smiles wide now and grabs her phone to show me pictures like she's a new mom. "He's so good and cuddly and sweet. I hate leaving him alone every day, but it's what I have to do for now. I'm looking into daycare, but—"

"They have daycare for cats?" I ask, accidentally cutting her off.

She nods with her brows lifted. "Oh yeah. It's great. You drop them off every morning and they get to play with the other cats; they have a snack, and I don't know, do what cats do." She shrugs.

The whole thing seems adorable but I don't let the conversation linger. Instead, I tell her again how cute he is before marching straight into his office before he has time to call me in. I'm on a tight schedule and I don't have time to wait till he's ready.

When I do, I breathe his rich scent in deeply and let it settle over me like a thick, warm blanket of comfort. Whatever the scent is, it's all his own. His entire office smells like him and it's intoxicating. He's seated at his desk, a serious look on his face as he studies the piece of paper in his hand.

He's wearing a dark-navy suit that has a slight plaid pattern to it in a blue that's almost the same color. He straightens his tie almost absentmindedly before running his hand through his thick, silky locks. Images of my erotic dream from this morning come flooding back and I feel an instant heat creep up my cheeks.

"Wren." He says my name without even looking up from the file in his hand and it causes a tingle in my lower belly. It's not his usual *office voice* as I like to call it, but deeper and rich, echoing through his chest. It's the tone I've only ever heard a handful of times and each time it sends me straight to the moon.

Keep Reading *Dirty Little Secret.*

ABOUT THE AUTHOR

Alexis Winter is a contemporary romance author who loves to share her steamy stories with the world. She specializes in billionaires, alpha males and the women they love.

If you love to curl up with a good romance book you will certainly enjoy her work. Whether it's a story about an innocent young woman learning about the world or a sassy and fierce heroine who knows what she wants you,'re sure to enjoy the happily ever afters she provides.

When Alexis isn't writing away furiously, you can find her exploring the Rocky Mountains, traveling, enjoying a glass of wine or petting a cat.

ALSO BY ALEXIS WINTER

Four Forces Security

The Protector

The Savior

Love You Forever Series

The Wrong Brother

Marrying My Best Friend's BFF

Rocking His Fake World

Breaking Up with My Boss

My Accidental Forever

The F It List

The Baby Fling

Grand Lake Colorado Series

A Complete Small-Town Contemporary Romance Collection

Castille Hotel Series

Hate That I Love You

Business & Pleasure

Baby Mistake

Fake It

South Side Boys Series

Bad Boy Protector-Book 1

Fake Boyfriend-Book 2

Brother-in-law's Baby-Book 3

Bad Boy's Baby-Book 4

Make Her Mine Series

My Best Friend's Brother

Billionaire With Benefits

My Boss's Sister

My Best Friend's Ex

Best Friend's Baby

Mountain Ridge Series

Just Friends: Mountain Ridge Book 1

Protect Me: Mountain Ridge Book 2

Baby Shock: Mountain Ridge Book 3

Castille Hotel Series

Hate That I Love You

Business & Pleasure

Baby Mistake

Fake It

ALL BOOKS CAN BE READ AS STAND-ALONE READS WITHIN THESE SERIES

Printed in Great Britain
by Amazon

25295899R00165